SARAH WALKED OVER THE MOUNTAIN

SARAH WALKED OVER THE MOUNTAIN

A NOVEL BY

RUTH MOORE

WILLIAM MORROW AND COMPANY, INC.

NEW YORK   1979

Library of Congress Cataloging in Publication Data

Moore, Ruth.
    Sarah walked over the mountain.

    I. Title.
PZ3.M7867Sar [PS3525.05666]   813'.5'2   79-14331
ISBN 0-688-03523-X

BOOK DESIGN   CARL WEISS

Printed in the United States of America.

2   3   4   5   6   7   8   9   10

For John Willey

I

The foundation on which the Scott family farmhouse stood was 168 years old. In its time, three different home places had been built there, the last one on sturdy, hand-hewn blocks of granite, lining ample cellars. But the first, a log cabin, had been put down on earth left by the mile-high cap of the Ice Age—a foundation which had been there for some ten thousand years.

Andrew Scott, from England, later a solid citizen of Gloucester, Massachusetts, built the cabin in 1784 to hold his title to a huge tract of wild land in Maine. It was the least effort demanded of him by his contract—a one-room structure with an earthen floor, twenty-two by twenty-two feet. Five hundred feet back from the shores of a narrow harbor, it stood on the edge of wilderness which, except for Indian trails, stretched for miles nobody knew how far north into the back country. Andrew's wife and children lived in it for thirteen years, starting in there before the town even had a name. The cabin burned down in 1798.

Walter, Andrew's eldest son, put up a frame house on the same site in 1811, using the material and profits from his and his brother Martin's sawmill. During the War of 1812, when the British destroyed what there was of the town, that, too, burned down. The third house of necessity started small, but when sawed lumber was plentiful again from the restored mills, the Scotts replaced it with a solid structure, long and roomy, with accommodations for many children. Built by men whose people had faced up to enemy attack by sea and Indian raids by land, the house from the beginning was as tough as a fort, a stronghold, its outer walls made, not of boards, but of four-by-fours set one on top of another. The early settlers owned the wilderness and the mills to saw it into lumber. This time, they built to last, and last their home place did, while the century played itself out and a new one came along, and a town grew up around it, with lawns and shade trees and new generations.

The early Scotts had cleared three hundred acres for farmland and pasture; the place had been a farm then and in 1952 still was, only, now, equipped with modern dairy barns and outbuildings. For old Mrs. Matilda Scott, who had grown up there, the time of history ticked in the walls with as authentic a beat as did the grandfather clock in the hall. Why, that clock is a youngster, old as it is, and so am I, even though I'm a two-great-grand-mother now, she would think.

Even after her marriage, she had remained a Scott, because her husband, Dennis, had been her cousin. They had inherited the place from their grandfather, the second Walter, Nathan's son; and the second Walter had known his great-grandmother, Sarah Thomas, Andrew Scott's wife. The second Walter had heard her story, first-hand from her and her sons, and had written it down. It contained much of the history of the town, which he had taken the trouble to document from old State and County records. Turning the pages, fuzzy at the edges now and so soft that they had almost the feel of worn cloth, Matilda would think, That history is what a real person saw. You can tell what it was like to live through them days and know the people we all go back to, both good and bad. Sarah Thomas was our beginnings in America—Sarah Thomas Scott, because, much as some would like to, we can't leave out Andrew. We had him, too. And after all the generations, we've still got a few mementoes of him now. Let's face it, as dear Grandfather Walter used to say.

II

The second Walter's document began:

Sarah Thomas was born in Wales of a poor family whose children had to go out and earn a living. Well, that's not unusual. We've all been hard-working. She went to England and found a job as a lady's maid on a big estate. She was there three years and the lady she worked for took a shine to her and taught her to read, write, and figure. She met Andrew Scott, a ship captain, in London, and they got married. He was a big yellow-headed Englishman, stood six-foot-four in his stocking feet and she had hair as black as mine used to be, so we can see how we come by our looks honest. Their little boy, Walter, wasn't a year old when Andrew lit out, took off for America. He'd go on ahead, he told her, set up a home for her and the baby to come to and then he'd let her know where to come. She never heard a word from him for the next two years. All she knew about where he'd gone to, he'd said he had a cousin in Gloucester, Massachusetts, and would start out for there.

She couldn't write him because she didn't know where in the God's world he was by then, nor the cousin's name. He hadn't said.

She'd saved her wages, had enough for her passage with a little over and she had her dander good and well up. So she packed her things and sailed off to America to find Andrew.

She was a neat girl and careful of her things. She had nice ones, too. She showed me a list of what she carried in her trunk, covers two pages, both sides. I can't recall half of what there was—rig-outs that I guess a nice, genteel lady's maid would have to look good doing her job.

Dresses and ribbons and laces and fancy petticoats. And stays, I guess, I can't remember. A whole trunkful of things like that, but not one single, solitary thing that would do her a mite of good in the howling wilderness she ended up in.

She had a rough crossing in not too stiddy a vessel and she and the baby was both terrible seasick. The outside cloak she had on was stained so bad where she and young Walter had puked on it that she never could get the spots out when she got to a place where she could try. The vessel put in to Boston, and there Sarah landed on the wharf, with her baby, her trunk full of furbelows, not much money left, and no notion in the world of where to find Andrew, except somewhere in Gloucester, Massachusetts. And where in the world was that? She said she had a terrible time trying to say "Massachusetts," it twisted her tongue all up, and that first day she said, "Massa-two-shits," so that the landlady at the waterfront boarding house where she stayed that night was real raked out with her.

The next day she asked around the waterfront and heard about a Gloucester vessel that was headed for there. She still had some grit left in her craw. The notion of another trip by sea, even a short one, turned her stomach upside down, but she took passage on the vessel.

On the way, she had a talk with the skipper, name of Coffin, and she found out that there was an Andrew Scott in Gloucester, not only well known, but for a newcomer, he'd done pretty well for himself. He'd gone into business with a cousin of his and now he owned a trading schooner, the *Amelia C.*, which made regular trips along the coast as far as Machias, on the east end of Maine, with supplies for the settlers and brought back cargoes of lumber, hides, seabirds' feathers, dry fish, and shooks—whatever they had ready to come.

There were other Scotts living in Gloucester, Cap'n
Coffin said, but he guessed that from what Sarah'd told
him, this one might be who she was asking about—big,
husky fellow, lot of yellow hair. No other Andrew that
Coffin knew about. Sarah agreed with him. She was feeling happier by the minute.

Another thing Sarah found out—but that was a long
time later—Andrew'd landed in a buttertub when he'd
arrived in Gloucester. His cousin, who'd been there for
quite a number of years, had got to be mighty well-off, a
ship owner and land speculator. He'd bought in millions
of acres of wilderness as far south as Virginia and north
to the Province of Maine. He was a widower with one
daughter and no son to take over when he was dead.
Andrew, after he'd been with him a while, had got closer
to him than a son.

He found out right away that the old man had a bull
by the tail with his tracts of land in Maine. The State of
Massachusetts was in a flap about getting the wild lands
settled so as to get revenue. They wanted to get towns
established fast, with settlers moving north in droves, the
way they had before the Revolution; but the War had
cut that off for years, while most of the men who would
have gone stayed back to fight in the Army. Then, for a
long time after 1783, the whole country was in mortal
hard times—even families who'd been well-heeled didn't
have much cash; shipping was at a standstill; most vessels, including old Ai Curtis's, laid rotting in the harbors.

That was Andrew's cousin's first name—Ai. Looks odd
wrote down, but it's a solid, pious one, straight out of the
Bible, and the way it's said is A-eye.

Old A-eye, who stood to lose his contract with the
State unless he got some settlers on his northern land,
had sent one vessel up along the coast with four or five
families, but when they got there and see what the

place was like and what they'd have to contend with,
they'd hauled-ship and gone on east to Machias, where
there was already a considerable-sized town and better
land available. And by gum, not to be blamed for it, either.

This town we live in now, you can look out the window and see the nice homes and the school and the church
and so on, but what you want to take a good long look
at is the highway that runs through here and out into
the world. In them days, this was one of the wildest
places on God's green earth and the only sensible way
to get to it was by water. Unless you wanted to take a
kind of Injun track over Black Mountain and be troddled
on by bears and loucifees, and the Injuns wasn't too
friendly in them days, neither. You can look out there
now and see Black Mountain, too, if you want to.

By the time Andrew arrived, Ai Curtis was about ready
to let the contract go. He was old and tired and not in the
best of health and he had more land other places than he
knew what to do with. But here came Andrew, young
and able, and with git-up-and-git enough for the both
of them. Andrew had a plan.

If the old man would let him have a vessel, he'd
guarantee to round up enough settlers to hold the contract, and see that they stayed put, too, after he'd sailed
them north.

In times to come, Andrew was to brag to Sarah how
he'd done just that and how he'd diddled old A-eye into
giving him the vessel and the contract to the lands in
Maine.

"Keep the land in the family, I told him. And you ought
to seen the old fuddy-duddy prick up his ears at that."
Andrew was a great hand to brag around the house, but
he never did brag about how close into A-eye's family
he'd really got to be. It was years before Sarah heard the
truth of it.

Cap'n Coffin told Sarah that he'd heard Andrew Scott say he owned a house downeast somewheres where he stayed whilst unloading or loading cargo. He was about to go on and add to it that Andrew had a grand house in Gloucester, too, when he see that Sarah had busted out crying.

She said she was sorry to be such a fool, but she was Andrew's wife, new over from England and this was his baby; she'd been scared she wouldn't be able to find where he lived now. He must've wrote her, she said, and the letter'd gone astray. Still crazy about him, she was, and loyal to him too. She wasn't crying, she said, because she wasn't happy, only that it was such a relief to know that there was a home for her and the baby to go to, and she hadn't much money left.

My grandfather, that was young Walter, her boy, told me it was likely the last time in her life that Sarah cried, though there was always plenty of reason to.

Except to say that the *Amelia C.* was due in Gloucester any day now, Cap'n Coffin shut up like a hen clam with a sore tooth. Because a year ago Andrew Scott had married his cousin's daughter, Amelia Curtis, at a society wedding. His vessel was named for her and they were living together in the big house he'd built for her in Gloucester. Coffin did manage to mumble something about Sarah's not to build her hopes up too high—it might not be the same Andrew Scott, but she didn't even listen, she was so sure. Then he offered to lend her money if she needed some, but she said no, he'd been kind enough already, all she needed now was to see Andrew. He did tell her about a decent place near the waterfront where she could stay—said he knew the woman who ran it would likely trust her for room and board for a while. He was a nice feller, Cap'n Coffin.

What Sarah did, she traded one of her fancy petticoats

for food and lodging. She found she could have traded
the lot of what she had, because ordinary womenfolks
in Gloucester, them days, was starved for pretty clothes
from England. It turned out she didn't have to. The
Amelia C. made in a few days before she'd used up the
first petticoat.

Andrew found Sarah and Walter on the wharf waiting
for him. If he was took aback any he didn't show it—
didn't turn a hair. He give them a happy greeting, put
them in his cabin aboard the vessel and they had a fine
reunion whilst he switched cargoes and sailed off up the
coast on his next trip north. He told her he'd been expecting her, but had about give up, figured his letter
must have gone astray. Where she hadn't got it, the vessel
carrying it must have sunk. She believed him. He said,
well, anyway, here she was, she must have second-sight
or read his mind, and she was happy as a bluebell till she
got a look at the place he took her to.

It was this place, this town, only it wasn't a town yet,
didn't even have a name. Andrew's deed from the State
of Massachusetts read that his land wouldn't be taxed
for twenty years if he settled it. He was to bring in
twenty-two families, each to build a house twenty-two-
foot square and get together setting up a church and a
school. Why twenty-two of everything I don't rightly
know, maybe something to do with permanence. No fly-
by-night shacks, but solid structures.

Andrew wasn't about to be caught in the same bind
his cousin had been, about people to settle. It was only
a little while after the Revolutionary War and a good
many soldiers were foot-loose and land hungry, looking
for a new place to go. What Andrew did, he offered a
hundred acres to any man who'd settle here, bring his
family, and help build a town. After seven years, the set-
tler would get a deed to his property, free and clear. He

didn't have much trouble finding people, either, on a deal like that. At the time of Sarah's arrival, though, the project had hardly begun; so far, only five log cabins had been built—Andrew's was one of them—though there were plenty more folks to come.

Andrew hadn't a notion in his head of living here himself, though his deed said he had to; he was doing too well with his trading vessel and some other irons he had in the fire. There was a fortune in lumber on the land and one of the first things he got the settlers to do was build a sawmill—a tide mill, it was—up at the inlet, where the tide goes hellity-hoot in and out of Cooper's Stream. Still does. You can see the old mill foundations there to this day, if you know where to look. Later on, they built a gristmill, but that hadn't been got around to when Sarah come.

According to the agreement he'd signed, Andrew couldn't hold his land unless he was to live on it, raise his family there, so after he'd built his cabin, he'd stop over in it every so often for a week or so and have a hunt. The wilderness, the real old wild, was alive with critters to shoot. He and his crew could set on a log outside his back door and gun down enough deer and moose to take a ton or so of dressed meat back to peddle in Gloucester. Lately, though, the State land agents had begun getting picky with him because he wasn't setting up housekeeping here himself; but here, now, was Sarah, a godsend—nice little wife and baby, legal, too—who could live in the cabin, solve that problem and be far enough out of the way so as not to interfere with his establishment back in Gloucester. If the land agents wanted to look into it, there she'd be. So he made her welcome as the flowers in spring and that was why he did, only she didn't tumble to it. Not then.

She landed into what had been no more than a hunter's

roost—a place where nobody but a rough crowd of men had ever slept and had left their tracks behind. There wasn't much in the way of furnishings—a few bunks full of straw, some bundles of filthy quilts; the fireplace had a crane with some burnt-out kittles hanging on it. Some seats was around, made out of lengths of split log with holes bored for sapling legs. The floor was nothing but plain, tramped-down dirt. And except for about an acre cleared from the cabin down to a kind of makeshift wharf where the *Amelia C.* tied up when she put in, the whole works was nothing but black-green wilderness to the back door.

The inside of the cabin made Sarah sick to her stomach, but she believed Andrew when he fell all over himself saying how sorry he was. The last time he'd been here, he said, he'd been going to make the boys clean the place up, but he'd had to light out of the harbor in a flap, ahead of an easterly, or he couldn't have made enough sea-room to weather the islands. It was just about killing him now to have to leave her in such a mess, but he had supplies for Machias that the folks down there needed fast because they was all starving to death. And so on and on, all lies. That would've been news to the Machias people, they'd have laughed their heads off, because they was doing mighty well at the time. They had quite a big, prosperous town going down there then, with trading vessels of their own, and Andrew was far from being their only contact with the cities to the west-ard. Sarah, of course, didn't know that then.

He told her he'd leave her trunk on the wharf, along with some decent bedding and food enough to get by on till he got back. One of the neighbors, he said, had an ox and if she asked him, he'd haul everything home for her. And off Andrew went like a whirling wind before she even had time to ask him the neighbor's name. Turned

out to be a man named Frank Cooper and he did haul
the baggage, but when he saw what Andrew'd left her to
cope with, he went in the air sky-high and rounded up
the neighbors.

They helped her out with what they could. Some of
them didn't have much more to do with than she had,
but they scraped up a copper boiler and a tub and a
clean cooking kittle. The womenfolks, they got together
on it with a bucket of soft soap. They helped her hoe out
the cabin. The men hauled down some scrap lumber
from the mill, fixed a makeshift floor to cover the dirt
one. When Andrew got back from Machias, the place
was span-clean, with even the hunters' rotten quilts
boiled out and made decent to sleep under. Frank
Cooper read Andrew out, give him partic'lar hell, but
all Andrew did was thumb his nose at Frank and light
out for down-coast, without even spending a night.

And that's the way it was for the next thirteen years
while young Walter was growing up. He said the *Amelia
C.* would put in every so often—she hadn't any regular
schedule—so his mother never knew when to expect
Andrew. But there he'd be, twice anybody's size, roaring
round and carrying on because Sarah hadn't made the
place more comfortable for him, and too many kids underfoot. He finally had to come to it and build another
room on the cabin, because every two years or so there'd
be a new baby. The neighbors made so much outcry that
he had tight plank floors put into both rooms. After a
while, he stretched himself and brought Sarah a cow
and some hens. When Frank Cooper asked him why he
didn't bring her an ox that could haul heavy loads, like
firewood, he said the cow could give milk to feed the
brats, and, for the god's sake, could be learnt to haul heavy
loads, couldn't she?

Five children she had by him during those years. She

took care of them as best she could with what she had, but she had mortal hard times. Andrew was stingy's a goat—half the time he forgot to bring stuff she needed, or didn't bother to, not having his mind on her, so to speak. Almost everything had to come by the *Amelia C.* in those early days, so if something wasn't there, it wasn't there. She went without.

Now, this is as far as Great-grandmother Sarah got with the story. She was awful old then, and tired, and she had to stop and rest. That was the last time I see her, because she died not long after. The other part of the story come from young Walter and his sisters, Rachel and Kate, my grandfather and my great-aunts.

Whenever the *Amelia C.* put in, Walter and his brother Martin would be about crazy to get aboard of her, see what she was like—talk to the crew, learn something about the world outside of the wilderness they lived in. They would have to sneak to do it, because if they came around, the crew would tell Andrew and he'd thrash the daylights out of them. The crew wouldn't talk to them anyway—been told not to, Walter guessed, and Andrew forbid them the vessel, even said to keep away from the wharf when cargo was being handled. They was nothing, he said, but a couple of damn frigs and he'd be tickled to death to drownd them both if they got in his way. They stayed pretty much out of his way, anyway, when he was over at the cabin. All the kids did, because he thought nothing of booting the baby across the room if it happened to crawl too close to him. He didn't give them much cause to love him. They didn't.

The boys, though, couldn't see why he was so touchy about the vessel. What harm would it do if they just went aboard and looked around? Walter was fifteen, going on for sixteen and Martin was twelve when they found out why.

Walter was a big boy, over six foot tall, took after Andrew in looks. He was already the man of the family who could take care of the heavy outdoors work for Sarah. He'd worked in the lumber mill since he was ten, earned good wages. Times in the winter, when supplies ran short, he'd gone over the mountain to Machias with a batch of neighbor menfolks, who teamed up and helped each other haul dogsleds up and down the narrow trail. The mountain track was narrow and steep, little more than a footpath, its S-curves following the contour of the mountain.

The trip had always been rugged, but generally it had been fun, the way a hunting party is. There was a block-house-type shelter just over the last peak on the Machias side, which in the early times had been built as a lookout for Indian raids where hunters or pilgrims or anyone who might need it could stay. The men had always put up there for the night on the way back from Machias to rest from the tough twenty-mile haul. The land from the foot-hills on the Machias side of the mountain sloped towards the sea, so that the loaded sleds had to be dragged uphill. The shelter had rough bunks and a stone fireplace and everybody would tell stories and sing songs, pass around the rum jug and have a righteous good time.

The year Walter was twelve years old he had come back from one Machias trip with a gun and had learned to shoot it, so that from then on he'd been able to bring in plenty of wild game for Sarah to put on the table.

Times, through the years, changed in the village. People got to be prosperous. They owned their own land now, where they grew corn and barley which could be ground into meal and flour at the gristmill. The Scott boys had cleared and dug a garden behind the cabin, had fenced it against the wild critters with cut poles. Martin had gone to work in Frank Cooper's boatyard and Frank had given him his choice of wages—he could take his pay in cash or he could have a rowboat that he'd helped Frank to build. He took the boat. So now his family could get plenty of fresh fish to eat; even the girls, Kate, eleven, and Rachel, twelve, could pull a mess of flounders out of the harbor when the boys were too busy working to take the boat farther offshore for groundfish.

Sarah had more time now to tend her babies—she still had two, Sidney, three, and Morgan, fifteen months. She was beginning to feel less like a work-machine and more like a human being when everything blew up around her.

In November that year, the *Amelia C.* docked on her way down the coast and stayed long enough to load cargo, but Andrew didn't spend a night at the house. He came up on an afternoon, got a list of things she needed from Sarah, told her that she always wanted too damned much. What did she think? He was two jumps ahead of the poorhouse. They'd be sailing on the tide in the morning early, so he'd have to sleep aboard. He took a look at three-year-old Sidney, who was black-headed, cussed some about having to raise another god-damned Welshman, and took himself off down to the wharf.

Sarah was just as glad he had. It was Sunday and the older kids were over at Paine's Pond ice-fishing; she always tried to get them out of the way when Andrew was around—it was easier on everybody. There'd been a light fall of snow which had melted some, and then a good hard freeze-up. One of the neighbors had gone over and tested the ice on the pond, so she wasn't worried about the kids. If they didn't get back till after dark, why, there was a full moon.

Rachel and Kate got home first, just after moonrise.

They had a fine string of fish. Sarah was about to say how nice that was when she discovered that they were both crying and mad.

"What is it? What's the matter?" There was always something when Andrew was around.

"It's Pa!" Rachel said. "The mean old devil's stole our skiff. He's got it hauled up on deck down to the vessel. The boys have gone to get it back."

Sarah got rigged up right away to go down there. She'd hardly put foot off of the doorstep when she heard a rumpus start up, Andrew yelling and some woman screeching her head off. Sarah began to run.

Walter said he and Martin had got aboard all right without anyone seeing them. The crew, seemed, had all turned in, but there was a light in Andrew's quarters. Martin's boat was lashed down on deck good and taut. They decided to cut her loose, then wait for the light to go out and Andrew to go to sleep. They knew how he slept, like a log in the water. They'd horsed the boat around times enough themselves to know that they could ease her over the rail and into the water, but not without making some kind of a noise. So they waited a while. They were both so roaring mad that it was hard to sit and do nothing. When they couldn't stand it any longer, they sneaked aft to peek through the cabin light, see if the old man had gone to bed yet. He hadn't. He was sitting at a table eating something and there in the bunk back of the table was a woman.

Walter said it hit him like a brick in the face. He was hard put to it not to let out a yell. He got a kind of dry, stinking taste in his mouth, he remembered that. And then someone grabbed him by the collar and yanked him away from there. It was one of the crew, a young feller Walter'd seen helping load cargo at the wharf.

"What d'you dirty-minded skunk think you're doing,

peeking in at the skipper's wife?" he said. He begun to shake Walter good and hard.

Walter hauled off and let him have it right in the breadbasket, knocked the wind out of him. He begun to gurgle and swear and here comes Andrew, blunt-end-foremost, up the hatchway. He took in what was going on and made a grab at Walter, expected he'd run, but Walter didn't. By that time he was so tearing mad, with all the hate that had gathered up inside of him through the years, that he didn't even think of running. He hit Andrew as hard as he could, right on the end of the nose and butted him in the belly.

Walter was a big, hefty boy and had lived rough; he'd been in fights before. Andrew went *ker-plunk* over backwards and laid there. The woman stuck her head out of the hatch and begun to screech like a loucifee. Walter could hear the crew moving, feet hitting the deck, and then he did run. He hollered to Martin to make time out of there and the two of them took off over the rail as fast as they could belt. They met their mother halfway down from the cabin.

Walter said his mother's face when they told her about the woman scared them both stiff. She didn't say a word, just looked around the cabin from one thing to another. She didn't say what she was going to do, either; but he wouldn't have been surprised if the blaze in her eyes had set the place afire. Then she stirred up and begun to pack. Walter didn't ask where they were going, because he knew. There was only one place they could go. Machias.

The *Amelia C.* was the only vessel due in this backwater now until spring, and they good and well wouldn't be sailing with Andrew. Wood roads had been cleared out back of the town, partway to Machias, where they petered out into old Indian trails that led every which of a way into almost impassable wilderness. Walter knew, because he and Martin had got lost in there one time and like to never got out. The only other way out of here was over Black Mountain. That wouldn't be so bad with a bunch of men along, all carrying guns and with plenty of muscles to haul sleds. But with two babies, two not very big girls and only him and Martin—he didn't believe they could do it.

They'd have a five-mile tote to the foot of the mountain, a steep climb up and another one down, then another twelve or thirteen miles to Machias. The light fall of snow would have melted some on this side, the south side of the mountain, so there'd be ice to contend with on the trail. He didn't say to his mother that she'd bit off more than she could chew. He was scared to. He figured she was as crazy mad as he'd been. She might cool down and be sensible later. What he did say to her was that if she was scared Pa would show up here tonight, she needn't be. He was laid out flat down there, and if he did come ranting around, there was the gun. Pa'd get his head good and blowed off. "I'd have done it, too," Walter said. "Been glad to."

Sarah didn't even answer him.

Then Martin, who'd been watching Sarah, got the idea of what she was doing, and he exploded like a firecracker. Martin was too young to have much judgment about things, but if there was something hard to try, he was always the boy to try it. "Hey, Walt! Ma's getting ready to leave here," he hollered. He jumped up, grabbed his mother in a big hug and spun her around. "Oh, my gorry, my gorry! This is great, Ma! This is a great thing we're going to do!"

And all at once, Walter said, he stopped being foolish mad and begun to feel free and wild all over. This *was* a great thing. Get away for good from under Pa's thumb and out where there was a whole world they hadn't seen and were going to see. Anything they run into couldn't be half as cussid mean as what they had here. So Walter quit holding back and started to help Sarah. The minute he did, he realized that she wasn't crazy, not by any means. She was cuffing around and making plans as sensible as the face of the moon that was going to light them on their way.

They couldn't take much. The dogsled they had was long and skinny, built to haul wood on narrow woods paths; it had stakes on it to keep the wood from rolling off. The babies would have to ride in it; any space left over would be what there was for bedding and food. Sarah had that all planned out. She told Walter to go out to the lean-to, put a good thick layer of hay into the sled and pack it down. Over that, she spread a square of canvas from one of the *Amelia C.*'s castoff sails that Andrew had left her one time when she'd asked for bedding. It was big enough so she could double it and have overlaps on all four sides. On that, she put a layer of quilts and fixed a kind of nest for the babies.

In the meantime, she'd made Martin kill and dress four hens, shoo the rest of the flock outdoors so the neighbors could find and take care of them. While she cut up the hens, she put Kate and Rachel to work peeling potatoes and turnips and carrots from the root-cellar. Then she chucked the whole works into her biggest cooking kittle, hung it in the fireplace to stew.

What she'd put in there about filled the kittle and smelt like heaven whilst it was cooking. Nobody had had supper and Walter said they all like to died before the stew was done. There was time to make cornmeal and barley flour bannocks; Sarah made a mort of them, had the girls bake and turn them in front of the fire as fast as she stirred them up and then stuff a sack with them. In another sack she put cups and spoons, some squares of clean sacking for diapers for the baby. What the other kids would wear was anything they had to stand up in, which wasn't much to write home about, unless you had a home to write to and say send warm underclothes. Sarah said they'd have to keep moving to keep warm.

Walter pushed an ax under the hay on the sled, took his hunting knife and gun and all the loads he had for it and he was ready. What Sarah took for herself was the last of all the nice things she'd brought with her when she came over from England—her string of carved wooden beads. She put it around her neck and wore it the time she walked over the mountain.

The stew took time to cook and what with getting the kids fed and ready, it was nigh midnight when Walter hitched the cow to the sled and they lit out. He'd wanted to let the neighbors know, but Sarah said they mustn't. She said the only thing against his father that Walter had ever heard her say.

"We must go in the dark. They'd never let us go if they knew what we are doing. The men here take care of women."

She did one other thing. When they left, she took a stick and raked the fireplace fire out into the middle of the cabin floor. Walter was horrified at first, because he had it in his mind that if they couldn't get over the mountain, they could always come back, but then he realized that she was fixing things so they couldn't. He had a lot of respect for her for doing that. It sure took more guts than he had handy at the time, he said.

They went along the flat past the harbor and up a hill and down, into the foothills of the mountain. The old cow pulled like a major; they got along fairly fast.

Walter carried his gun and walked ahead leading the cow. Martin had a bundle of dry firewood, in case they needed a fire in a hurry. Sarah took turns with the two girls lugging the kittle of stew, which was still scalding hot. The cover on it didn't fit very well, so that the stew slopped a little, now and again; Walter said he kept getting a whiff of it, and the girls kept running their fingers around the slop. None of them had ever tasted chicken before. Hens were a scarce article in that wilderness; nobody hardly ever killed one to eat. There were plenty of wild birds around—partridges and seabirds—and if a hen got too old to lay she could still get broody and set on eggs.

All the people had kept asking Andrew to bring more hens so's they could build up flocks and he'd say that he'd started out with a good batch of them in coops, but hens always got seasick and died. One of his crew bragged around though that they aboard the vessel et chicken dinners all the way up from Gloucester.

Walter said he got to thinking about the five or six he'd shooed out into the cold, seemed such a waste. The idea of it made him look back. There he saw a big orange flare of fire against the sky. He said to his mother, "Look, they got a big fire back there," and she said she didn't doubt they had. That was all anybody said about it as they went up into the foothills of the mountain.

It was a while before daylight when they got to the base of the mountain. Nobody had a timepiece, but Walter judged from the looks of the sky that it might be four o'clock. They made a kind of camp in a thicket of trees on the edge of a forest of spruces, walloping big ones— you don't see many of them nowadays, they've about all been cut down. Walter took the ax and hewed limbs and dry brush off a dead one for a fire. He wanted to save the dry wood they'd brought, because he wasn't sure if he could find any on the bare peak of the mountain. When, or if, they got as far as the hunters' shack, they'd likely find some, because whoever used it last was always under promise to leave wood for the next man, but Walter wasn't taking any chances.

He and Martin brought armloads of green boughs to sit on; the girls put the stew kittle on the fire to warm up again. Sarah pulled some hay out from under the babies, fed the cow and milked her. She gave the baby some warm milk—there was enough for him but not much more. That was one tired old bossy and she wasn't giving down anything she didn't have to. Sidney got the rest of the milk, but he was three and could eat stew. Then they rested and ate, fixed a bed so the kids could sleep till daylight.

They, all but Walter, packed in like a batch of puppies on top of the sailcloth from the sled, spread over the green boughs, with quilts spread over them. Walter tried to get his mother to lie down, but she wouldn't. She sat holding the baby, staring into the fire, not saying anything. Walter could guess what she was thinking—if any of them got hurt, or worse, on this journey she was starting, she'd never forgive herself. So he figured that the fire better be kept going. He tended it for a while, but he was tired to death and full of stew. Twice, he almost sagged over with his face in the coals. The last thing he remembered was dumping on a big armful of wood and sitting down on the pile of boughs next to his mother. When he woke up, he was lying there under a quilt with his arm around her. She and the baby were both asleep, leaning against him. It was daylight and the sun was coming up.

Anyone who ever climbed Black Mountain before they built the road up over it knows what that trail was like. It begun to climb slow, wound around somewhat the way the road does now, got steeper as it went up. The village men had worked on it in the worst places, so that hand-hauled sleds could be taken over it, or an ox hauling one, if they were careful and it wasn't too icy, but it was meager going for a tired old cow pulling a load. There was some snow on it, melted after the sun got higher, icy in spots and steep. In some places, Walter said, he and Martin had to scrabble on their hands and knees with a rope around their chests tied to the cow's halter so she wouldn't fall over backwards and land on the sled.

Sarah took the babies out, in case the cow did slide down onto them. She and the girls took turns lugging them. They had to stop and rest often. Sometimes he or Martin would have to anchor the cow, whilst the other one went back with Sarah to where the girls had got cast with the babies and hadn't the strength to struggle up the slope. It took all day to get to the peak where the hunter's shack was. When they did, they were beat out to a frazzle and the dark was beginning to come.

The shack was tumble-down and drafty, but the fire-place worked. Some holy Christian had left a stack of dry wood. They made do with the rest of the stew, but everybody was too tired to eat, anyway. But the thing was, the worst was over—the rest of the way was all downhill. They'd have been all right if sometime in the night a bear hadn't winded the cow.

They heard her bawling and before Sarah could stop Walter, he lit out of the shack with the gun and shot at the bear. He hit it but not bad enough to stop it coming at him. He had to fight it off with the ax. He killed it, but not before he was bad clawed up and the cow was dead. Sarah got him back inside, bandaged him as well as she could with strips torn from a bread sack. In the morning, he couldn't walk, so she and Martin stretched him out on what was left of the hay in the sled. Then Sarah took the cow's place and started off with him down the mountain.

It was Walter's sister Kate—my Great-aunt Kate she was —who told what happened then.

Martin had wanted to be the one to go, put up quite a battle, but Sarah said no, she would have to do it. Someone had to get the girls and the babies down the mountain, take care of them on the way; Martin could shoot the gun where she couldn't. She told him to take Walter's knife and slice some meat off the cow, get the liver if he could, bring it in the empty stew kittle along with what bannocks was left. She said to follow her tracks as fast as they could, because she wasn't going to stop, she was going to get Walter to the town and find help for him quick.

Sarah found out right away that she couldn't go ahead of the sled, the way the boys had done on the way up. The slope was steep; she had to hang on behind and act as a brake. For a while, they could see her on the turns as she took the sled down the naked side of the peak. The last they saw, she and the sled skidded out of sight amongst the trees that started halfway down. Their Ma was hanging on for dear life with her hair and skirts streaming out behind like in a gale of wind.

The minute they lost sight of her for good, Kate said, she and Rachel got scared half to death. It had been bad enough with Walter and their mother there, but they didn't have much faith in Martin's being able to fight off the wild critters if they was to come around. He was about half Walter's size, skinny and small for his age, and they could tell he was scared, too. They tried to get him to forget the meat from the cow, start on down out of there quick's they could. The old cow was a horrid sight, clawed up the way she had been—they didn't believe they'd ever be able to eat anything that come off of her, anyway. Turned out, they'd misjudged Martin. He might be scared, but he'd been left in charge of things.

"You kids shut up!" he said. "You do what Ma told you, dammit! There's long miles ahead of us, and she looked ahead to them and thought how us kids was going to eat, tired and tore out as she was. So you two start down with Sidney and Morgan, and don't be scared, no varmints going to tackle you in the daylight. I'll catch up with you, soon's I can. If you think old Bossy looks bad now, you better not stick around and see what she'll look like when I get done. So git!"

The girls shivered and shook, expecting another bear to come along any minute; but one didn't, and after a while the worst thing was, they were cold. Kate said that ever afterwards she never put on a warm pair of woolen underdrawers without feeling that they was something holy, because before, she'd never owned a pair of drawers in her life.

Butchering wasn't too hard a chore for Martin. He'd helped dress out too many deer and moose not to know how and what to take from the poor old cow. The girls had got almost to the foot of the mountain before he caught up with them. They were some old glad to see him. He was a bloody mess and he'd about lost his breath from running, but he had the stew kittle full of meat in one hand, the gun in the other, and the bread sack slung onto his back. He was good and proud of himself. First thing he said was, "I got the old girl's liver."

They went on down the mountain.

After a while, they heard somebody holler. Martin said, "That's Ma. Come on, maybe she needs help," and away he went. The girls came hobbling after with the babies as fast as they could, which wasn't fast. And here came Sarah, climbing back. She had a man with her and a big, comfortable-looking ox, hauling a sled like theirs, only longer. Turned out he and another man had come over from Machias on a hunting trip after deer, which were plentiful on the lower slopes of the mountain. They'd spotted Sarah coming down lickety-split just in time to get their rig off the trail before she went past them like greased lightning.

They could see she had somebody hurt on the sled, so they had gone back down and caught up with her at the foot of the slope. Seeing how bad hurt Walter was, they didn't lose any time. They wrapped him up in a couple of bearskin robes they'd brought along to sleep on, put him on the extra sled they had with them to carry meat back on, and one of them took out full tilt for town where there'd be shelter and a doctor.

They tried to make Sarah go with him, but she said she had five more children up there on the mountain and they'd be scared and need her worse than Walter would, now he was took care of. She told Kate afterwards that both of the men acted as though they thought she was crazy, but finally the second hunter said he'd come up the trail with her and help find them. Kate said he swore good and loud when he saw the babies. He was bound to load everybody on to his sled and haul them all back to town.

Sarah said no, their own sled was down there; they could make do, they had so far, except for the bear. She told him that, if he was out after meat, there was a dead cow and a bear's carcass, fresh killed, up by the hunters' shelter, both of which he was welcome to. He was hard put to it to know what to do. A bear's carcass, before some critter got at it, would be a treasure because of all the fat on it, and Sarah told him he'd better get up there quick then. She thanked him for his help, but first things first. So he larruped up his ox and went off up, and she and the kids finished walking over the mountain.

Down below, after a few low foothills that didn't amount to much, they came on to the flatlands that sloped towards the sea. The trail was icy and packed-down snow, so that the sled mostly went by itself. They took turns riding on it, with Martin steering. They made good time. By afternoon, they could see smoke from the chimneys of the town rising up over the trees.

Sarah was awful anxious to get there to find out how Walter was, but the babies were howling hungry and everybody else was starving, too. So when they came to a nice, clear brook that wasn't all froze over, she called a halt. Martin ripped off the stakes from the sled, whittled kindling and got a fire going. They roasted slices of meat on sticks; Martin took good notice of the fact that neither one of the girls had any trouble eating part of poor old Bossy. He went on about it at a great rate till Sarah shut him up. He was always an awful tease, Martin was.

Sarah fed the babies with bannock mashed up in water from the brook. She hoped it wouldn't kill them, and it didn't. Then she made the kids wash their hands and faces and comb their hair as best they could. She said she wasn't going into town looking like a witch-woman with a lot of goblin children, though there wasn't much they could do about that; they all looked awful tatty, especially Martin.

Later, when they'd got nearer to the town, a bunch of menfolks came out to meet them with a team of oxen hauling a big woodsled. They said Walter was terrible sore and clawed up, but he was all right except the doctor had had to take off two of his fingers. He'd come to enough to tell people about the journey over the mountain, though some hadn't believed him until they met Sarah and the kids on the way into town. They sure gave her a rousing welcome then.

They'd expected to find the second hunter on his way back, seemed nobody hunted on that mountain alone. It wasn't considered safe, so they always went in pairs, or more. When they found out where he'd gone and what for, some of them took the ox team and sled and went to meet him; the rest helped Sarah get her tribe and her sled into town.

The Machias people made a great fuss over her and the kids. They couldn't imagine how she'd done what she had, but there she was. They took care of the children till she got rested, helped her out with clothes the kids were all desperate for, and a man and his wife took them all in to live with them, and never charged her a cent, until a vessel put in headed for Boston, which is where she wanted to go. Some awful nice folks lived in Machias them days; still do.

She spent the rest of her life in Boston, worked mortal hard at first to earn enough to keep her family going. She had a job in an eating-place for sailors first. Then she got a chance to keep house for a doctor who had an invalid wife. She was bound and determined to raise her family decent and educate them, and she did. Along awhile before the War of 1812, when the British was ravaging around on the high seas, Andrew's vessel was overhauled by one of their frigates, and being the kind of high-class fool he was, he put up a fight. They sunk his vessel with him and his lady and most of his crew. A few survivors got picked up by another vessel. They got back to Gloucester to tell the tale.

And then she got, I will say, what she surely had coming from Andrew Scott. She and her children inherited everything he had, a fortune and a fine, fat one. She sold his house in Gloucester—wouldn't go to live or even die in it, she said. By rights, it should have belonged to old man Curtis, whose money had built it, but he was dead and so was his daughter, and no living relatives except Andrew's. So she took the cash she got for it—a good round sum it was, too—and sent Walter and Martin north with it, to give it to the neighbors who'd been so decent to her in the place where she'd fought her lifetime battle.

"Tell them thank you," she said. "And say it's to pay for the hens that Andrew cheated them out of all those years."

Walter was twenty-nine then and Martin twenty-five. They'd both got married and had growing families—Nathan, Walter's first boy, was eight years old, and they'd seen quite a lot of the world that they'd been so crazy to get away from here and see, because they owned their own vessel now—one of several that had belonged to Andrew, and they'd been around some in her. In the thirteen years they'd been gone, this town had grown some—more settlers moving in, building frame houses instead of cabins, and the wilderness cut back. They decided that, without Andrew to put up with, this would be about as pleasant a place as any they'd run into on their travels. Besides, they still owned three hundred acres of it. So they bought a sawmill, built a house where the old cabin used to stand and, in time, raised their families here. When the British come along and burnt it, they all turned to and built the one our folks have lived in ever since. Neighbors helped neighbors, in them days, to rebuild a town. I don't doubt they would now if we had the same British and Injun troubles they had.

The boys tried to get Sarah to come back here and live with them, but she never would. She put her foot flat down. "You can thank Frank Cooper and the neighbors for naming the town after me," she told Martin. "But go back there? Not in my casket would I go."

The money she'd sent for the hens came in handy and the people of the town were pretty glad to get it, because after the British frigate got through with the settlement, they needed a new schoolhouse. So they built one with Sarah's money. To pay her back they named the town

Thomasville. I guess most anyone could see why they didn't care to call it Scottsville.

And that was how Grandfather's manuscript ended.

Time ticked over in the walls of the house. In the night, Matilda Scott could hear it. It was only a beetle, whose small sound was faster than the slow, ruminant *tick* and then *tock* of the grandfather clock in the hall, measuring time now, but the time in the wall seemed, somehow, more truthful to go by. She could remember, dimly, Great-great-grandfather Nathan, born in 1803, only four years after George Washington died. Someway it had always seemed strange that his one life stretched from her own time almost all the way back to Washington's.

She herself had lived almost a century, from 1862 to 1952. Through Grandfather Walter she had known Sarah Thomas, the beginning; and down the road was her great-grandson Walter's house, where his boy, Henry, was eighteen months old.

A *tick* and then a *tock* measured time for children, slow and lasting, as if forever. "God love you, Tilly," Grandfather Walter used to say. "Time hasn't even begun to move for you yet." But time for her now slipped by like the shadow of a cloud on a mountain. Tomorrow would be her ninetieth birthday.

"Oh, that old soap opera!" Aaron Falls said. "She walked over a mountain with her goods and her kids piled on a dogsled hauled by an old cow and none of them had any underdrawers, not even the cow. You honestly believe that, Aunty?" He grinned at his great-grand aunt, and she glanced back at him with one eyebrow cocked. She was used to his kidding, often gave him back as good as he sent, and the members of the family who had come to her birthday party settled back to see how she would do it this time. The consensus was that anyone ought to think twice before he needled Gran Matilda, but of course young Aaron was a show-off—he liked to be in the limelight, particularly in a crowd of people, and quite a number of relatives had showed up for her ninetieth, some of them from out of town.

"Well," the old lady said placidly, "it doesn't seem to me that Sarah's story spreads around quite so much suds as soap operas do. All the dust-ups and tough luck and so on that happen in them ain't too different from what happens to real people, only not often for entertainment. And it's a fact that her boy Walter did have two fingers missing from his left hand. Around here, those days, they called him Eight-fingered Walt."

"I heard," Aaron said, "a bear bit them off."

"There was a bear. He wasn't walking over the mountain to see what he could see. He was after the cow."

"Why wasn't he tucked away for the winter? Come on, Aunty."

"You go stuff up your gob with cake and quit being picky." She glanced around at her family, her eyes sparkling. "You hear him?" she said. "According to the old folks tell, the fault of being a loud-mouth has come straight down from Andrew Scott himself. We get one in every generation, it's like being yellow-headed. Are you all going to sit around and listen to him Scott-up a good story?"

A roar of laughter went up; someone whistled, and a voice called out, "That settles you, Aaron, you old yeller-head!"

Aaron grinned at the old lady and patted her cheek. There was never any ill-feeling over these passages between them. She always expected him to make fun of the ancestors, say their old stories were for the birds. "God love you, you old white-tailed hornet," he said. "I better give up before you start in on my love life."

He sat down next to his girl-of-the-moment, Annabelle Franklin, who was firmly established near a big platter of birthday cake with two of his cousins, Paulus Scott and Amanda Willis. "Scoot the cake over here, will you, somebody?" he said, a trifle glumly.

Annabelle said, "You got your gob good and well stuffed up that time; you don't need cake."

Paulus grinned, stretched a long arm for the platter.

"Look out!" Annabelle said. She slid her hand under Aaron's wrist, but too late. The sleeve of his smart gray jacket had drabbled into the frosting, which was nearly an inch thick and gooey. It had left a sticky streak halfway to his elbow.

"Oh, hell!" Aaron said. "That'll look great at the dance tonight." He grabbed a wad of paper napkins and started rubbing at the streak, getting nowhere, because the paper at once disintegrated; paper shreds stuck to the material only made matters worse. "What to hell was that made out of—putty?" he grunted, meaning the frosting. "You'll stick to me for keeps, Annabee, if I don't get that off."

"I've no intention of sticking to you for keeps," she said. "You're in love with a boat. A great, big, fishy-smelling dragger." She smiled at him. "So what chance have I got?"

Cora Willis, Amanda's sister-in-law, spoke up from across the table. "I made that frosting and it ain't putty. If you want to know, it's a masterpiece. If you'll stop in the house after the party's over, I'll take that off for you in a jiffy, just to show I ain't got no hard feelings, you blaming me because you Scott-ed that one up."

Aaron, comforted, grinned at her. "You're the only one here that loves me, Code. I'll come in, happy to, and I won't blame you for sticking me into the same cubbyhole with I-don't-know-how-many-greats, old Granpop Nathan."

No one, nowadays, least of all Aaron, took seriously the tattered piece of folklore, dating from Nathan Scott's time, about some of the early Scotts being well-known butterfingers. Somewhere in the past, the family had had an extraordinary run of hard luck. Houses burnt down, vessels sank, or, being launched, fell off the ways. Large projects and small had somehow got bumbled up and had come to grief. This series of catastrophes had been ransacked out of old newspaper records by a patient reporter on the Thomasville *Times*, who had used them to point up his article about Nathan Scott's loss, through an oversight, of the barque *William Carey* in 1863. For a while, in those days, a family mistake or plan gone awry might well have been commented on by a neighbor, "Well, Scott-ed that one up, didn't they?"

Grandfather Walter, recalling the story of the *Carey* for young Matilda, began it with a snort of disgust. "So they was butterfingers, was they? Well, enough of it rubbed off of their fingers to leave us all setting in a buttertub, when we come to heir the money they left. What happened to the *William Carey* wasn't Nathan's fault. Wasn't anything to blame, except the weather. She was a British barque of London, bound from Callao to Saint John, New Brunswick, via Saint Thomas. In the Gulf of Maine, she run into one of the worst tornadiums the folks of the time remembered, and she anchored outside our harbor here, three miles off, distress signals flying. Nathan called for volunteers, got together a crew for a dory and they rowed out and boarded the *Carey*. Had quite a time doing it, what with the tide and the gale smacking into each other, head-on.

"Nathan took charge, told her skipper to slip chains and he'd take her into one of the safest harbors on the coast. They come in flying hellity-hoot, past the outside ledges, before the wind like a bird on the wing.

"Now, the *Carey*'s skipper, it turned out, in his scramble up the coast, had had to let slip a number of chains, leave some anchors behind him; the only one left was a small one, but he'd thought that coming into one of the safest harbors on the coast he wouldn't need more than that. He didn't tell Nathan so, and Nathan hadn't thought to ask him or to tell him that in a southerly the wind bulled up this harbor like through a funnel. That light anchor didn't even make the *Carey* hiccup. She piled up high and dry on the west harbor beach. All hands was saved along with her cargo, but she went to pieces there. Total loss. Quite a lot of the townspeople benefited—got wood and furnishings out of her. You can see the things now, if you know what to look for in some of the old houses."

Matilda, Gran Scott now, with two greats before her name, looked down the picnic table and smiled a little, to herself.

There's no doubt, she thought, that some of us, mostly on the yellow-headed side, has been butterfingers in a big way. Without our black-haired ones, I don't know where on earth the family'd be.

There were Paulus and Amanda, brother and sister, her two remaining grandchildren, slim and limber as witherods, hair black as coal and curly, the way her own had been once; and there, at last year's birthday party, had been their older brother, Ralph, dead now, whose hair had been yellow as a marigold. And there sat Aaron, a splendid sample of the yellow-headed side.

He had blue eyes, pink cheeks and a wild thatch of

reddish-gold curls which pushed off his head any hat that wasn't a sou'wester with a strap fastened under his chin. He was big-boned and heavy; his feet thumped when he walked. At thirteen, he had stood six feet tall and had weighed two hundred pounds. At twenty-eight, he had slimmed down some, but his mother, Sarah Falls, said that hearing him come downstairs now you might expect to see a barrel of apples.

Years ago. Morgan, who had felled a pine tree on top of himself and had died under it. Nathan and the *Carey*. A whole list of catastrophes, which Grandfather Walter had remembered, or had found in old records. And last January, Ralph, who had somehow managed to go overboard in New York harbor from the deck of the cargo-boat on which he'd been third officer.

She mustn't think about Ralph. Not today. Bumbler he may have been, but there'd been something endearing about his bumbling, even when you knew that you could probably count on it. Of all her grandchildren, he had been her favorite, the nearest one, the apple of her eye. Not that she had ever shown it. She had brought them up, Ralph and Paulus and Amanda, after their parents had died in a flu epidemic, and never in their lives had she shown that she loved one more than another. She had loved him best, perhaps, because he so desperately needed loving. The other two had always been all right in themselves, confident and brainy, able to cope.

Don't dwell on it, she told herself firmly. The sad things are over and done with, nothing you can do about them now. People have come here today to see me and to have a good time. And grief is heavy but it is fragile, too, like a bubble ready to burst and show. Today, anyhow, is the younger generation's day. And Ralph's boys, looks like, are going to need some help, as much as he did. Not Walter—he was twenty-one, on his own now, with a fine wife and child of his own. But George, fifteen, and Jesse, twelve—now that their father was gone, neglect showed on them like a disease.

She glanced down the table at their mother, Ralph's widow, Gladys. Gladys was in black, but obviously not in mourning. Her expensive dress was sparkling with costume jewelry of one kind and another; earrings dangled; rings glittered; bracelets clacked together as she reached now here, now there, rummaging in the platters of goodies. Her plate was piled high, surrounded with the debris of her eating—peach and olive pits, banana skins, nut shells and such. Most people had finished, but Gladys was still happily plowing through the picnic.

She eats, Matilda thought, like a starving hyena. Thank God Paulus will be home for good at the end of July.

Arrow-straight, the old lady sat at the head of her table in her simple black dress with the white vest and choker and the necklace of carved wooden beads she always wore to parties. Her hair, once shining black, caught light from the shifting shade of the big maple tree under which the long trestle table had been set. A tiny woman, too frail it would seem, to be the only living source, the genesis now, of this husky throng of family—the yellow-haired and stocky, the black-haired and slim, the intermediate dark and light children.

Paulus had once remarked that Sarah Thomas and Andrew Scott must both have had damn powerful genes, if her black curls and Andrew's shock of yellow ones were still showing up after the family had been married into for so many generations. Aaron kidded Gran sometimes, saying that he knew for a fact that there was a Penobscot Indian mixed up back along there; she said no reason to believe there wasn't. Out on the water or in any strong sunlight, the fair ones would sunburn and peel; the dark ones never did. Their lean cheeks tanned

leather-brown; they were fast on their feet, splendid run-
ners and dancers. The men stood tall and slim, like Paulus.
They were all great story-tellers and singers, who, as the
old lady did, tried to recapture the past, bring it back
to life.

Paulus was thirty-eight. He had joined the Navy at
eighteen, before World War II, and now, after twenty
years of service, was retiring soon on his Chief Warrant
Officer's pension. He had managed to wangle a few days'
leave to come home for Gran's party.

"Damned if you ain't going to look funny out of that
monkey jacket," Aaron told him. "I don't recall ever seeing you without one. Well, so there'll be another of you
black-headed tribe loafing around here whilst the rest
of us poor slobs got to work. Only, with you, you'll be
off the Town Poor List. That old Navy pension, hanh?"

"That's right. You can come and watch me loaf with
my feet stuck in the oven."

"You looking forward to it?"

"Yes and no," Paulus said slowly. He glanced down at
his neat Navy dress uniform. "Yes, I guess I am. Been a
long haul. Long enough for your cake to taste of salt
water because I touched the platter."

"Would I know it if it did? Kee-riced, you war mongrels
ain't the only ones drink salt water, boy. I make my
coffee with it."

The party was breaking up. The smaller fry were already tired and restless; mothers were rooting the younger
generation out from under, on top of and around the
table. Other women, including Gran, were scraping and
stacking dishes. Gladys was eating serenely on, from a
row of platters pulled close to her plate.

For some time Paulus had been aware of a small, un-
obtrusive presence which occasionally hovered near him—
behind his back or at his elbow. It was Jesse, he knew,

Ralph's youngest, who apparently wanted to say something, or, perhaps, to get acquainted. Paulus had been so long away, home only on his leaves, that he hadn't known Ralph's boys very well, mostly as an absent uncle who had forked out a tip or brought home a present. But today, each time Paulus had looked around, Jesse had vanished, either into the lawn shrubbery or around the back of the house. He did this again, just as Paulus opened his mouth to say, "Hi, Jess."

"Now you see it, now you don't," Aaron said. "Gladys better put a rein on them two kids of hers. That George is a hellion; he raises Cain all over town and Jesse tails him. They always look like hell, too. Ma says Glad-rags lets them run like that, so's folks'll realize how poor she is, now Ralph's gone. You'd think she'd dress 'em up halfway decent for Gran's party; looks like she's got plenty to put on her own goddamn back."

Paulus had, without seeming to, been watching his brother's sons, who had stood out like dirty tramps among the other children. Of course, it was an outdoor picnic and nobody was really slicked up, but most of the play clothes were clean. George didn't seem to give a hoot about the filthy rags he had on. He had flashed around making noise with some cronies his own age and had left with them as soon as food was served and eaten. Paulus could hear them wrassling around in the yard back of the house. But Jesse obviously minded the sight of his kneecap, a white, skinny knob like a smutty egg, poking out through the hole in the leg of his pants. He kept twitching the hole to one side so it wouldn't show; and Paulus was touched, remembering himself at that age—the shame and embarrassment he'd always felt at the notion of standing out in a crowd, being conspicuous, being different.

George, he thought. George looks like Ralph all over

again, but Jesse, with his looks, he could be mine. He could be my own son, if I'd ever had one. If I'd ever wanted one.

Needed a haircut, both kids did, and George's spectacular dirty neck could be seen across the lawn. The neatness Paulus had learned in the Navy had made him fussy, he guessed. A kid was almost always a dirty kid, so what? But a neglected kid, that was different. Wonder what Walter thinks about this, if maybe he ought to take a hand.

No. He supposed Walter wouldn't. He would have nothing to do with his mother, had not been near her house since she had thrown him out of it. He had come over here to the farmhouse to live and had been like a son to Gran and Amanda, seeing his father when Ralph had made one of his rare visits home, but otherwise taking very little interest in Gladys, her works or ways. Whether or not he bothered with his young brothers, Paulus didn't know. He glanced over at Walter, who was sitting with his wife and baby as far away as he could get from Gladys, and Walter, catching his eye, grinned and waved a hand. His son, Henry, joined in sociably, pounding on the table with a spoon; Walter grabbed away a glass of fruit juice just in time.

A voice with a clang to it, unmistakably Gladys's, called out, "Excuse me, Gran Matilda, but them old stories you put out and around, I don't see how they could be anything but made-up yarns, unless you was there yourself. How could you know all them facts unless maybe you was?"

The old lady did not look up from the plate she was scraping. "Which story bothers you?" she asked mildly.

"Well, that one about the vessel somebody's old ancestor wrecked, you'd have had to be aboard of her, wouldn't you?"

"Not really. We know quite a lot about the *William Carey* from old newspaper accounts. She was built of teak, a wood that never decays. The stair-rail and banisters in our house are made from it. The captain's dresser with all the nice little drawers in it came from the *Carey*. You've sat in front of it all the numberless times you've come to meals in our dining room. Surely you must have seen the newspaper clippings the day you went upstairs to my room and fossicked around in my scrapbook. If you're afraid you'll spoil your dress helping us clear away, I could lend you an apron."

Aaron snorted and choked back a roar. "God, I love that old gal," he muttered in Paulus's ear. "Talk about a gob-stopper!"

Gladys had indeed eaten numberless meals at the farmhouse. She would appear just as the family was about to sit down, sniffing at the food smells and peering at the kitchen counter to see what was for dessert. "Oh!" she would cry. "Fish and potater and pork scraps, Amanda, I do love it so!" or "Oh, a biled dinner! And don't that corn beef look good!" Uninvited, she would pull up a chair, paying no attention when Walter and Cora Willis, Gran's housekeeper, took their plates to the kitchen.

Amanda did not mind feeding her so long as she brought George and Jesse with her—she was glad to give them a square meal whenever she got a chance to. But more often than not Gladys came alone, and when she did, Amanda would wish, devoutly, that nobody had ever started the family tradition, unbroken for generations, which hung, carved on a wooden plaque, over the dining room mantelpiece:

NOBODY EVER LEAVES THIS HOUSE HUNGRY

Gladys, if challenged, would have said that she had a perfect right to eat meals at the farm, or to look through the rooms in the house when she had a mind to, because she was Ralph's wife and he was one of the heirs, owned a third of the whole property. She had never been known to recognize a snub, or a gob-stopper, either. She smiled pleasantly at Gran, and said, "No, thank you, for the offer of an apron. I've got to get home. I've got a sayonce this evening, people coming, I can't stay. Where's Jesse? Anybody seen him?"

For years, she had been a practicing medium and a successful one. She charged high prices for a séance and what she called a "thing-reading"; she had a loyal following of local ladies, and clients came from all over the area to take advantage of her second-sight. In summer, she always reaped a harvest from the tourists.

She got up to leave, making a circle to pass the place where Paulus sat. "Hell-o, Paulus," she cried out. "How lovely to see you. And don't you look handsome in your blue uniform!"

"Thanks," Paulus said.

"I want to talk to you-oo, before you go back."

He knew well what she wanted to talk about—any money that Ralph possibly might have left, in case Paulus could tell her where it was. Ralph had willed her his house, free and clear, but his safety deposit box at the bank had contained only a few keepsakes and a paper, signed and witnessed, making Paulus the legal guardian of his sons; nothing whatever about the farm property.

"Yes. All right. But there's no time now. You'll have to wait till I get home for good in July."

"Now, look. I'm just getting along by the skin of my teeth. You saw my boys today. I can't even afford decent clothes for them."

"So it would seem. Tell them to go over to the store and Amanda'll fit them out with new shirts and jeans."

"Oh, you ain't got any idea how they *eat*. I ain't able to begin to pay for food for them."

Paulus glanced at the stylish black dress.

"Oh, I know. My dress. I got to keep up appearances in my business, you know that."

"Look, Gladys, you're not destitute. I talked to Ralph in New York, just before he—"

"Ralph, for heaven's sake! You never could believe a word he said, even if you caught him when he wasn't half-sloshed. What I want is his share for the farm that that old woman's trying to do me out of."

Paulus's temper had a low flashpoint, and this was enough. "You stow that kind of talk," he said between his teeth. "We all know what was the matter with Ralph and it wasn't booze." He walked away and left her standing. In his fury, he almost bumped into Joe Falls, Aaron's father, who fell into step beside him.

"Hard to believe," Joe said. "There's people all over the works that pay that gloriosa daisy good money for telling their fortunes and fetching their dead to life. Look, I've got to talk to you about her kids, Polly. Is there anything you can do about getting them to come live over at the farm, the way young Walt did? Because if they keep on the way they're going, they'll be in trouble with the law and I'll have to take steps."

Joe was, among other things, town constable. In his younger days, he had gone lobster fishing, but now he owned a small commercial greenhouse and made part of his living selling flowers.

"We can't get hold of them legally unless she heaves them out of the house, the way she did Walt." Paulus had already gone into that side of the question with a lawyer in New York. "You can't part children from their mother, seems, without a hammer and a chisel. She's got to be proved immoral, or the kids show signs of abuse."

"Well, there's a flock of female flitterbugs would rise up and call her holy if you called her immoral," Joe said. "She's respectable, Gladys is, if nothing else. But them kids, my God, Polly!"

"What have they been up to, Joe?"

"George is light-fingered with cigarettes and candy around the stores, I know that for a fact. There's been some talk about his lugging off lobster traps that get cast up down along the shore, which is against the law. Some traps been found sunk in the pond behind the cove beach. Latest thing is, they been running with a batch of young sprigs that've got the notion of hassling the tourists. Started out with yelling at them, go home, fatso, nobody wants you here, like of that. Holler-and-run stuff. I run in young Rod Colcraft for it, and the Judge put him on probation. Since then, there've been worse actions, like splattering some poor guy's windshield with red paint."

"I see," Paulus said slowly. "I'll do what I can, Joe, but I won't be home for good until July. You said anything to Walter about this?"

"Not much use to. I guess you know that. He don't see much of George, don't think much of him. Says he's his mother's business, not any of his mix. And Jesse, well, he sees Jesse. Every time Walt and Aaron get in from fishing, Gladys sends Jesse down to ask how much they made on the trip."

"Oh, for godsake!"

"Crazy, ain't it? Well, now, Polly, I'll hold off if I can till you get home for keeps. But I d'no. Some of the storekeepers is oary-eyed about kids bothering the tourists. Ain't very good for business."

"No, shouldn't think it would be." Paulus was thoughtful, remembering himself at fifteen . . . George's age. "Didn't you ever feel like hollering at the tourists, Joe?"

"Jeezis, yes. I live for Labor Day." Joe grinned. "You don't appear to change much, Polly. I d'no but you'd be a pretty good one to give them kids a talking to. Okay?"

"Okay," Paulus said. "I'll have a go at it, Joe." And a fat lot of good it'll do, he told himself.

The property which Gran Matilda had inherited from her grandfather was considerable—a working dairy and stock farm, with hayfields, pastures and woodlots. A smart businesswoman in her day, she had added to it a big general store in town, which now included the Post Office. Later, when old age began catching up with her, she had deeded the entire property to Paulus and Amanda and Amanda's husband, Frank Willis, now dead; she had planned the original deed to include Ralph on equal shares, but Ralph had refused pointblank to accept any of it.

"Look, Gran," he'd said. "You must know that anything I own Gladys is over like a tent. I won't have her sticking her nose into the farm business, which she would like a shot if I owned a third of it. Lord God, she'd be up here living, séances and all, drive you all crazy. Take over, and no legal way to stop her. So thanks, old girl, but no. I'm all right the way I am, getting along fine."

She wondered if he were. She had watched for years the change which the disaster of his marriage had made in him. For all his bumbling, he had been an amiable and humorous young fellow, and some of his casual ways had still showed, but each time he had come home, which was seldom, he had seemed more exhausted, more wrung dry. At thirty, he had begun to look like an old man. Gladys had put it out and around town that he drank like a fish, but Gran didn't believe her. If he did, he hadn't ever come to see her with liquor on his breath. Irresponsible? No. This was a valuable property he was turning down.

"You sure, Ralphie? You're entitled to a third share, you know."

"I'm sure."

"Then let me give you your share in cash. I could, without too much of a wrench."

"Don't do that, either. She'd have it out of me before I could get to the bank with it."

"For heaven's sake, you don't have to knuckle under like that. Why not slap her sideways and have an end to it?"

"No one does that to Gladys, Gran, not without paying for it. Look, I'm seldom home. Even if I stayed, I couldn't . . ." He paused, then went on with a slow, desperate patience in his voice which seemed dreadful to her, remembering what he had once been like. "If I don't toe the line with her the way she wants, she takes it out on the kids, and she knows I know it."

"Then they ought to be taken away from her. We'd love to have them here."

"God, I wish they could be. But they can't, not without Gladys." His voice wavered and stopped. He sat looking at the floor.

"Ralphie, there's more to this than meets the eye. Tell me. I used to be able to help."

"That's right. There is. I guess you've forgot that down under all this sog, I've got a black temper that I can't handle once I lose it. Remember the time I damn nigh killed Eph Stevens for putting kerosene on a cat and setting her afire?"

"Pity you hadn't," Gran said. Yes, she did remember. It had taken three men to haul Ralph off of Eph and then still hold him back. It had been the only time in her life she had seen Ralph mad. No wonder she'd forgotten his temper.

"If I ever started in on Gladys, my hands would take over," he said slowly. "I'd murder her."

"Yes, I believe you would." Gran did believe it, remembering what she had seen.

"If you want to help me, you could put my share of the farm in trust for my kids and fix it so that Gladys can't ever touch a cent of it."

"Of course I will. Through the bank here, I'll set up a trust, in Paulus's name. Your share of the farm isn't peanuts, honey, and the income from it is yours as long as you live."

"No. I want the kids to have it all. The way things are, they'll need it, every cent."

"All right. It'll go to the children. With strict instructions that Gladys can't touch a cent of it. Unless you tell her she won't know anything about it."

"Good. That takes an awful heavy load off my mind. Good-by and God love you, Gran."

After that, Ralph came home only rarely—perhaps once in two years. The time came when he would never come again. Members of the cargo steamer's crew had heard a cry and a splash. They had thrown life jackets overside and, as quickly as they could, had launched a boat, but could find no sign of him. It was January; the East River current was running fast with floating icecakes. He hadn't had a chance. They knew it and gave up.

Ralph's disappearance had made up Paulus's mind about retiring from the Navy. He had always loved the farm, had thought about it with loneliness in weird places all over the seven seas. But could he find work enough at home to keep him busy? After all, he had been a wanderer since his boyhood, a citizen of nowhere but the world, had gone where the Navy had taken him for twenty years.

Thirty-eight wasn't any age for a man to give up the job he was good at, which was in the engine rooms of battleships. Engines of one kind and another had been the love of his life. At the farm, he'd be as lost as a stray dog and about as much use as one. He couldn't see running the farm or helping Amanda in the store; he'd go nuts. Both of those jobs were well taken care of anyway. Amanda and Gran said they needed him around—a man in the house—but the thing was, they didn't really, not that he could see.

For years, Amanda and her husband, Frank Willis, had taken care of things at home, Frank working the farm, Amanda as storekeeper and postmistress. After Frank's death six years ago, their neighbor, Set-Fire Linscott, who had been foreman for Frank, had offered to run the farm for Amanda. Not as a hired man—he made that plain. He didn't care to work any longer for wages, it stifled a man—but as a partner on a share basis.

"That'll depend on whether I can show you I can make the farm prosper," he'd told Amanda.

Under his supervision, the farm had prospered as never before, and nobody had ever regretted the arrangement.

Set-Fire, whose given name was Chester, had got his nickname because his byword was "Set fire!" and because he was a moderate man who was seldom known to move fast. Some joker had once remarked that it took Set-Fire ten minutes to round a sharp corner. But work he had to do got done and done well and didn't take too long, either. Backing up his brown, craggy face and modest manners was a brain as sharp as a gimlet—a brain the joker would have been pleased to own if he had known he didn't have it.

After Set-Fire's wife had left him and had taken their two children with her, he had lived alone in his house next to the south boundary of the Scott farm. "She up'n took off'n gone," he had once told Amanda. "I found I could use the room she took up." But he had missed his children. He showed Amanda snapshots of them which he carried in his wallet. "Lord, they'd be growed up by now. Ain't heard a word of any of 'em since Lily divorced me. No idea in the god's world where they might be."

Set-Fire was now forty-five. He liked children. Any kids were welcome to track around with him. If they raised hell, he said, he didn't care, it only showed they were kids. After young Walter's final row with his mother, he had left home in the clothes he stood up in and had gone, first, over to Set-Fire's house.

"Good, you come and batch it with me," Set-Fire'd told him. "Time I had something young around here besides calves and piglets."

During Paulus's absence, Set-Fire had suggested to Amanda that they add pigs to their other stock. "Plenty of room for them in them big sheds back of the barn. But what I'd like to do is build modern pens and yards along the south line, let the critters run free till fattenen time, in my fenced-in north field. And not any low-grade pigs, neither, but a good breed that'll grow sweet pork on'm. A pig, now, is fun. He's brighter'n some humans and he's a clean critter too, if he's took care of clean."

The pig-farm had expanded. Set-Fire was now known all over the State for the pedigreed, healthy pigs he bred and traded. His cows furnished milk and butter for his own and Amanda's households, as well as for the dairy section at the store; his herd of Black Angus provided them with beef. The meat department specialized in fresh and salt pork, prime beef, chickens, and home-cured hams. He himself supervised the butchering, pickling and curing. His delicately flavored hams melted in the summer people's mouths at summer season prices. In any season he could have sold twice his supply, even though he kept increasing his stock. The farm now kept two, sometimes three, hired men busy.

No place for me there, Paulus told himself. I'm no farmer. What I'd be, I guess, as a civilian, would be a good mechanic.

The only hobby he had besides reading—he had always been a great reader of anything he could lay hands on and lug aboard ship, from comic books on up—was antiques. He'd always had an eye for them, had been fascinated by things past and old, and had a pretty good collection of things which he had picked up here and there in his travels and had had shipped home to Amanda. But the mental picture of himself running an antique shop seemed absurd.

He had almost made up his mind to sign over for another hitch in the Navy when he had had the talk with Ralph, five months ago, in New York. His own destroyer was lying in the harbor and he was delighted to find that Ralph's ship was there, too. He was also delighted to see that Ralph looked like a new man. His haggard, stricken look was gone; the color was back in his face and his wide grin was the one Paulus remembered, before his brother had got hung up with wife trouble.

"God, I'm glad to see you, Polly," Ralph said, grabbing at his hand. "You look like a million dollars."

"So do you." Paulus slatted his hand, which felt as if it had been wrung off at the wrist.

"Do, don't I? Must be the sea air. Come on, there's a good little bar along here with booths, where we can talk private."

He went charging along the pier and Paulus followed reluctantly. Damn the bar, he thought. I don't want to sit around and see the old boy get tanked up, I want to talk to him.

But Ralph, it seemed, had no notion of getting tanked up. He ordered double whiskeys and tasted his, then left the glass sitting. "Let me take a load off your mind, Polly," he said. "I ain't gone on the wagon. Thing is, I ain't ever been off it. You ain't seen me anywheres but at home for years, have you?"

"That's right," Paulus said. "But sometimes, around there, I've wondered. . . ." There had been talk, too.

"The ship I'm on, the way the skipper is, if I was ever a lush, I'd've been chucked off of her years ago," Ralph said. "We've always been pretty open with each other, Polly. I don't recall ever lying to you."

"You don't have to say that."

"No, I know it. Fact is, I ain't ever forgot what Gramp used to say about liquor." He grinned. "Remember him and the wine?"

Their Grandfather Dennis had taught them both to respect liquor. He himself had respected it and had used it moderately as a fine thing a civilized man was entitled to. Gramp had been a talented man and he had passed to his grandsons one of his talents, which was how to make wine out of the available fruits of the countryside. It had been excellent wine—apple, raspberry, elderberry, blackberry, dandelion—the old man had tried about anything there was around and most of it had come out a masterpiece. Two kinds hadn't: parsnips had made wine but it hadn't tasted good to him, and spinach, experimented with once, had been abandoned forever. Paulus grinned, recalling Gramp's face when he'd tasted what had come from spinach. "Good God!" the old man had said. "It's come out turtle piss!"

Ralph went on. "Gladys was always more comfortable to live with if she had something rotten about me she could put out and around to the neighbors. So whenever

I come home I had a rum bottle I hid around the house for her to find. Took a swig once in a while and breathed on her. That was all it was."

"She put it out and around all right," Paulus said. "I will say I had trouble believing it. Gran never believed it."

Ralph nodded. "I know she didn't. Well, leave that. I've got things to tell you you've got to know. First place, I've made my last trip home. I ain't ever going back there."

"Not even to see your kids?"

"They've learnt not to miss me. I wouldn't want any one of them to see me kill their mother, or have it to remember that I had."

Jolted, Paulus stared at him. "Good Lord, Ralph, I know she's got something coming, but—"

"Wait. Walt's all right, he's on his own, making his own way. Gladys can't get at him, he's over twenty-one. George has got too big to lick. It's Jesse I worry about. She's always made the kids help her with them goddamn séances. It never bothered Walt or George to hide in the cubbyhole and go tunk-tunk and scratch-scratch to let the fool customers know the spirits was coming. They're both tough-skinned enough to think it was fun. But Walt's left home and George's outgrown the cubbyhole, so Jesse has to do it. And Jesse ain't tough-skinned. He's like them seabirds, them shags that sink in the water if their feathers get too wet, except they can get out and dry their wings. Jesse can't. He sinks."

"If she's that much of a fake, why don't people know about it? Why haven't the kids told us? Even Walter, he's never mentioned it. My God, Ralph."

"All right. Leave that, too, for now. Fake, sure. A healthy crow's got more second-sight than Gladys has.

Her mother in Nova Scotia had it, I guess some people
do, and she and her sister was brought up on séances.
Learnt the ropes enough to put on a show, without any of
the gimmick to go with it. Her sister, lives in California,
got quite well known as a medium, Madame Preston her
business name was, but she had to haul in her horns and
cool off some when her husband, Hank Preston, got shoved
in the slammer. He had a racket going with her of rounding up girls in the family way who wasn't married. He'd
tell them where to go to have the baby unbeknownst and
to leave it there, no questions asked. They used to peddle
the babies around to people who couldn't get one any
other way. Made a lot of dough before the law caught up
with them. The Madame testified at his trial, said she
hadn't a notion in the world of what he was up to. Said
if any of the girls who attended her séances, which, after
all, was snow-white, holy religious services, had been in
the family way, she hadn't known it. She got out of it
but Preston died in jail. You look somewhat sick, Polly."

"Well, I could puke if there was a basin handy. How'd
you know all this, Ralph?"

"Gladys has always been wovelled up with her, hand
in glove. They write to each other. Twelve years ago,
when Jesse was born, Gladys was bound and determined
to take him to Madame Preston, said we could get a fortune for him. I told her then that if she did, I'd kill her.
I guess I made it stick because she backed down on it,
never brought it up again. Except she's made it plain that
she hates my guts because I done her out of a fortune.
She hates the kids, too, treats them like dirt.

"Now she's had three-quarters of my wages sent regular to her every month, for years. She's told the boys, got
them to believing it, that I've never sent a cent home,
that all that keeps the place going is what she makes in

her business, fake or no fake, that it's up to them to help her and keep their traps shut, because if she goes under, she'll ship them off to the orphanage, and that's that."

"Ralph, this is . . . Walter would have told us."

"Walt good and well knows what a hell she can make of life at home, when anybody crosses her. He's staying out of it and I don't blame him. He won't do anything to make it tougher than it is for George and Jesse. Besides, he's had to swallow Gladys so long that he's like me—it's all through him like rank poison."

"You could divorce her, at least get the kids away from her, couldn't you?"

"Uh huh. I've tried. Gladys is pure-glass respectable, she helps people. She conducts religious services. Even then, thanks to her, I was a well-known lush, didn't even try to support my family. I'd have to prove that about Madame Preston, and I couldn't. It was word-of-mouth between Gladys and me. You see?"

"I sure do. How can I help, Ralph?"

Ralph reached in a pocket, pulled out a key. "This is to my safe deposit box in the bank at home. In it is a paper making you legal guardian of my kids, in place of a father. All right with you?"

"Of course it is, if it's something you need. You aren't going to do anything foolish, are you?"

"I ain't going to kill myself, if that's what you mean. I'm leaving for good, is all. Going to the place where I've always wanted to go and settle down there."

Paulus nodded. "The South Pacific? That place you always used to talk about, right?"

"God, I hate to ask you. Dump my responsibilities on you all in a heap. But—"

"Look, Ralph, I don't blame you, not a damn bit. I'd rather think of you safe on the other side of the world than in jail for murder for the rest of your life. Go on out there and find yourself a nice tan girl with no tongue in her head, who'll make you happy for the rest of time. Godalmighty, you've got it coming."

Deeply concerned and more than a little appalled, Paulus was trying hard not to let anything show. "Hell of a father I'll make, old boy; I don't know a kid from a bagful of monkey wrenches. But I'll try my best."

Ralph got up. "Then God bless you forever, Polly, if I don't see you again."

Paulus stared after him as he went out and closed the door behind him. Well, that was one solution, probably the best one. There was no doubt whatever that Ralph had meant what he'd said. If he had gone home again, he would have killed Gladys.

The booth seemed bleak and lonely now that Ralph had gone. His all but untouched glass of whiskey was on the table, as if he had stepped out a moment and ought to be coming back.

If I weren't getting out of the Navy, I might get to the South Pacific again sometime and see him, Paulus thought. Absently, he finished his own drink. He's going not because he wants to, but because he's got to. He's chucking the whole lot of us, and it's as rough on him as it is on us. Maybe his way isn't the best way, but he thinks it is and, after all, it's up to him. He's got to get somewhere in peace, put himself together again. Easy to see that just the idea of going's helped him start to do it, too.

And I'm needed at home. That's for sure.

The bartender, passing the booth, looked in. "Guy didn't like his booze?" he asked, all ready to defend the brand.

"Had to leave in a hurry," Paulus said. "Don't worry,

it's good whiskey." He picked up Ralph's drink, held it a moment as if making a toast, then drained the glass.

"Forget his key?"

"Nope. That's my key." Paulus picked it up, thrust it into his pocket. Slowly he made his way back to his ship.

Gladys had called on her second-sight and was able to tell the world that Ralph had fallen overboard while drunk. She told the sewing group at the Ladies' Aid, where she was popular with some, that she had been in touch with the Other World about it. Ralph had never showed up, she said, in any of the Sacred Places; if he had, she would not have spoken to him. Her spiritual companions were very high-class people, kings and queens of yore, once in a while a princess. In her opinion, Ralph had landed in hell. Not in her whole life had she called up a spirit from hell, nor would she stoop to. Evidently, it made no difference to her that Sarah Falls, Ralph's cousin, was there and couldn't help hearing her. Seeing that she'd got no reaction at all from Sarah, Gladys went on to nail her statements down.

"And I've talked to Andrew Scott's spirit, too. He says Ralph is certainly not in Heaven."

Sarah looked up from the intricate design she was embroidering on a pillow slip. Sarah was outspoken, usually, loved to raise issues, and had a fine instinct for a row which she might enjoy. "Andrew Scott? In Heaven?" she asked casually.

"Of course he's in Heaven," Gladys said, unaware of the trap into which she was heading. "He was a *good* man. He's asked me to tell around that all them yarns about him is lies."

"Why, listen to that, girls," Sarah said, very deadpan. "Gladys is saying that all us Scotts go back to the royal kings and queens of England. Andrew's in Heaven and he's got to be a king, because she don't speak to anyone else."

Gladys stared over at Sarah, who got on with her embroidery. "Them kings know what they're talking about. They keep it all in their Great Book of Records. And they don't lower themselves to talk to ordinary people, either. They keep company with one of their own. Sometimes they make an exception with special people, like they done with Andrew Scott."

"My goodness, Gladys." Sarah bit off a thread. "It must have been quite a comedown for them to come across one of their princesses running a fish market in Shubenacketie, wasn't it?"

"If you are trying to make fun of my spiritual powers, let me tell you here and now that all my people has had second-sight. My sister, Madame Preston, is a nationally known medium and a thing-reader as well, like I. We can pick up a thing that belonged to someone we never heard of, maybe died a hundred years ago, and hold it in our hands and it goes hum, hum, hum against our fingers. Tells us anything we want to know about who owned it."

"I be dag," Sarah said.

"You had better be something, dear, trifling with Sacred Powers you don't know nothing about. Great suffering or a turrible sorrow soaks into the thing like dampness, never does go away. That's how we come to have haunted houses and ghosts in the cemetery. The material soaks up the suffering spirit."

Sarah let go with a hoot. She possessed a notable one and some ladies jumped. Others looked shocked. After all, a number of those present were loyal and pious believers in Gladys's powers. "Oh, shoot, Gladys! Honest to God, did you ever see some poor unfortunate go tarryhooting around the graveyard in a white nightdress? Which I don't believe a sensible spirit would do. If any of our menfolks ever come back after such a journey and in whatever shape, it wouldn't be the graveyard they'd head for, it'd be for the dinner table and the nearest cup of coffee or where's the rum bottle."

"If you are speaking of Ralph, a truer word was never spoke. I could pick up one of Ralph's rum bottles that he left all over my house and let it hum to me about where he really is. But I would not touch a rum bottle, even if empty. I have my principles as all the world knows. All I need to do is talk to them old, old kings. They know who's got royal blood and who's worthy of Heaven. Ralph was dead drunk and fell overboard, Scott-ed things up for good, and there ain't no mystery about where he landed to."

"Well, now," Sarah said. "Royal blood and the way it shows up on people sometimes might depend on which one of the old kings you talk to, wouldn't it? Take George the Third. He Scott-ed things almightily up, didn't he?"

The night following the birthday party, after supper, Paulus told Amanda and Gran about his talk with Ralph. "I didn't write this home," he said. "I was going to, and then I thought twice. I don't know how Gladys does it, but seems there isn't a letter that comes into this house that she doesn't get her hands on sooner or later. And I think old Ralph had better stay dead. I felt like hell, putting you two through it, but I couldn't see what else to do. I'm sorry, Gran."

"Well, it's over now," she said briskly. "I think you did just right. And so did he, God love him. You say he looked better, like himself again?"

"Sure did. Looked ten years younger."

"Well, thank God. I feel some younger myself. As if

the stone had rolled away. You think we can do something about the boys?"

"I'll try. I don't see stirring Gladys up now and leaving you two to cope, and I'll have to catch the plane tomorrow, but July's coming. I've done what I could in the time I've had—had a talk with Joe Falls and one with Set-Fire. He and I both think that the reason George is squirreling away busted-up lobster traps is because he wants to do what Walt did, have a boat and traps of his own, earn his living that way. Can't see how else to do it. So I've told Set to keep his eye open for a good stout skiff. If George wants it, Set'll lay in some trap-stock, show George how to build his own traps, forget the busted-up ones. That's a beginning. I don't think either one of the boys can be pried away from Gladys, but she certainly can't object to George earning his own living."

Amanda snorted. "She'll take every penny he makes, the way she tried to with Walter. And she doesn't need to. Walter told me that he sneaked a peek at her bank book one time she forgot to lock the drawer it was in. She's made a mint from those fake séances, got it all tucked away."

"She'll have to be stomped on," Gran said. "She can be. Your grandfather did, the time she caught him and Ralph brewing up a kittleful of dandelions in the kitchen, and went and put out all around town that that sinful old man was a drunken bum. That rumor stopped. Then, at that time, it stopped cold, after Dennis went down and stomped on Gladys."

"Well, I'm not too good a stomper on anyone, I guess," Paulus said. "I'm still the peaceable boob who got so scared off Iwo Jima that I wasted a good steak dinner off the destroyer's fantail."

"Thank God you still ain't," Gran said. "But I expect you did all right, when the time came. Two war medals went through this house like a scared cat before I even had time to see what they was for. I wish you'd leave them out so I could."

Paulus grinned at her. "You'd hang them on the wall in plain sight, wouldn't you?"

"I certainly would. But I don't expect I will. I'll settle for you being smart, dear. You're a comfort to me."

"Good. What we do now is, I guess, you two keep an eye on Ralph's kids as well as you can, till I get home for keeps. If Gladys comes around hassling you about Ralph's share of the farm, tell her he haunts it and you've seen him."

The next morning Paulus stopped by the bank and arranged to have some cash from the interest from Gran's trust put into a checking account. He wrote a sizable check for Walter and drove down in one of the farm jeeps to leave it at his house, which was out on the point on the western side of the harbor. The mooring where he and Aaron kept their fishing dragger was empty, so he judged that Walter wouldn't be home, but his wife, Suzy, was there and his son, Henry, was working over a flowerbed in the side yard. He had pulled up half a dozen budding petunias and was covered with mud to his eyes. He greeted Paulus with a delighted grin, came staggering across the lawn with open arms. Suzy caught him just before he grabbed the leg of Paulus's neat uniform pants.

"Oh, my soul and body!" she gasped. "Look at him! I leave him for five minutes and—where'd you get hold of water, you yeller-headed little bumblepuss?"

Paulus laughed. "Seems like he piddled in the garden and sat down in it," he said.

"Yes, and made mud pies in it. Oh, Polly, I'm glad to see you. We were going to hunt you up today, but Aaron came by last night all fierce to go out, and you know

Aaron. Won't take no for an answer. So they're off on a two-day trip outside the Three Brothers Islands. Come in whilst I hoe off old Hank, here. He really isn't too bad to look at when clean, which is seldom."

For all Paulus had been home so rarely, he had known and approved of Suzy for a long time. She had been Walter's high school sweetheart; apparently neither of them had ever looked at anyone else. Off and on, Paulus had wondered how they would make it, she being sociable, talkative and full of energy and Walter such a sobersides, but they had got married as soon as they could manage it after their graduation, and by Christmastime of the next year Henry had been on the way.

She flipped Henry out of his filthy clothes, sat him in a small tub in the kitchen sink and turned the faucet on him. "It's the playpen for you, you frigment," she told him, "whilst I talk to Polly. You can see why," she said over her shoulder, trying to make herself heard above Henry's yells of delight and splashings. "I swear this kid gets dirty on purpose so he'll get a bath."

Henry, however, had other ideas. Clad in a snowy diaper, he made a beeline across the floor to Paulus, latched onto his trouser leg with both hands and started to climb. His mother pursued him. "No, you don't," she said, pulling, while Henry clutched harder.

"It's all right," Paulus said. "Let him, if he wants to."

"Give him a chance to pee on that lovely uniform? No way. Oh, Jesse! Thank goodness, am I glad to see you! Take Hank outdoors a little while, could you? I do want to visit with Polly."

No one had seen Jesse arrive. He stood just inside the kitchen door, leaning against the jamb, in the same dirty T-shirt and torn jeans he had worn at the party. He was breathless and panting, as if he had been running hard, and for a moment couldn't get a word out.

"Honey, what's the matter?" Suzy said. "Are you all right?"

Jesse nodded. "I thought I'd come down . . . and see Hank," he croaked. "Run fast, so I'd catch . . . Uncle Polly, maybe ride back . . . with him."

"Good," Paulus said. "I'll be heading back pretty soon, Jess. I wanted to see you, and George, too, before I started off this afternoon. You know where George is?"

Jesse nodded. He said, "Okay, c'mon, Hank. Where's his playsuit, Suzy? Sun's hot; he'll get sunburnt."

Through the screen door they could see him patiently struggling with Hank, who didn't want any part of a playsuit on.

"That poor little duffer," Suzy said under her breath. "He looks like a sick chicken. I'll bet he's half-starved, right now. Walt says his mother never cooks anything, she just goes and eats out, herself, leaves a package of hotdogs or cold cuts on the kitchen table, if she remembers to. Jesse cooks the stuff, or they eat it raw. I feed him whenever he comes down, which isn't very often, usually when she sends him to pump Walt about how much he made on a fishing trip. Oh, I do so hope you'll be able to do something about those two kids when you get home for good, Polly."

"I've got a legal chance to try. Ralph made me their guardian, you know. Speaking of him, he left you and Walt this, to help out where it's needed." He handed her the check he had written at the bank.

Suzy spread it out on the table in front of her and looked at it. "God love him," she said softly. Tears came into her eyes and she mopped them away. "I wish I could tell him thank you. I never really knew him, he was gone so much and Walt never seemed to care about him, I guess because he never sent any money home to help the family out. Only, last Christmas he sent me a beautiful pair of marine binoculars, wrote that I might like to watch for Walt when his boat came in sight between the Three Brothers Islands. The way his letter sounded, I wondered then if he didn't think lots of us, not just didn't give a darn, the way Walt's mother said."

"Look here, Suzy. I think Walt ought to know that his father sent most of his wages home regularly every month. Gladys just tucked the money away; didn't mention it. He wasn't a drunk and he was crazy about all three of his kids. Now, those are the facts and I know. You two keep them under your hats till I get home, okay? There's no use stirring up that mudpuddle of lies until we can get those two kids away from her. Because she's nuts and there's no knowing what she'd do."

"Oh!" Suzy said. "Yes, of course, Polly. I'll tell Walt. I guess I'm right to be scared of her. We never see her— she's never spoken to me, or seen Henry. If I pass her on the street she gives me this funny look that gives me a cold chill. We aren't likely to stir her up in any way whatsoever."

"Wish I hadn't told you, if it's going to worry you," Paulus said. "But I figured it was time Walt knew."

"Oh, I won't worry. Things won't be any different from what they've always been. I'm glad you did tell me, it ought to make Walt feel better about his father." She followed him to the door. "You hurry back, Polly. You're going to be a comfort to have around."

Both kids made a beeline for him as he crossed the porch. Jesse stood, beaming, with his shy smile; Henry repeated the performance of gripping a pants-leg and trying to climb up.

Suzy laughed. "I'll be darned," she said. "What are you, Polly—the Pied Piper? Hank doesn't usually make friends that easy. And you don't either, do you, Jesse?"

"Oh, most kids like a jeep," Paulus said. He thought, a

little uneasily, as he headed out into the highway, Pied Piper, my God! What do *I* know about kids?

Jesse was mostly silent on the way back. He spoke only once, which was when Paulus asked him where George was. "He's up to Foss Bailey's garage."

George was delighted to leave the job he was doing for Foss, which was sweeping out the showroom. He tossed his broom at a corner and was out of the door before Foss could catch up with him.

"Hey! Come back here, you flutterbug!" Foss yelled. "How about finishing up?" But George was already tumbling into the jeep.

Foss peered after him, saw Paulus and waved a hand. "I'll make it right with you, Foss," Paulus called. "Don't know as I ought to take you away from your job," he said to George.

" 'S all right. He'll finish up himself," George said. From him arose a rich and overpowering smell of dirty clothes and unwashed youngster that seemed almost visible, like steam, in the jeep's closed cab. He sprawled on the seat, his big stern wedging hard against Jesse, who folded up like an accordion. "Where we going?" he said.

"Well, now," Paulus said. "I was going to take you over to the store and dig up some new jeans and T-shirts. But Amanda'll flip. You know womenfolks. She won't let you put on clean clothes unless you get washed up first."

"I know," George said, cheerfully. "We stink, don't we?"

"Yes, you do, bud. Jesse, now, he smells kind of like cucumbers, but damned if I know how to classify you, George."

Jesse said, unexpectedly, "Cucumbers! Wow! That's rattlesnake smell. *Zzzzt!*" He gave George a solid poke in the ribs. "You been bit, kid. You'll flop over any minute now. We could pick up the things first and then go out

to Paine's Pond swimming. That'd get us clean enough."
He glanced doubtfully at George. "Not without soap,
though."

Paulus laughed. He slid the jeep into gear. "Amanda'll
be tickled to death to throw in some," he said. He
wouldn't in the least mind a good swim himself.

At the store, Amanda not only provided jeans and
T-shirts, she tucked into the package soap, towels, and
washcloths.

George protested. "Aw, we don't need all that stuff, do
we? We can soak it off and dry in the sun."

Amanda eyed him. "Soak nothing!" she said, and George
took her word for it.

After the scrub and the swim, they didn't touch
Amanda's clean white towels, though. They all three
dried off in the sun. Paulus couldn't recall when he'd had
a better time; he hoped the boys had, too; they certainly
seemed to be enjoying themselves. George had plowed
around, raising a bow-wave like a tugboat, showing off
how well he could dive and swim, calling out to Jesse,
"C'mon out over your head, don't be so chicken; I'll hold
you up if you sink." But Jesse wouldn't. He said, "Yah,
you'll only duck me, you fat mud-turtle," and stayed
where he was, sitting with only his head out in the shal-
lows where the sun warmed the water on the sand. "I
can't swim as good as he can," he said. "Tell you something, I don't like to. I can run faster than he can, though,
and I can jump-jim-crow. He falls over."

Paulus settled down beside him. "You and George remind me of your father and me when we were kids," he
said. "That's about how it stacked up with us, too. He
could swim circles around me, but he couldn't run very
fast." He stopped, seeing the sudden change in Jesse's
face, before the boy turned it away from him, and began
to talk very fast.

"I learnt how to drive Set-Fire's jeep faster'n George did, but he catches more fish in this pond than I do. He sets stiller'n I do. I can't set still enough. I'm clean, I guess I'll get out now, dry off." He surged up out of the water, ran away along the pond beach, scattering sand and pebbles. Paulus watched him out of sight behind a small promontory that jutted into the lake.

George swam in, borne along by a mighty overhand stroke that stirred up the lake mud under him and carried him high on the beach, scraping along on his stomach. "Where's old wonky gone?"

"Drying off," Paulus said. "Guess we better start to. We've got just about time to stow away some steaks at the restaurant before I have to leave for the airport."

George turned red. He stepped down into the water and, back to Paulus, began rinsing the beach sand off his stomach.

Now what? Paulus thought. Stepped on another sore spot, have I? It's like walking on eggs with these fellas.

George said carefully, "Which rest'runt we going to?"

"Why, Cooper's, I guess."

Jeest. He would. Pick the best one, George was thinking. And that one. Where Jess and me wouldn't dast to walk in at the door.

Where, one night not long ago, he and Jess had broken a back window and made off with four big thick steaks and some bread from the restaurant kitchen. Where someone had seen them and hollered, but they'd got out fast and hadn't been caught. It had been close, though. A pickup truck had been stopped on the corner waiting for the lights to change and they'd piled in the back without the driver knowing. They'd hid amongst his load, which was bags of something, with the ice-cold steaks plastered under the fronts of their jeans and T-shirts—like to froze their balls off before the feller slowed down enough again so they could jump off. He was barreling out the highway, headed straight for Machias, and they'd thought that was where they'd have to go, too; but he'd had to haul over to let a big semi-truck-and-trailer pass him, and they'd made it into the bushes. They found they weren't far from the pond road that led down here to the pond, so they'd come down, built a fire on the shore and cooked the steaks, and had they ever been good! Ma had had one of her puckery times when she hadn't left the package of hotdogs on the kitchen table. And jeest, we had to have something. Jess always got sick if he didn't eat. But Cooper's Rest'-runt, jeest, no. Can't push our luck too far. So now I got to lie to this nice old bugger, and I wisht I didn't have to.

George came out of the water, sat down on the grassy bank behind Paulus. "Wisht you'd said you was going to buy steaks, we coulda brought 'em along, cooked 'em on our fireplace we built out here," he said.

"Wish I'd thought of it, if you and Jess would like that better. Still, I don't guess there'd be time for a cookout, anyway, just about enough to throw the party at the restaurant. Steak and french fries and ice cream, okay?"

George gulped. "Thing is, Jess is awful bashful and we ain't ever et at a rest'runt. Jeest, he wouldn't be able to eat a thing. He likes cookouts. We got a hell of a nice fireplace out here, too. Want to see it?"

"Sure. Where is it?"

"Right behind you. Can't see it, can you?"

"No." Paulus had already spotted the fireplace—in the same place and probably built on the foundation of the one he and Ralph had made years ago. Only, they'd never bothered to hide it. A small evergreen tree, roots and all, stood in it now.

George reached down, lifted the tree and there it was, steak bones and all and the remains of the loaf of bread.

Jeest, he'd forgot they hadn't cleaned that out, been too sleepy and full to, that night. He clapped the tree back fast, hoping Paulus hadn't seen. "We got to hide it, a lot of kooks come out here, eat, and stuff it full of their cruddy garbage," he said. "When I can manage to come up with a steak, we bring it out here and cook it, can't cook it at home, Ma eats it, and I can't, uh, you know, come up with one very often, I got to scramble to get one—" Suddenly realizing where his gabby tongue was taking him, he ground to a stop, and breathed again as Paulus said, "Must be quite a tote, all the way out here when you're hungry." Good, he hadn't noticed.

"Oh, we can almost always hitch a ride. Or I can borrow somebody's bike. I mean, we always take the bike back," George said. "We can get fish out here, too, them ones that's pink inside, where they've been out in the salt water. Jeest, are they good!"

Steaks hadn't been on the list of items Joe Falls had said George had lifted from the stores, but Paulus guessed that they very well could have been. By the god, he told himself, as he drove the jeep back to town, those kids are half-starved and I don't blame them a damn bit.

He didn't mention the restaurant again. Instead, he stopped the jeep outside of Foss Bailey's garage.

George moaned a little to himself. Damn fool, I am, he told himself. I done us out of a good meal, and now I got to go back to work hungry, and Foss'll be like a cat with a sore tail.

But it wasn't like that at all.

"Foss," Paulus said, "can you spare George the rest of the day?"

"Any time," Foss said. "I'm used to being without him." He shook his head, staring not very pleasantly at George.

"Good," Paulus said. "I want these two fellas to have

their own bikes. They can pick out the ones they want, no strings. Okay?"

The kids stared at him, speechless. Foss said, "Okay, if that's what you want." He turned and went into his office.

George recovered first. He breathed, "Jeest, Puh-Polly! You mean it? Honest?"

"That's right. Go ahead. Pick one out." Jesse was still staring at him. "You, too, Jess."

He watched them at the racks where Foss kept the new bicycles, going from one to another, pointing out this and that, discussing in low voices. Slow and careful, he thought. The way the policeman picks his shoes.

In the office, Foss sat at his desk looking black as a thundercloud.

"Use your phone?" Paulus asked.

"Help yourself."

Paulus called the store. "The kids'll be over after a couple of steaks and stuff for a cookout," he told Amanda. "Okay?"

"Of course. Didn't you eat at Cooper's?"

"No. Kids don't like to eat at a restaurant. Look, tell Set-Fire to send one of the boys down to Foss's and pick up the jeep, will you? I'll have to step on it now, if I'm going to make the plane."

Behind him, Foss said, "You sure will. I got your taxi waiting, if you can get around to take it. Clyde might make it, I d'no. You know how he drives."

"Then I'll make him let me drive," Paulus said cheerfully. "What's eating you, Foss?"

Foss snorted. "Ain't a storekeeper in town won't cuss you baldheaded for putting them two hoo-ha's on wheels. Including old Cooper at the rest'runt. He's gunning for them."

"You tell old Cooper to hold his water till I get home."

"You think you can make a difference? Hell, their own mother can't handle 'em. She told my wife the other day the only place for that George is in the reform school. And all them bikes will do, it'll make it easier to get away from what they're up to."

"You gave George a job," Paulus said. "If you feel that way, why?"

"I always liked Ralph, that's why. And I might's well ha' hired a fox in a hen-house." He reddened a little. "And my wife Sal says Gladys is having a rocky time keeping going. I thought any money Ralph—I mean his boys—could bring in might help."

"Sal go down to Gladys's raise-up-the-dead shows, does she?"

"Sure she does. Misses her mother. It's a comfort to her. What's the harm, if it's got her over them crying spells she had so long, after the old lady died? Makes it a damsite easier for me and the kids at home. Gladys only charges what she thinks each lady can afford to pay, and a lot of nice ladies go there. Why, Judge Cramer's wife and sister's always there."

"Well, God bless the nice ladies," Paulus said. "I expect you know what Sal pays. Say ten, fifteen or even twenty nice ladies turn up to a time, that ain't hay, is it? Without any overhead, like, say, you've got. You mull that over, sweetheart, it'll brighten your day. Lend me your pen, will you? I'll write you a blank check for the bikes. You can fill in the cost of the bikes when you find out which ones the kids pick out." He wrote and handed over the check and started for the door.

Foss sat staring at the check. "Polly," he said, "you're one hell of a nice guy, you know it? Don't go off mad."

"Nope. Seldom do. I like you, too. Might even come to work for you, later on, after I get squared around, see what there is."

"By the god, I wish you would. I don't know anyone knows more about the guts of a gas engine than you do."

The boys had their bikes out on the sidewalk, checking tires at the air compressor hose. George said, "Jeest, Polly, we picked out the good ones. Is that okay?"

"That's okay. I called Amanda. She's got steaks and stuff for a cookout for you, and tell her some new sneakers. We forgot those. And look, you know the fireplace Set-Fire and Walt built down to the cove? You could go there, if you don't want to hack it back out to the pond. Remember, I'm coming home for good. If you need anything while I'm gone, will you go see Amanda?" He produced a five-dollar bill. "Slide this into your jeans and keep it till you need it, okay?"

George gulped, but no words came. Unable to wait any longer, he spun off down the street, his new wheels glittering in the sun. But Jesse lingered. He started to say something and stopped.

Holy cow! Paulus thought. I'll never make the damn plane now.

Jesse said, "All this . . . this new clothes and bikes . . . you want something back for all this?"

"No strings, Jesse, you heard me say that. It's all in the family now. You make George take it easy till I get home, is all." He tucked the five dollars into Jesse's pocket.

A tall boy in the universal uniform of jeans and T-shirt stopped and stared, first at Paulus, then at Jesse and the bike. "Hi, Jess," he said. "You in trouble?"

Not friendly, Paulus thought. Sarcastic. A smart-ass.

Jesse returned the stare with a long, level look. "Nuh," he said. "But you're going to be."

Paulus missed his plane, as he had guessed he would; it was in the air over the Machias airport, heading west, when the taxi drew up at the gate. Old Clyde Trent, the driver, snuffled a little. " 'N there she goes," he said reprovingly. "Told'ja I couldn't make it. Late start. You might's swell stayed home." He went on to enumerate exactly the number of times he'd made the trip over from Thomasville, the time the trip took, how it never varied between seven and ten seconds in all the years he'd drove a taxi, except once with a summer lady who was took to pee and run into a hornet's nest in the bushes; how Paulus should've known better than to ask him, Clyde C. Trent, licensed taxi-driver, to let a passenger drive the taxi, seemed like a growed man and him in the uniform of the You-nited States Navy ought've known it would've been breaken the law . . . and dammit, how was Polly, anyhow, it was a sight for sore eyes to see him home again.

Paulus listened with delight to the lecture, delivered in a gentle monotone and without rancor, while the Boston plane scurried out of sight into a cloud beyond Black Mountain. He was well acquainted with the stubborn independence, the works and ways of his fellow townsmen, particularly of the elderly; the slow, unhurried talk was the sound and flavor of home.

Clyde came to the end of his leisurely discourse, glanced over at Paulus. "Well, boy, what you setten still for? There's reason to hustle. You better hyper in, see'f they got a seat left on the night plane, grab it before someone else does. Otherwise, you'd be better off riding home with me."

Hiding his grin, Paulus went. The ticket agent seemed glad to see him. "Coming, we're all jammed up," he said. "Going, we ain't."

"All set," Paulus said, going back to the taxi for his bag.

"You ain't et, Polly. I better drive you down to a rest'-runt."

"Good enough. Find one with a bar. I could use a hooter or two. Couldn't you?"

The old man gazed at him with a glint in his eye and outrage on his tongue. "You young squirts nowadays ain't got one mite of a notion about the law and the order. Me take a drink and drive taxi? Hanh!"

"Lord, I forgot that. Of course you can't."

"And drinkin' in the middle of the day, that ain't decent."

This was surprising and something new with Clyde, who, Paulus remembered, had never been known to refuse a drink in the middle of the day or any other time. "You gone on the wagon, Clyde?" he asked.

"Had to, driving taxi. Don't touch a drop now." He drove briskly down into town, stopped at a pleasant-looking eating place and parked the taxi. "Come to think of it, I ain't et, neither."

"Come in, then, and eat lunch on me," Paulus said.

"I d'no b't I will." Clyde hopped spryly out of the car; he was out of sight through the restaurant door before Paulus moved.

When he had got into the taxi in front of Foss's, Paulus had noticed Clyde's dinner bucket and thermos in plain sight on the back seat; at some time or other, both had been neatly covered with a spread newspaper.

Why, the old cuss! Drove slow, so I'd miss the plane and he could wangle a free meal, I betcha. Us Scotts! Nobody ever leaves our house hungry. I'll fix him.

He had in his bag an unopened bottle of rum which he had brought along in case supplies ran dry somewhere along the way. He rooted it out, wrote on the label: *Or thirsty either, Clyde, old son,* and shoved it under the newspaper with the dinner bucket, knowing Clyde would get the message, find out that Paulus had been on to him. As for the "don't-touch-a-drop-now" bit, that had an odd side to it, too. Let's see what happens down *that* back alley, Paulus thought, grinning to himself.

They had a fine dinner, as might be expected from the best restaurant in town. On the way back to the taxi, Paulus said, "I better get something to read on the plane. You know where there's a bookstore, Clyde?"

"Well, now, le'me see. I *think* I do. Might be, we'll have to hunt round a little, Polly."

He drove slowly along Main Street, looking here and there, came to full stop in front of the liquor store. "Now where . . ." he said, peering severely at the stores on either side of it. "Now where did I . . . h'm . . ."

"Candy store, laundromat," Paulus said cheerfully. "No bookstore. Try down the street, Clyde, that one on the corner looks hopeful."

"No, it ain't. That's the Christian Science place, hands out all them tracks and newspapers free. No. Le'me try round the block again, come up on her same way. Maybe it'll jog my mem'ry."

They went around the block at a clip which made the policeman on the corner look twice, came full stop again in front of the liquor store. "Now, ain't that some god-damned old funny," Clyde said. "Where'n hell d'you s'pose that cuss moved to, run the bookstore? I could've swore . . ."

"Never mind. I'll grab a couple of magazines at the airport. I expect you'd like to get back home."

"I ain't in no hurry. Ain't you got some shoppin' or something? I just as soon wait. We're right here, now," he added delicately. "In the middle of it."

"No, don't need a thing. You know, Clyde, when Ralph and I were boys, sixteen, seventeen, we got hold of an old Model-T we overhauled and fixed up to ride around in. One time, we took her down as far as Portland, got lost in the city. We finally come up on the Soldiers and

Sailors Monument, drove round it, looking for a way out, didn't see any. Went round again, still didn't. The third time we started to, out comes a cop. He says, 'That there is the Soldiers and Sailors Monument. You fellers drive round it again and I'll run you in.'"

Clyde gave in with grace. "Well, now, Polly. I can't think of what in the ever-lovin' God's world made you think of that." He grinned, slid the taxi into gear and headed for the airport.

The night plane didn't leave until nine o'clock. Paulus had expected a long wait and had almost looked forward to it. He was tired; the first day of trying to handle Ralph's responsibilities had been a strain. He had made a beginning, at least he hoped so, with the boys. But there's a damsite more to it, he thought glumly, than buying presents and saying lean on me. I'll likely Scott this one up. Two little hellions, and what do I know, anyway?

All he could do was try, remembering that when he was George's age he had been something of a hellion himself. But how did I feel then? How did I function? Try as he would, he couldn't remember. Of course there was Walter, who had gone over to live at the farm and had turned out damned well. Even then, Gladys had had the notion of trading a youngster for money; Paulus recalled Amanda's letter telling how she had come over hot-foot and demanded payment in cash for Walter. Paulus had carefully held back from Gran and Amanda any mention of Madame Preston; no reason to weigh them down with that, which still made him sick to think about.

Well, Ralph was out of it, well away, wherever he'd gone, with a chance now for a decent life there; and the draining grief for him had been lifted from Gran; and from the rest of us who love him. Someday the boys could be told what their father had done, that he was still living; that they might, perhaps, see him again. But not yet, not until they were older, because there was no knowing how well young kids could hold their tongues, and Gladys must not know.

Dammit, I'm needed at home all right, Paulus told himself. Gran and Amanda and even Set-Fire had told him so. Could be, Ralph's boys had told him so—how was he to know?

Suddenly he caught himself wishing he were going back aboard ship to stay—to the life he knew something about, to the job he was good at. And he couldn't help resenting the weight of Ralph's responsibilities, dumped on him all of a heap, which already seemed too heavy to handle.

The plane took off at the end of dusk, when the moon was beginning to climb the eastern sky. From his window, Paulus could look down on the place where Sarah Thomas, for thirteen years, had fought her battle against odds. The wilderness was gone. Where it had been were streets, stores, houses; but the geography of the harbor was the same. Between its eastern and western points, the narrow slit of sea led back to Cooper's Inlet where the grist- and sawmills had been, and then to the salt marsh that meandered across the flats to Paine's Pond. The harbor shores were lined now with the business places of a fishing town—wharves and sheds, floats, walk-ways down to the lobster dealers' flat-topped storage cars; the fish-processing plant was going full steam, under lights, working overtime. Some boat with a hefty catch must've been late getting in; could be, Walter and Aaron.

And coming up, ahead of the plane, its naked peak whitened with moonlight, its secret, inaccessible places dark as night, was Sarah's mountain.

A mountain's a mountain, Paulus told it. But it doesn't need to be you, you chesty old black devil.

IV

Young Walter had prospered in more ways than one after he had left home at the end of his third year in high school and had gone over to live at the farm. His mother had thrown him out of the house. "Get out and stay out," she had said, which she had not really expected him to do. But he had gone and had not come back.

Since he had been old enough to pick up odd jobs around town, he had tried to earn enough to keep himself and the kids decently dressed for school, to see that they got a good meal once in a while, but Gladys had demanded every penny he'd made. On every payday, he had had a raging battle with her, which he had always lost. He had come to realize that if he stayed with her, he'd be finished in the same cold-hearted way his father had been—through the years, more worn out and wrung dry.

He had gone to Set-Fire's house at first because it seemed to him the place where he wouldn't bother anyone, put anyone out. Amanda was busy all day long at the store; Gran was frail; and Cora Willis, the housekeeper, had a lot to do—he wouldn't want to make extra work for her. With him and Set-Fire batching it, it wouldn't make much difference because he could help Set with cooking meals, or whatever there was to do. But one day, both Gran and Amanda came over to find him. "We've got something over to the house that we want you to see," Gran told him.

They had had the spare room on the second floor done over, repapered in bright colors and hung with window curtains that featured speed boats and galloping horses —had turned it into a boy's room with extra bunks. "In case you want to ask your friends to stay all night,"

Amanda said. There were a closet for his clothes and
a pine dresser with a key. "So you can lock up your
treasures if you want to," Amanda said.

If the speed boats and galloping horses were designed
more for the taste of a younger boy, Walter didn't care.
In fact, he had liked the room the way it had been, with
its big old spool bed and heavy oak furniture. But nobody in all his life had ever done such a thing for him
and he choked up so that he couldn't say a word. At first,
it had seemed unbelievable that he could invite friends
home with him—his mother had always refused to have
any of them in her house; some of the younger ones were
scared to go there anyway, because they said she kept
dead people in the closet. At last, he managed to bring
out, "Won't I be a lot of work for you, being here?"

"Shoot!" Amanda said. "Cora'll be tickled to death to
have a man in the house to feed. Bring your things." And
he was embarrassed, because he had no things to bring,
only the clothes he stood up in.

At the farmhouse, Walter had learned how it was to
be valued and loved; for the first time in his life to have
his own place where nothing was ever gone over and
interfered with, taken away or sold; to earn his own
money and do what he liked with it. At first, Set-Fire
had put him to work on the farm, paid him a hired man's
fair wages; then, using one of Set-Fire's old skiffs and
his outboard motor, and a string of traps built in his
spare time, Walter had spent weekends and summer va-
cations supplying lobsters and crabmeat to the seafood
department in the family store.

After he had been settled at the farmhouse for some
months, Gladys came over, carefully picking her time—
a day when Cora Willis had taken Gran down to visit
with Sarah Falls. She explored Walter's new room from

closet to dresser, finding there what she had hoped to
find, and she was coming down the front stairs, humming
to herself, when Cora walked in at the door. She had not
intended to spend the day at Sarah's, only to drive Gran
down, then came back to get Amanda's lunch. She
stopped dead in the middle of the floor and stared at
Gladys, whom she detested.

"What do you think you're doing, snooping around the
house when nobody's home?" she asked.

"Oh, mercy! I ain't been snooping, not around the
house. I'm Walter's mother, dear, remember? I've got a
perfect right, I guess, to visit my own son's room.
Amanda's done it over real pretty, ain't she, but what
a funny place for a TV. My Lord, if I could afford one,
I'd keep it in the living room."

"Walter likes to look at it, *dear*, sometimes when the
rest of us don't," Cora said. "Besides, that TV belongs to
him. It's his. H-I-S, his. So's the room. You got no right
in the god's world to go up there and underrun it, in this
house or anywheres else. You better get straightened
out about that."

"Walter ain't of age, dear. Everything he owns belongs
to me. And that includes two nice pretty ten-dollar bills
I found in his bureau drawer."

Amanda, arriving home for lunch, heard this as she
came through the door. She saw Gladys flick the bills
under the end of Cora's nose. She stopped to see what
might happen.

Cora was a big woman, stoutly built, whose muscles
had been toughened by years of hard work. She was also
short on temper, especially where Gladys was concerned.
She caught Gladys's wrist and squeezed hard, snapped
the bills away from her, tucked them deep in her apron
pocket. "Steal a young boy's hard-earned savings, would

you, hanh? How stinkin' mean can you get? And now you clear out of here, before I walk you Spanish down over the front steps!"

If Gladys was furious, she didn't show it. She stepped back a little, rubbing her wrist. "As to that, dear," she said, "if we're coming out into the open, I ain't about to be ordered out of Ralph's own house that he owns a third of, by a hired maid-servant who ain't got as much right to be here as I have. You tell Amanda that I own Walter and what he makes, and if she don't pay me what he's worth to me at home, I'll come after him with a court order."

"All right," Amanda said. "You've told me, Gladys. While we're coming out in the open, if that's what we're doing, you threw Walter out of your house, he's come to live here, earning his own living, paying his way. How is he to manage that, if you take his money?"

"Well, I want him back. I need him. I can't get by without what he makes."

"Don't come that on us," Cora said. "Frank's cousin, runs that gift shop over to Machias, told me you was in there the other day, bought that fancy handbag. Cost you twenty-five dollars. That don't sound poverty-struck to me."

"And let's straighten out something else," Amanda said. "Ralph doesn't own any part of the farm and neither do you, and if you drive Walter into leaving here, you never will, and that's final."

"Why, Amanda, how you talk and carry on! I never thought you'd be put out, your upstairs is always neat's a pin. Only, on the way up-attic, I noticed that pretty room, all fixed up, like for a young boy. S'I to myself, Amanda must be expectin'. Pregment, but by who I can't think, unless Set-Fire? Don't look at me like a meat ax. I know you ain't got no sense of youmor."

She left, tittering a little, and humming softly to herself. She took the handbag with her.

"My God!" Amanda wrote to Paulus. "How can you get through that rhinoceros hide? I think the woman's crazy, and I hope she doesn't tackle Walter."

She did. She confronted him on his way home from school on that very same day. "You get your ass home," she told him. "Or I'll have the District Judge issue a court order."

"You do that." Walter stared at her, steady-eyed. "And I'll burn your house down and you with it. It'd be worth going to jail for."

That did get through the rhinoceros hide. She stared at her tall son, who towered over her by a head. The cold glitter in his black eyes scared her; she felt chilled to the bone. She turned on her heel and walked away from him. He means it, she thought. Why, the black-headed little bastard! He means it. He'd do it. Well, just let him wait. I'll fix him. And I'll take care of Miss Old Amanda, too. Let her wait and see.

Amanda heard nothing about this confrontation. Walter was a quiet boy, a sobersides, who talked very little, and never about his own affairs. If he carried his hatred for his mother like a stone in his chest, he said nothing about it.

Gladys did not bother him again and apparently she harbored no hard feelings against Amanda. She came more often to the farmhouse, arriving always at mealtime, sometimes bringing the two younger boys; she never failed to speak pleasantly to Walter, calling him "my dear son" or "my dearest Walter."

If whoever left the lighted cigarette in an ashtray on the edge of the Post Office counter, so that the live end burned off and fell into the wastebasket underneath, had been more than forgetful or criminally careless, that did not occur to Amanda. She smelled the smoke, doused the smoldering papers and moved the ashtray.

When Walter finished high school, Aaron Falls at once offered him a chance to buy half-shares in his new fishing dragger, the *Sarah*, named for Aaron's mother. Walter could pay for his partnership as fast as he earned the money and could spare it. He wouldn't have been able to buy a boat of his own for years, certainly not a big dragger like Aaron's, and Aaron's offer was generous— 50 percent for the boat, gear, and expenses, the remaining profit divided equally between himself and Walter. It was a great chance for Walter and he took it. Aaron was an expert, a high-line fisherman and a driver. He knew where to find fish, and with his skill and *Sarah's* equipment, he made money. After the first two years with Aaron, Walter was able to make a down payment on a house of his own.

The house he bought had once been a substantial old-timer, but Pansy Plummer, its owner, widowed and old, hadn't been able to keep it in repair. She had died at eighty-five, alone in the house with parts of it falling down around her. Her relatives were either dead or living out of state and Walter had got it for a song. Everyone, except his father and Paulus, had thought him crazy to have bought it at all. Walter's intention, which he did not share with anyone except Suzy, was that he would rebuild the house himself.

Paulus had a passion for old houses; he was familiar with most of the ones left standing in the area. He knew that the Pansy Plummer place was as old as, if not older than, the Scott farmhouse. On one of his leaves he had gone over the house from top to bottom with Walter. "It'll be a headache to fix up," he'd said. "But with a roof job to keep the rain out, it's livable right now and you can take your time tinkering with the rest of it. And look where it is, and what you'll have when you get it done."

The house stood a hundred feet from the tip of Western Point, its windows looking out on the harbor, the many islands to the south and the horizon and open ocean to the east. The view was magnificent; but Ralph, who was at home that year for one of his brief visits, didn't even glance at it. He had seen horizons, he said, until they were coming out of his bellybutton, but the house, at least one aspect of it, was something else again. He had vanished after a while, that day, and Suzy and Walter had found him in Pansy Plummer's old summer kitchen, with his feet thrust almost to the knees in the oven of her ancient, woodburning cookstove. There was no fire in it, of course—he was merely trying it out for a practical use, had discovered that its oven door opened sideways instead of flopping down from the top. A man could warm his feet there in the winter without blistering the backs of his calves on a red-hot oven door.

"By the god, Walt," he said. "This stove's a treasure. And look at that old Dutch oven. Buy the house and live in this kitchen."

Walter, who had never spoken his father's language anyway, and who had no sense of humor at all, glowered a little and grunted; the old man, he thought, was likely half-sloshed, if all he could say about the house was to praise up the wreck of an old stove and a Dutch oven. But Suzy laughed and patted Ralph's shoulder. "We'll keep it for you for when you come home in the wintertime," she said. And that was the year Ralph had sent her the binoculars—"so you can spot Walter's boat when it comes up over the horizon."

Since the summer kitchen chimney had been built long before the days of woodburning stoves, its ample Dutch oven had been set into the brickwork of a fireplace, but it would heat quite well from the cookstove which stood there now. Walter, who had set up his woodworking shop in the summer kitchen, had built fires to warm up the shop at first, but soon had discovered that the lime-mortar between the ancient bricks was crumbling—that the whole chimney was unsafe. He had given up fires in the stove, but after a while he had found a pleasant use for the Dutch oven.

Repairing the house, Walter had found, was an endless job. It would have been, even if he had had more time to work at it. But Aaron was a driver, sparing neither himself nor his gear, nor did he spare Walter. The first winter Walter went with him he found out all about Aaron. Some of it was hard to take. Aaron's boat, Aaron's gear, his skill in handling both, were the best there was. He had maps in his head, telling him where rocky bottom was, or any other obstructions that would tear up a dragnet. There wasn't a patch of good fishing ground anywhere that he didn't know. About the weather, he didn't go by forecasts—t'hell with them, he'd have been dead and the *Sarah* sunk forty times over, if he ever paid any attention to that crap. Some guys, the damn fools, were futzing up their boats with a lot of electronic gear—radar, zoobar, stinkbar, whatever they called the stuff —even telephones. Not Aaron, by the god.

"Hell, what I need that trash for? My gal *Sarah* can tell me more in half an hour's running, any direction. She gives me the word, say, how she feels about the wind and tide bearing on her, and I match it up with a squint at the sky. There we got it, back and forth."

He talked quite a lot to the *Sarah*. Sometimes he roared at her and swore, but in a tight place, he spoke gently, never raising his voice. "Like smoothing down a woman," he told Walter. "Kee-riced, she *is* a woman. A boat always is a woman. You handle one right, you don't have any trouble."

Walter, the realist, listened without saying very much. He had learned early on that it wasn't any use to; what Aaron believed, he believed and he wasn't interested in any opinion but his own. Arguing crossed him up and he had a low flashpoint, anyway. If all that bragging got to be tiresome—a hell of a bore once in a while—Walter reminded himself that that was the way Aaron was; he had to convince himself, as well as everyone else, that he was that special. Not that he needed to. He might be feisty, short-tempered, and stubborn, up to a point that at times affected his good judgment, but no one could deny that most of the brag he put out about himself was true. He had worked on the water since his boyhood, and, Walter knew, there was no doubt that he *did* have maps in his head.

"Now, right along here," he might say, on a blustery morning, with the snow driving in thick and visibility ten feet or less, "used to be one of the best spots they is for gray sole. But down there is what's left of a German submarine the Navy stove to pieces in World War Two. She's full of dead Huns who I wouldn't care to have come up in a dragnet. The stink they made when they was fresh was enough to curdle the gall in a man's liver."

He didn't wait for Walter to ask how he knew exactly where the submarine was, he went on telling. He liked a good story, not to leave one half-finished. "I saw that happen and I got the location fixed in my mind. About two miles east of the Three Brothers Islands. I took marks. It was daylight, just about, and I broke out past the reef on the Third Brother, and there was a hell of a hoop-te-do going on—three-four airplanes dive-bombing something in the water. Couldn't see what it was for the spray flying, but whatever the god's name it was, was shooting back. Then there was one old dag-snorter of a *ker-blam*, pieces of stuff blew up all over the works. The planes hung around a little while and then they went off. I started to sag over there to see'f there was anything worth hauling out of the water, but then I see there was a Coast Guard cutter heading me off, lickety-tilt. She hove to alongside and an old cuss in a monkey jacket read me some act of God about being out there, when all the fishermen had been warned off not to, till the Navy got the subs cleared out of adjacent waters, and I says, 'Look, Grampop, I ain't let to fight in the War because I got to stay here and catch fish to feed the people. You want 'em all to starve to death?'

"Oh, I got that old son told, le'me tell ya. Look, it's breaking away in the west. Told ya this snowsquall wasn't going to last. Was I right, or was I right? Le's get cracking."

Two, three hours later, miles offshore, they would put over the dragnet, while Aaron got the fish told.

"Come alive down there! You half-eyeball critters going to get a sorry surprise today! Think you're cuddled down for the winter in the nice soft mud, don't ye, hanh? Well, watch it, bubbas! Aaron Falls is coming!"

The half-eyeball critters were gray sole and flounder, who wore their eyes on one side of their heads. "You eat a gray sole dinner in Boston, Walt, it'll cost you your uppers and lowers, kid. Want to bet me ten cents we get weather enough for a two-day haul, hit top market price?"

He would head offshore in weather that would tear the coattails off of most fishermen, who had it over among themselves about the ungodly chances he took. "T' hell with that," Aaron said, when the talk got back to him. "My coattails, ain't they? The more times you guys hang

yours up in the shed dry, the better price I get for my
trip out. You go right ahead, set with your feet in the
oven and don't glut the market."

"He's some fierce out after the money," they said of
him.

This was true, and it was true of Walter.

Money. From early boyhood, money had been Walter's
goal, the only way he knew to decency and independence
—almost to salvation. He had earned it, in his time, the
hard way, little by little and never enough: dimes and
quarters for running errands, opening up and sweeping
out stores, starting furnace fires for people on icy mornings, washing mountains of restaurant dishes. Now, with
Aaron, he was making it—good pay for a man's honest
work. Pay enough for what he was worth.

Putting up with Aaron's temper, his bossiness, his
know-it-all, might get tiresome, but it was certainly no
hardship. Not to Walter. He could grin behind his hand
at Aaron's foolishness about jinxes and Jonahs—what was
unlucky aboard a boat, or who could set foot on her. Any
man who'd ever had an accident on the water couldn't,
that was for sure. Any tool that got dented or damaged,
he deep-sixed—wouldn't even let Walter take home one
that was still usable and easy-fixed. And once, when to
Walter's surprise, a new punt had appeared on their
mooring, he found that someone, for a joke, had left a
dead gull in the old one, and birds were unlucky. Aaron
had sold the old punt and bought a new one.

If Aaron had quirks about old wives' tales, so what?
Walter didn't. A boat to him was a boat. And a woman,
he would tell himself, is a woman. And a house is a house.

The *Sarah* might be smashing through the tide-chop
with the northeaster building up behind her and her stern
dragging water under the weight of a hold crammed full
of fish. But, in this weather, she just could be the only

boat out and the market price for those fish could be high. And Suzy would be waiting, with Henry, safe in the house that was theirs, where no one, by the god and by law, could interfere with them or bother around. The house that Aaron's so-called unholy chances were helping to pay for.

Walter had had the years up at the farmhouse and he had liked it there. The family had been good to him and he loved them all, dearly. They had said he'd been like a son to them, and perhaps he had been. But now he was on his own and nobody's son. The words "mother" and "son" still ground fiercely against his grain whenever he thought of them, which wasn't often. Let Aaron sound off and be quirky all he wanted to. Hell, that was nothing. Walter was content for the first time in his life.

Being gone so much, he didn't have all the time he wanted to finish the repairs on the house. All he could do was work on it when he could. Paulus, on his leaves, helped rebuild, paint, and patch; Set-Fire in his spare time shingled the roof, so that Walter and Suzy could move in dry. Suzy pecked cheerfully away at the desolate rooms, sometimes wondering if she could ever get them clean and repapered, but the work went faster when Sarah Falls could come over to lend a hand and the two of them made the dirt fly.

At the time of Ralph's disappearance, the house was still mostly unfinished upstairs, but the downstairs rooms were furnished and livable; Suzy's new kitchen, with modern appliances, was done. She could stand on the newly repaired porch, holding up Henry, so that he could wave to his father as the *Sarah* flashed by up-harbor, headed home. Henry would wave frantically and yell with delight, because that was Dad, and he always brought presents.

Whenever the *Sarah* put in to a town down-coast,

where the market price for fish was higher than at home, Walter would go shopping for something nice to take back to Suzy and Henry—an electric blender, an interesting toy or two. After a while, he began to include a present for Jesse, because sooner or later, Jesse would show up, sent down by Gladys to find out how much money Walter had made on the trip. For all Walter had made up his mind to have nothing to do with his mother or his brothers, he couldn't help but see how tough it was for Jesse to say what he had come to say. He was always torn with embarrassment and would turn red and stutter, unable to find words. And Walter, in spite of himself, was touched.

Suzy's light-hearted kidding helped, and Henry helped, too, because he dearly loved Jesse. Often enough, Jesse's visit would end up with him and the baby playing together, having a fine time, the stress and strain forgotten, the question easily asked.

"Come on, Daddy Warbucks," Jesse might say. "Give. How much? I don't dast to go home unless you tell me."

And Suzy would name a figure so absurd that even Walter would burst out laughing.

"And what did you bring home for Suzy?"

"Oh, our refrigerator was over a week old, so Walt bought me a new one. Lugged it up from the shore on his back."

"Tell her the first one's on the town dump, if she wants it," said Walter. But always he sent the boy home with a reasonable figure, to keep him out of trouble. And after a while, there was always a present for Jesse.

Once, in town, Walter found something for Henry that he thought was great—a big wooden lobster on wheels, painted bright red and fixed to be pulled by a string. As it moved it waved its claws and clapped them open and shut; some kind of a ratchet inside it went *clack-clack*, quite a loud noise. "Take a look," Walter said, as he un-wrapped it. "Ain't that a gasser!"

"Somebody cooked it," Jesse said, referring to its color.

He and Suzy both thought it was a fine present, but Henry didn't. He was a stout baby, nearly as broad as he was long, with hair as bright a red-gold as his Grandfather Ralph's had ever been. He bumbled along on his feet, fell down often, but always got up by himself and seldom cried. He looked at the lobster with misgiving, finally took the string in his hand, started towing it across the floor. At the first *clack*, he looked behind him in horror. This couldn't be anything but a Thing coming to eat him up. Bellowing, he flew for his mother's lap, forgot to drop the string, fell down and got tangled up in it, so that the Thing chased him, claws snapping all the way to his safety.

Walter shouted with laughter. "Hey, Henry! You sure Scott-ed that one up, didn't you?" Afterwards he tried to convince Henry that it was a plaything, but Henry would never go near it again.

It wasn't George's fault that he looked like Ralph and was, in some ways, like him—easygoing and clumsy as a bulldozer. But, Amanda told herself, boys of fifteen are clumsy at times, and George had other qualities to recom-mend him. He was stubborn, with a stout backbone of his own; standing up for someone or something he believed in, he was a stone wall, not to be moved. He had a clear, logical mind, and a common sense which made him say what he thought without taking off in all directions at once; he had a kind of blunt-ended courage which might get him into trouble now, but would be a good thing for a grown man, with more judgment, to have. If she had a real problem to meet, she'd rather have George to depend on, young hellion though he was, than most people she could name. She loved all of her nephews, but she had an especially soft spot in her heart for George.

She was appalled when, about a week after Paulus had gone back to his ship, both boys appeared at the store in what looked to be the same old ragged jeans and T-shirts they had worn at Gran's party. George had a swollen cheek with a black eye in two shades of blue-green and Jesse was pale-faced and limping.

"For Heaven's sake, George, what's happened to your face? And those awful pants! Have you two been in a fight?"

"Ma hit me. And these jeans is all we got now."

"What in the world! Where are your new ones?"

"She took 'em down to the second-hand store. Said she had to find the money to feed us somehow, and she latched onto the five bucks Uncle Polly give us. We hid it in a new place but she found it. She always does."

Jesse said forlornly, "She took the bikes back to Foss's."

George went on. "Foss wouldn't give her the money for'm. Told her they belonged to P-Polly and he'd keep 'em till Polly got back. So she come home mad because she never got the money. She didn't buy anything to eat and when Jess said he was hungry, she started to bat him around and he fell down and was sick all over the floor. So yesterday he couldn't help with the séance, and to get her off'n him, I offered to. I helped," George said, with a glint in his one usable eye. "I helped with that ole séance, but good." He grinned, a lopsided grin that hurt his sore face, Amanda could see.

"She hit you—like *that?*"

"She sure did. Once. An old walloper right in the mush.

Polly said if we needed anything to tell you. Well, jeest, we ain't et since yesterday morning, I ain't been able to . . . uh . . . raise anything, and Jess gets awful sick if he don't eat something."

"Go straight over to the house," Amanda said. "Cora'll feed you and put something on that eye. I've got the afternoon mail to sort, but I'll close up as early as I can, and we'll have a slambanger of a supper. I expect you'd better have clean clothes."

"I know." George started to grin, winced, and thought better of it. "We stink again, don't we?"

"Yes, you really do, this time, lamb. Let's see. What sizes? You know, either of you?"

Surprisingly, George did. He moved over to the rack where the jeans were. "These is what Polly bought us. They fit all right, didn't they, Jess?"

The boys went off, each carrying his bundle of new clothes. They looked tired out and downspent and Jesse was limping really badly.

I could put back my head and howl like a wolf, Amanda told herself, watching them go. But maybe this is it. Maybe the law will have something to say about this kind of abuse. Could be, Paulus and I'll be the ones to get out a court order.

Sarah Falls, who helped in the store when needed and had been sworn in as assistant postmistress, came in, glanced at Amanda, and gasped. "My soul, Amanda, what's the matter? You look like the line storm coming up. If it was September, I'd say one was, too. The sky over in the west is black as a coal. What's happened?"

"Gladys," Amanda said. "She's really lived up to herself this time. She's pounded the daylights out of both of those kids. You should see Jesse. He can hardly walk."

"That isn't the story I heard all over town," Sarah said.

"What's that? Something Gladys put out, I'll bet a

cookie. The kids have just left here, I heard their side of it."

"Not the same, h'm? Well, Gladys tells this one. Seems George and Jesse got into a fight with Rod Colcraft's gang over the bicycles Polly bought for them. That's how they got beat up, according to her. Says she had to take the bicycles back to Foss Bailey's, so it wouldn't happen again."

"That's a plain, coldhearted lie. She was sore because Foss wouldn't give her the money Polly paid for the bikes, anyway, and then she boiled over because George did something at the séance—the Lord knows what, he didn't say, but it was probably awful."

"Oh. Oh, my yes! Haven't you heard about the tussie-mussie down at the séance?" Sarah chuckled. "She had our George crammed into the cubbyhole to make the noises, and when the spiritual kings and queens began to hover, he didn't go tunk-tunk and scratch-scratch the way he was supposed to, he let go with one old whacker of a fart."

"Good for George!" In spite of her anger, Amanda couldn't help laughing. "Oh, dear me, it's not funny, it's so terrible."

"I heard all about it from Fan Dunning, she was there."

"I hope it broke up the party."

"Didn't make much of a dent, really. Oh, one lady, a Mrs. Fowler from somewhere out of town, kind of took against, said that her first husband had made that nasty noise around the house for years, and she wasn't about pay good money to hear his spirit make it. So she took her money back and left. But the other ladies all stayed and sympathized whilst Gladys shed tears and told how awful her boys acted, and she couldn't handle them and didn't know what to do they were such hellions—look how George had just tried to bust up the religious services.

. . . And so on. Break your heart, wouldn't it?"

"Not mine," Amanda said grimly. "Now that I know what poor old George got his black eye for. Can you come back and tend out from four to five, Sarah? I'd like to get home early."

After Sarah left, Amanda thought over what Cora might have cooked in the house. A light supper planned for her and Gran and me. Plenty of sandwich filling, but nothing that would satisfy what those kids' appetites would be by suppertime. She called up Set-Fire and explained the difficulty.

"I could bring home some steaks," she told him. "But those boys are both tired to death and half-starved. I think some kind of a stew would set lighter on empty stomachs. If you've got a couple of hens handy, could you have one of the men kill and dress them and bring them over to the house?"

"I ain't too busy at the moment," Set-Fire said. "I'll do it myself. You know how Cora and I cook, lumberjack style."

When Amanda got home, the house smelled like a visitation of domestic angels. She wouldn't try to guess how many hens it had taken, but Set-Fire had a regular Sarah Scott chicken stew on the stove, with dumplings, and Gran and Cora had made three kinds of pie. The boys had had sandwiches and milk to hold them until the stew was done; they had both had baths and were asleep upstairs, George with a piece of red meat on his eye.

"We're real worried about Jesse," Gran said. "Cora had to help him take his bath and she says he's got terrible black-and-blue spots. His poor skinny little stern is a sight. We'll be lucky if he doesn't take sick."

But Jesse didn't. At suppertime, both boys felt fine. They ate huge platefuls of stew and, outside of what the others had, cleaned up every morsel of pie.

* * *

Amanda's letter, telling about the latest development, caught up with Paulus in Hawaii, on his way home.

Gladys is stewing up the same old storm about Ralph's share of the farm. I expected her that evening, probably for supper, and sure enough, in she comes, dressed up as if she was going to New York, happy as a clambake, sniffing out a free meal. "Oh," she says, "I believe I smell chicken," and Gran says, "You do, but the boys were so starved we ate early and they cleaned up everything we put on the table." Gladys says, "But I'm so upset and hungry myself I feel faint," and Gran says, "Too bad. This is a hungry house tonight."

Gladys went right on, telling how poor she was and how wronged, and how easy it was to toll her boys away from her with food, because she couldn't afford to clothe and feed them. Gran said, "The boys had new clothes and some money from Polly and you know where everything went." So Gladys said we didn't understand, dear, she'd had to sell the boys' things to get money for a decent meal, and Gran said, "You'd have got more if you'd sold some of your own," and walked off upstairs to bed.

Gladys said, "Oh, old people, all they ever think of is themselves." Deliver *her*. So where was Jesse? She needed him at home, he had to help her. I said maybe she did, but she wouldn't have him long, he'd be dead or crippled if she gave him another going-over like that last one.

"Why!" she said. "Did them little liars tell you *I* done that? That George is just like his father, you can't believe a word he says. I can't help it if they got hurt in a fight with the gang of hoodlums they run with. Let me tell you, I'm through for good and all with George, he's never going to set foot in my house again." So we can keep him if we want him, only we'll have to make over Ralph's share of the farm in trade for him. Some trade! So where was Jesse, if I'd be so good as to tell her.

The boys had both gone off to spend the night with Set-Fire, tickled to death to; he'd said if Glad-rags wanted them back that night, she'd have to tangle with him. The way I was feeling tired and mad and droopy as a broody hen, I figured Set could tangle with her better than I could, so I told her, and she said, gentle and sweet as a mother dove, "Why, ain't that nice of Set-Fire to help me out taking care of them. But you tell him that if he doesn't send Jesse home, I'll come after him, and you know I'd really hate to do that." And off she goes, not exactly with her nose in the air, but with it elevated a little, and I wouldn't call it a matter to mourn if she kept it that way.

We're in the middle of one old walloper of a southerly storm, and I pray to God you aren't anywhere out in it.

Love
Amanda

The storm which had roared in up the Gulf of Maine was an old walloper indeed. It lasted for three days, dropped nearly eight inches of rain in a single night and flooded the countryside. Set-Fire said to hell with it, he wasn't going to dump his rain-gauge after it filled up once; enough was enough. George and Jesse watched fascinated when the wind-indicator on Set's kitchen wall clocked up to seventy-two knots an hour. Brooks which had been dry for years came to life and washed out highways. Trees blew down all over—a big catspruce fell across the gravel road that led into Set-Fire's place, taking with it half a dozen smaller trees, completely blocking the way, but Set didn't seem to care. He admired a good blowdown, he said. Gave a man an idea of what God could do if He set His hand to it.

"Besides," he told Jesse, "your Ma ain't about to climb over that and there's six inches of mud—not to speak of puddles—in that road now, which you can't be expected to waddle out through, when any time another tree might fall on your head. So forget it. Your fellers want to do something useful, you can get dinner, whilst I'm out and around the farm."

"Hey, we can't cook anything fancy, Set," George said doubtfully. "Only hotdogs or steak, is all we know how to."

"Well, they's ways to learn. I got a whole cooked ham in the icebox and baked potaters and boiled carrots ain't nothing very fancy. What I'm really hankerin' for is a good caramel cake, and I ain't had time to build one. There's a cookbook. Look up the receet in the index."

"Jeest, Set! That's awful fancy. I dunno. Take a woman to make cake, wouldn't it?" George admired Set-Fire and would be glad to accommodate him in any way he knew, but the idea of baking a cake really threw him. "Wouldn't want to spoil . . . uh . . . a lot of good stuff."

"Godfrey mighty! What if you was on a camping trip or a cookout, both of which is kind of fun without no wimmenfolks around, and all you had to eat was something good you'd made swill out of because you didn't know how to cook it? Any man who don't know how to fix his own food good is a uncivilized damn fool." And Set buttoned his oilskin jacket and went off to see about the farm.

The boys looked at each other and grinned. It wasn't as if they hadn't been fixing their own food for as long as either one of them could remember. When Set got back, dinner was ready and it was good. Deadpan, they produced a cake. They had had some trouble with the recipe in the cookbook—George couldn't figure out what *tbs.* and *tsp.* meant, but Jesse could; he had put the mixture together and George had beaten it. "Beat until light," the recipe said.

"How'n hell do I know when it's light?" George said. "Feels light to me right now."

"Well, beat hell out of it anyway," Jesse said, and George had.

Set-Fire said it was light as a feather. Wasn't a woman he knew of could turn out a better one.

In the late afternoon of the third day, the storm let up and the sun set clear. George right away made plans to go beachcombing early the next morning to see if he could find any castaway lobster traps and gear. Jesse'd better go with him, he said, no sense going home, everybody was housebound because of the storm, wouldn't be any séance that day. "Let her come after you, if she wants you," George said. "And not find us here, hey?"

Jesse lay in his cot that night wondering how in the world he was going to be able to wake George up before daylight in the morning. The way George slept was enough to kill you. He would fall into bed and lie there like a rock at the bottom of a well. Shaking him and hollering at him—no way. Set-Fire had kidded them about it, saying the thing to do was turn George's cot upside-down and jump on the bedspring, but Jesse doubted if even that would work. He couldn't ask Set to help, because if Set found out where they were going and what for, he wouldn't think much of it.

It was against the law to touch any fisherman's gear; even if it was all stove up on the beach the man whose name or number was on it still owned it. But George was crazy-wild to get traps and a boat so he could go lobstering, make money enough to get loose of Ma, the way Walt had. In back of Eastern Cove beach just beyond a thicket of bushes was a deepish pond. What they had to do was try to get to the cove before anyone else did, horse all the traps they could find up over the beach and sink them in the pond. They had eleven there now and hadn't got caught.

That George! He'd gone to bed like a tree falling down, never a thought in his head about how he was going to wake up in the morning. Turning his cot over would make a heck of a noise. I couldn't do it, anyway, with him in it, Jesse thought, and briefly was put out with George. Then he thought of a way and went to sleep giggling softly to himself.

He woke up at three, wide awake, went into the kitchen, got some ice cubes from the refrigerator; he put them into a tumbler full of water and poured ice water into George's bellybutton.

George woke up, all right, with a squall that brought Set-Fire out of bed hollering what was the matter.

"It's okay, Set," Jesse called back. "Old George has a bad dream sometimes." Put that way, it wasn't telling Set a lie. Now, if George didn't forget to step on the sides of the stairs going down, they were off and running. Those old stairs creaked like a son-of-a-gun.

Jesse waited till he could hear Set-Fire snoring. Then he dressed fast, got downstairs without a creak. Old Shadow! Never did make creaks. He went out through the kitchen, taking time as he passed the pantry to lift the rest of the caramel cake out of the cakebox. They'd made it themselves, it was theirs, so it wasn't stealing. At the back beach, he sat down on a boulder, took out his jackknife and sliced the cake into equal halves. He and George always shared equal what there was. Besides, George was going to be sore about that ice water and a hunk of cake would help.

It was nice here, eating cake and looking. Maybe if he

could have cake like this once in a while, he'd start to grow some, not stay little and skinny as somebody's mouse.

Out over the water, the east was already lightening, a sick-looking yellow color, saying that the sun might come up sometime. There was still some rote from the storm making thunder on the outside ledges, but here in the cove the sea had calmed down fast, only six-inch rollers now, scooting edges of foam up along the sand and beach-rocks. The little rocks, sucked back by the undertow, made a soft rattle-sound, nice to listen to.

It had been an oary-eyed old storm while it lasted. Shifted the beach round a lot. Cast up a holy mess of rockweed and raveled-out pieces of kelp, all jumbled up with cultch. A rauncher of a flood tide with the wind behind it had lugged a lot of stuff all the way to the top of the beach, in some places over it. Near him, he could make out starfish and horse mussels and white plastic jugs, and what looked to be a whole village of big old sea-cucumbers that had sure got a sorry surprise when the storm rollers had begun to reach down to where they lived and *sa-natch!* out they came from their homes. He wondered how it would be, if he'd been one of them.

He swallowed the last of his cake, licked the frosting off his fingers and picked one up. Why! Poor old duffer was still alive. You could feel him pump in and out in your fingers. Leaking, too. Oozing out his life. Gummy, looked like they all were.

He moved around, picking up any he could see. Didn't have to hunt, there were hundreds of them. One by one, he began heaving them off into the cove, as far as he could. Not much use to, with the tide on the ebb, they'd all be out of water again in a while, but maybe they could soak up enough life to last them till the water came back again. Or maybe they could swim, go scooting off home.

He paused, wondering. "Can you old buggers swim?" he asked of the one in his hand.

There was George coming. You sure could hear old George pounding over the blowdowns.

George arrived with a thunderous rattle as his rubber boots hit the beachrocks. He let out a blat. "What for gaasake you doing, you gaadamn little kook?" So, he was still mad.

"Heaving sea-cucumbers," Jesse said. "Piece of cake there on the ledge, if you want it."

George wanted it. Through it, he complained thickly about the ice water. "You good'n well knew it'd make me holler, you ass-end of nothing."

"How'd I know that? I never heard you make that kind of a yowl in my whole life; didn't know you *could*. Hey, look, there's one trap I can see."

This diverted George somewhat, as Jesse had known it would, but he wasn't sure for how long. Of course, when he had time to cool off, he'd realize that Jesse'd done the best he could think of, but while he was still put out, he had a long forgetter.

Jesse meandered away along the beach, picking up here a bait pocket or a trap-head, there a tangled piece of warp. He passed four traps, all smashed beyond repair. Too bad. No use bothering with them wrecks. Then, at the end of the beach, where the ledges began, he made a real find. In a deepish tidepool, the sea rollers had swirled a massive tangle of trap-warp in with the kelp and rockweed. Jesse turned his back on it. Leave it for George to find—it'd sure make him feel better. "Traps any good?" he asked, as George caught up with him.

"All stove to hell. Nothing worth getting up early for. The way you moped along, don't look as if you'd found anything, either."

"A few bait pockets," Jesse said, showing them. It

would take George a minute to spot the mess of rope in the tidepool.

"Hey, look at that!" George brightened up considerably. "Right under your nose, too."

"What is? Oh, my golly! I bet there's five miles of warp wovelled up in that. Lot of it looks new, too."

"Well, don't stand there. Grab that loose end and give it a yank." George already had his jackknife out and was slashing at the tough rockweed.

"Some monkey puzzle," Jesse said. He grinned a little to himself and sat down to help.

Some of the warp was in short pieces and some raveled out into fuzzy fans, but a good part of it was new rope. Nobody ever got a chance to pick up that much of it for free.

It did take time. The edge of the sun was tipping the horizon when George got up, took a kick at the few remaining ends and said that was enough. "Come on. Let's git. This is one sweet batch of rope and we better haul it out of here before someone comes along and swears it's got his name on it. Thing is, it ain't got nobody's name on it, and we've picked up something good without havin' to steal it, this time." He strode back along the beach with the big coil on his shoulder.

Jesse walked along behind, whistling to himself. Tide had gone down a lot. He could see three or four of the sea-cucumbers he had thrown into the water out there where the ebb had left them. Didn't help much, did I, he told himself. He walked down the wet sand to see if any of the critters were still alive. Limp as kelp; had even stopped pumping. Good and dead now, poor old sods. Oh, well.

He stood looking out at the cove's water, nearly calm now with the ebb tide, ledges outside it beginning to show black and streaming. Storm rollers were coming in on the two points that sheltered the cove, but not so wild as they had been—a breeze from the northwest was begining to cuff their tops off backwards in fans of fine spray. Away east, the horizon was hubbly. The whole sweep of the ocean, stretching off, was picking up little glitters of light from the sun. Tinkling-bell light, he thought.

George came tearing down the beach on the dead run. He had gone up to hide his fat coil of rope in the bushes, but hadn't. He still had it on his shoulder. "Hey!" he said. "Look out there on that ledge—the far one. That's a punt!" He dropped the rope on the sand, began to shuck off his jacket.

The ledge, an old barnacle-back, was just beginning to show. It was full in the sun's glitter, and, squinting, Jesse could see something black on it—he couldn't tell what the thing was. It was as big as a punt, a small one, he could make out that, but it didn't look quite like one to him. He said so.

"Yah, you blind? It's somebody's punt gone adrift in the storm, grounded out on that ledge. What else could it be?"

"But who around here's got a black punt?"

"Could've come from anywhere." George went on undressing, flinging off his shirt and pants.

"What in the crazy old hell d'you think you can do about it, if it is? That water's like ice, you crumbhead. You can't swim out in it that far, you'd freeze your balls off."

"Then I'll be without 'em." George stood naked, shivering a little in the cool morning breeze. "I'm going to swim a rope out to her, tie it on. Then when the tide comes in, she'll start to wash off and around some and we can haul her in." He began clawing at the coil of warp, hunting for a loose end. "Come on, git movin'! Help me straighten this out, tie some ends together."

Oh, my Lord, Jesse thought. He's gone and got a thing about this. I got to think of some way to stop him, that cold water'll kill him. Try to talk him out of it, as if that ever done any good. He said, "If the bottom ain't stove out of her, which it prob'ly is, and she's worth saving, why, she belongs to someone and all you'll do is hand her over to him."

"For gaasake, shut up! Have you forgot how bad we need a boat? I get a rope on her she belongs to me and that's the law. Now, you listen. You pay out to me as fast as I need it, and if the rope ain't long enough, you tie a rock on it. Not a big one, one I can tow. It'll keep the end from flopping around and I can fish it up when the tide's out. You got that?"

"I ain't going to help you do no such damfool trick. No way. You could drownd out there, or ain't you thought about that?"

"You do what I say if you don't want to sink me, then. You want a sock in the snoot? Because I'm going and you ain't big enough to stop me."

"I know I ain't." Scared stiff, Jesse watched George tie a slipknot in one end of the rope, slide the loop over his head and under his arms. "For gaasake, George! Tie a bowline. That one'll cut off your wind."

"Not on me, it won't." George walked into the water, grandly trailing rope.

Nekkid as a apple, Jesse thought miserably. And blue around his mouth to begin with. I ought to run like the devil, get Set-Fire down here right now.

But there was no time. He found he had all he could do to pay out, straighten snaggles and kinks in the rope fast enough to keep up with George. George was a good strong swimmer and he was lashing through the water. Damn rope was stiff, too, wet with salt water.

Jesse suddenly was furious. "Okay, bubba," he yelled. "Long's I got my hands on this rope, I got more to say in this than you have. I see you petering out or in trouble, I'm going to haul you back here flapping, and you go ahead and cream me if you can catch me." His voice gave out in a croak. Yelling wasn't any good anyway, because George couldn't hear him—or if he could, he wasn't paying any mind. He didn't peter out and he didn't look to be in any trouble. He'd made it almost to the ledge when Jesse got close to the end of the coil of warp.

Tie a rock on it, hell! I ain't going to. I'm going to hang on, see'f he can tow me.

Then Jesse saw that he wasn't going to have to do that. The rope had stopped moving. There was George, heading back in, tearing up the water as if the old come-to-git-you himself was after him.

The sun's glare had shifted with sunrise. Behind George, the ledge was outlined clearly against the water. The punt had risen up on little stubby legs. It moved. It turned all the way around. For a moment, Jesse saw the length of it against a white splotch of surf that splashed up against the ledge; then it walked over and slid out of sight into the water.

It's big's a punt, Jesse thought wildly. But it sure-god ain't one. He began hauling on the rope the way he'd been going to, only harder.

George came thrashing through the water like a fish on a hook. He spraddled out on the sand, belly-down, arms and legs still swimming.

"For chrissake, George, what was it?"

George didn't say anything—he couldn't, he was too busy puking up salt water. The slipknot had tightened around his chest and his face was purple as a sea-cucumber. Jesse slashed the loop with his jackknife, pulled off his windbreaker and tried to rub George dry with it. There was a lot of George—it took time, but after a while he got up without a word, started to pull his clothes back on.

"I'm some glad I had a-holt of that rope," Jesse said.

"I ain't," George croaked. "You like to drownded me, you cussid fool. Yanked my head under five times."

"I hustled. I thought that critter was coming after you. The way you ripped up the water comin' back, seemed like you thought it was, too."

"Uh huh. So you got the living bejeezus scairt out of you, done just the wrong thing."

"Sure I was scared, who wouldn't be, and you was a lot nearer to it than I was. Did you get close enough to see what the cussid thing was?"

George had been scared, too. He stood looking off at the ledge, his eyes bugged out, as if he couldn't believe what he'd seen.

There was the water, icy-cold, greenish near the shore where it rippled over light-colored sand. There was the barnacly ledge, more of it showing now, and out beyond, the rollers, deep blue and hubbly for miles and miles, back to where they seemed to reach up and touch the sky. And nothing anywhere. Nothing alive. Nothing moving.

George said, "Gaadammit. Gaadammit to hell." But it didn't sound to Jesse like cussing, it was more a whisper-like.

Earlier on, George's yelp had waked up Set-Fire, who was a light sleeper. He'd snored a little before he'd got up. Kids were off on some prowl of their own, probably beachcombing, didn't want company. He'd planned, himself, to go down this morning, check out what damage the storm

had done to the beach. His building down there was old
and rickety—probably blowed flat, and that high tide and
gale had likely raised hell with the only handy landing
place on the cove.

At daybreak, he was starting up his breakfast when it
occurred to him that the kids would be starving by now,
and anyways, it was a nice morning for a picnic. Up at
the barns and pigpens, he could see that the hired men
were already starting work; he wouldn't be needed yet for
a while. His coffee pot was already hot; he loaded it, along
with a frypan; some thick slices of ham; a loaf of bread,
sliced and buttered; and a big bagful of doughnuts, into
a blueberry-picker's basket. Wouldn't be a dry stick of
wood left on the shore after that rain and storm tide, he
knew, so he took along a basketful of that, too.

Walking along the bank behind the bushes, he could
hear the kids arguing about something, but he didn't see
them until after he had started a fire in a dip of the ledges,
where there was a much used old fireplace built out of the
wind, and had got his coffee pot set in a niche where it
would keep hot. Then he climbed the ledges and peered
out over them just in time to see George's critter slide off
the ledge and George himself swing around and come
thrashing back for the beach.

Set-Fire's jaw dropped. I be darned! he told himself.
First one of them conundrums I ever see loose in these
waters. But what did them crazy little devils think they
could do? Catch it? His first impulse was to hustle down,
make sure George got in all right; then he saw the boys
were managing by themselves. He waited a while longer.
He always tried not to horn in on the kids' business unless
there was a real reason. Didn't seem to be one now.
George was good and cold, but he didn't look to be hurt
any. He seemed to be madder than anything else.

They both swung around when they heard the beachrocks crunch under his boots. He said, "You fellers just see a rare thing. Them big sea-turtles don't often come into these waters. You got blue feet, George. Better haul your socks and boots on."

Jesse let out a squeal. "Is *that* what that thing was? Oh, my golly, George, what you got so scared of, nothing but a turtle! A plain old turtle, only a big one. He thought it was a punt gone adrift, Set. Oh, wow! You sure Scott-ed that one up, Georgy, boy!"

George, who was sitting on a rock yanking his socks on, began to blaze with fury. Set-Fire glanced down at him. "Well, I don't know's I'd say that," he said. "If he thought it was a punt, he made a darn good try to salvage it. I got a bucket of breakfast over there in the ledges and a fire going. Let's go see what's in the bucket, get some hot coffee into you, George."

"Oh, boy, breakfast!" Jesse shot away, taking care to give George a wide berth.

"Him and his big mouth," George muttered. "Darn little wonkhead was as scared as I was, cuss him."

"Reason to be, both of you," Set-Fire said. "Man who has to do with the salt water is damn dumb if he ain't careful of something he runs acrost in it that he don't know what is, or why it's there, or what it might do. I see a mermaid, once, and she was pretty what I see of her, but I wouldn't want to be any closer to her than I was."

"Oh, come on, Set!" George grinned in spite of himself, already loosening up. He got up and came along, following Set-Fire across the beach.

"You see what you think you see, sometimes," Set-Fire said.

"I thought I saw a punt. It had to be a gaadamn turtle," George said. "How'd I know? I never see anything like it before."

"Few around here ever did," Set-Fire said. "I figure

this one was lost. That tommycane's been tootling up the coast for a week, likely drove him north out'n his own waters, so he come to rest on that ledge till he could get back enough juice to set out for where he belongs to. He's had a hard chance, that old feller. We was lucky to see him." He slid neatly down over the ledges to the fire, where Jesse already had the frypan on, the slices of ham spitting as they browned.

"Some luck," George muttered. He thought, Why couldn't I been lucky just this once? Scott luck, I got, like them old-time buggers. If that had been a punt and I'd've got to her, brought her in, everybody'd've thought I was smart. He gave Jesse a glare that fairly bounced. "Mother's little helper," he said nastily.

Set-Fire, noticing, slid a fork under a slice of ham and turned it over. "Let 'er cool off a little, Jess," he said. "Ham's better if it's browned slow." He went on talking. "Long ago's when I was a boy Laze Wyman caught one of them big turtles out by Three Brothers Islands. It got wound up in the warp on one of his traps. He towed it in alive and anchored it on the shore, so's people could see it, and it laid there mourning and sighing just like a person."

"For goshsake, what kind of a louse would do that?" Jesse said. "Why couldn't he let it go?"

"Well, it was something seldom seen round here, so he thought he could make a cent or two, charge people ten cents a look. Turtle only stood it an hour or so before it up'n died on him. Stunk something awful before he could get it moved, and then it cost *him*, because it took four men to lift it, and he had to pay them. That ham's done, Jess, dig in."

George dug in at once, but Jesse sat where he was. Set-Fire saw, without seeming to notice, that he had water in his eyes. Funny kid. Had more of a feeling for critters, almost looked like, than he had for humans, especially hurt critters. Couldn't stand it if any of the farm animals got sick or banged up. Took care of them like a mother, if he got a chance to, cried his heart out if one died. Made pets out of them—him and that big sow, Janine, he's named her, is closer'n brothers. And there he sets, all tore out about an old turtle dead twenty-five years ago.

He slid a thick slice of ham between two slices of bread and handed it to Jesse. "That's a beautiful sight," he said. "Now, if God is as right-minded as we been told He is, there'll be a table loaded with that inside of the pearly gates for the newcomers to mug up on. Eat it before it's cold, Jess boy."

Jesse stared at the sandwich.

George grunted. "Look at old drizzlepuss. Can't eat his breakfast because some old crudfoot was mean to a turtle."

"Dead and forgot, years ago," Set-Fire said. "So's old Wyman. Had a stroke in the barn and laid there all day, mourning and sighing, just like that old turtle. His wife thought it was the hoss took sick. She was scairt to death of a well hoss, let alone a sick one, so she didn't take any steps till Laze didn't show up for supper. She was Fan Dunning's granmother, runs in the family to be scairt of critters. Fan don't scarcely dast to feed the hens, afraid one'll fly into her hair. Quite often things get evened up one way or another." He stopped talking, seeing that Jesse had started on his sandwich.

"Evened up, nuts!" George burst out. "Look, I bust a gut trying to get me a punt, and what's the gaadamn thing do, it turns into a turtle. How's that even up anything?"

"Well, now, George, it's let me know how bad you want a boat to go fishin' in. I gather, from the traps you got squirreled away in the pond, that that's what you want one for. You seen the skiff Moses Allen brought back from Nova Scotia, last time he was up there?"

George's jaw dropped, revealing a bite of doughnut, unswallowed, on his tongue. Seemed Set had known about those traps all the time! "Sure, I seen it. It's a dandy. For sale, too. Seein' it don't help me any." He sat with his head bent down so that Set couldn't see his face, which had turned red.

"Well, I was talking boat with Polly when he was home. He was saying how good Walt done catching lobsters and crabs for the store summer trade, in my old peapod, which ain't usable anymore. We used to make money out of that, and so did Walt. Polly said why not look around for a good stout skiff that'll take an outboard motor, and lay in some trap-stock, or you could overhaul some of Walt's old traps that's still stacked up in my old fishhouse over there on the bank. They're old, but some of them ain't in bad shape."

"Jeeze," George said and choked a little. He did not look up, but Jesse rose with a yell. "Oh, gosh! Oh, gorrying, Set!" He started off across the ledges in a wild dance, yelling, "Woo! Woo! Woo!"

"Look at that crazy kid," George said in a croak. He yelled after Jesse, "Cut that out, you cussid little fool, you'll bust your gaadamn neck!"

But Jesse didn't. He plunged out of sight down the ledges, and they could hear his joyous racket fade away along the beach.

"That skiff of Mo Allen's is too good a chance for us to miss," Set-Fire said. "I ain't got time to go over to his boatyard today, but how'd you like to do it, find out how much he wants for her, and what an outboard would cost? Tell him, he don't want the cost of a set of uppers and lowers, Paulus'll buy her."

George gave him a straight look. "Does P-Polly know about the traps in the pond?"

"Joe Falls does. He's been holding back because he

growed up with your father, always liked him. If I was you, I'd fish them traps outa the pond, line them up top of the beach, so's them that owns 'em can find 'em."

"Jeeze," George said again. He got up. "Darn kid left us with all the stuff to pick up and the fire going."

The dregs in the coffee pot weren't enough to put out the fire and to get water meant, with ebb tide, a slippery trip down over the rockweed-covered ledges. George unzipped his fly. He produced a splendid stream. The fire died without a crackle.

Set-Fire hid a grin. Not that, wet like it was after the storm, there was any danger from a beach fire, but it was a good idea to douse any outdoors fire, any time.

Well, there were all kinds of ways for a boy to brace up his manhood. Aloud, Set said, "My gorry, George. Sammy Cole's got you matched for distance, but I never see that volume beat in my whole life."

Paulus arrived home for good and on schedule. He found George at the farmhouse, living in Walter's old room, but Jesse had been forced to go home with Gladys, who had appeared at the house with the threatened court order. Jesse hadn't wanted to go, though he hadn't fought against going, and Amanda had known no legal way to keep him. Polly would have to cope when he got home. He tried to, going to the District Judge who had issued the order. He found there was nothing to do about Jesse, Gladys having got in first with her tale of woe.

"You surely can't want to take the last of this poor woman's sons away from her," the Judge said. "And you have no legal grounds for doing so. Mrs. Scott is not immoral, she is one of the most respectable ladies in town. Oh, I know she goes in for a dab of spiritualism, but a lot of people believe in that and she's got a bunch of loyal followers, my wife among them who'd rise up, mad as hornets, and call her holy, if you tried to prove immorality against her. As for her abusing her children, I see no proof of that. My wife tells me that youngster, Jesse, acts as a doortender, an usher, at his mother's séances, and you couldn't ask for a politer kid or one better dressed. She puts him in a little jacket kind of thing with a Buster Brown collar and the ladies all go crazy over him."

"My God!" Paulus said, staring. "She also puts him in a closet to make thumps and noises so the customers'll know the spirits are coming, or didn't she tell you that?"

"Heard about that, did you? My wife was there that day, saw what happened. The older boy hid in a closet and made vulgar noises. Tried to disrupt the services."

"Services? It's a religion?"

"Certainly, to people who believe in it. That boy is a known thief, and I'm pretty sure it's only a question of time before he comes up before me on a charge of petty larceny. You've only his word, no proof, that she sells the clothes you buy or that she beats him and his brother, abuses them. Personally, I wouldn't believe a word he says."

"Is that right?" Paulus said. He was already hot under the collar, trying to control his temper.

"I understand you've got him living over at your place, now."

"Yes. His mother blacked his eye and threw him out of her house. Both boys were hurt. The younger one was black and blue all over."

The Judge nodded. "The Colcraft gang," he said. "There's another town plague the law'll catch up with sooner or later. Well, maybe you and your sister can straighten young George out." His tone said he didn't believe that could be done.

"I'd like to make it permanent," Paulus said. "Adopt both boys. Their father, as perhaps you don't know, appointed me their guardian in his place."

"H'm. Their father. Not too responsible a man, was he? No. You've got no grounds for legally separating them from their mother. The only way you can do it is with Mrs. Scott's written permission. You understand I've got a good deal of eyewitness information in this case. Unprejudiced, I might say."

"Unprejudiced? From Gladys Scott?"

"From my wife, who was present the day young George tried one of his irresponsible tricks on his mother. It seems to me also that your attitude towards her is influenced by ill-will. And ill-will often makes for injustice."

"I admit that my family and I are influenced by what we know to be facts," Paulus said slowly. "As I have tried to explain to you. And I won't listen, even from you, to any goddamn slander about my brother Ralph, regardless of the lies his wife's put out about him. He was a decent man, who supported his family as best he could. I don't doubt the bank has a record of some of the checks he sent home, a good part of his wages for years. If you're interested in justice, you can find out. It doesn't seem to us that a fake medium parlor, where young kids are forced against their will to take part in the fraud, is a very healthy place to be brought up."

"These children should be brought up by their own mother, it's only natural, with her doing the only thing she has she can make a living by. I'm afraid you haven't convinced me, Mr. Scott."

"I'm afraid I haven't. Thank you, sir, for wasting my time."

And has that jowly, sanctimonious old bastard had one hell of a snow job worked on him, Paulus thought, as he drove slowly home. Well, Gladys was one who could do it. She was no fool, and she had many faces she presented to the public. The motherly, wife-of-God one she showed to her clients, as bearer of pleasant messages from Heaven —and she must put on a good show, since she was able to convince so many of them; the one she had turned on for the Judge, of a good woman, deeply troubled, struggling against odds to raise her hoodlums of kids, who were going to hell in a hack, no matter how hard she tried, and with no help from anyone—she, attractive and good-looking, too. . . .

Paulus, in spite of his fury, burst out laughing. My God! he thought. The poor old Judge. Because Gladys *was* good-looking and most attractive when she wanted to be. She could put it out the way a squash blossom puts out pollen; her voice which could clang like a busted bell could also coo. Paulus knew; she had tried it on him; it was potent stuff. Bet she had the old gasbag mumbling comfort and patting her hand. As if he'd had a chance.

"I guess she's got us over a barrel," Paulus told Amanda. "There's nothing we can do, except wait to see if she takes her hand off her number."

That Gladys, herself, thought she had, showed almost daily. She refused, gaily, to sign anything. "Who knows, I might just want George back again someday." She had obviously got the message about Jesse. He was always clean now, natty in decent shirts and jeans. She brought him often to the farmhouse, as if to show how well she was keeping him. If Jesse had begun again to droop like a wet chicken, at least his clothes were neat. With signs of inner triumph and with Jesse trailing, she would appear at mealtimes.

"I've brought Jesse to see his darling brother, he does so miss George at home. Oh, you're eating, Amanda! Sayonce day, and I always just lose track of the time." She would lean toward the table, the sides of her nostrils, thin as paper, working in and out as she smelled the food. "Oh, beef stew. I can't think of when I've had a good one."

If you want a beef stew all you've got to do is to cook one, was on the tip of Amanda's tongue, but she didn't say it. It was worth it, having Jesse here, knowing that, today at least, he was getting his dinner, but sad, seeing his disappointment because George wasn't home. George was a busy boy these days; he not only had his new skiff, but he had a sparkling new outboard motor; he was putting in all his time getting his lobster traps ready to put in the water. He was staying down at Set-Fire's place, eating and sleeping there because it was closer to his work. Jesse would look around and, not seeing George, would dawdle and eat next to nothing, not even Cora's dessert, something she knew he liked and fixed especially, hoping he would turn up today. Often he would leave it on his plate, get excused, and go out to wander around the farm, not finding Set-Fire either, who would be down having his dinner at home. Jesse would end up over at the pigpens, visiting with Janine, his pet sow.

Gladys never noticed that George wasn't there, or that, sooner or later, Cora would begin to sneeze. Cora was allergic not only to Gladys, but to the perfumed stuff put on Jesse's hair to keep his curls neat. "My Go-ud! That boy *reeks!*" Cora would say, pick up her plate, and depart to finish her dinner in the kitchen. Gladys's full attention was always on the laden plate Amanda passed her; she would not look up until it was empty, polished clean with a piece of bread. Then she would sit craning her neck at the kitchen counter to see what was for dessert.

They could always tell by the smell of Jesse's hair whether or not he could stay for the afternoon. On her séance days, Gladys anointed Jesse with a perfumed concoction which made his hair stand up in neat little black sausages all over his head. It smelt like a combination of all the ladies who came to Gladys's sessions; George, who had had it used on him—but only once since it hadn't worked on his wiry thatch—said it tasted worse than it smelt. He had swiped a bottle to experiment with and reported that it was like a tutti-frutti ice cream cone mixed with a girl's lipstick.

Jesse would wash it out as soon as he could after a morning séance, but if there were to be an afternoon one on the same day, he would have to leave it in. On those days, he would barely have time to rush over to the pens and say hello to Janine, scratch her a couple of times along the ears, before his mother came hollering after him. She didn't care where he went or what he did when she didn't need him; but summer was her busy time with all the tourists, services twice a day.

Back with her he would have to go, shoulders hunched, to make the tunks and thumps and little moans to let the customers know the spirits had heard the call and were coming through.

Such a handsome little boy, the ladies said—quiet and with such nice manners to answer the doorbell and usher them to seats in the darkened living room. A picture child in his Buster Brown collar, all love and sweet innocence, who surely would not be there or would be different, if what they had come for was nothing but a wicked fake, as some people believed it to be.

What could be wrong with wanting even a moment's relief from the desperate longing, when words spoken and a touch light as an angel's wing on a tear-stained cheek were proof that a lost loved one was not lost forever? Dear Mrs. Scott, transformed, as she said, out of herself, to a sacred vessel the beautiful messages from

Heaven dropped into—she was like a universal mother bringing comfort and hope. "As if," one lady whispered to another, "she might be God's wife."

And that sweet little boy, who never looked up when he let you in—he must be shy, the lamb—fitted the services much better than that great lump, George, not here any-more. Why, when he had tended door, he'd stare at everyone in a real smartypants way, not nice at all; and once when somebody asked him why he did that, he said he was counting the house.

Jesse had heard all this talked over, at one time or another, and he did not look up at the ladies because he could not bear to. Because Ma was taking those sorry-acting women for a ride, for what she could get out of it, and they *was* sorry, awful sorry, poor old buggers, they really meant all that howling they did. They wanted so bad to believe in what Ma said she could do, when she didn't and couldn't, and he had to help her make fools of them, no way out that he could see. And he was alone in the house with Ma, now George was gone. And George was really gone. Jesse couldn't get used to the empty bed across the room from his own.

He had looked forward to Uncle Polly's coming home, sure that he would do something to help, but, so far, Uncle Polly hadn't. All that had come of that, George had the boat and the outboard all to himself, and was too busy working on traps and setting them to do any-thing else, even to take time off and give a feller a ride in the boat. And if he did, he wouldn't let you run the engine, just humped over it like a fat old broody hen, put out a lot of glop about no fisherman could afford to have his engine fooled with. If you ate over at the farm-house with Ma, half the time George wasn't there, he was either eating down with Set-Fire, or he'd taken his lunch and gone off in the boat for the day. Made you

feel like in a desert with nobody else good around. Nobody friendly. Seemed the only friend he had now was
Janine—at least, she'd let you scratch her back and come
into the pigpen with her.

For all the séance ladies knew, Jesse, too, might be
counting the house, but he never looked up at them and
no one saw the panic in the black eyes under the lowered
lids.

VI

Paulus found, after he was settled in at home, that he
would have no trouble finding things to do—there were
enough jobs lying around to keep two men busy. George
could use help getting his string of traps in shape; Walter,
using what little time he had, was still plugging away at
the Pansy Plummer place—if anyone needed help, Walter
did at the height of the fishing season. Either of those
two would welcome him with open arms.

He was thrifty and smart; over the years he had saved
what he could of his Navy pay and he had his retirement
pension. He decided he could afford not to tie himself
down to a steady job—he'd take a kind of working vacation, help out the boys, potter around at auctions, look
the situation over. Summer was antiques season in the
area; there were auctions and yard-sales all over the place.
He went to any auction he heard of and generally came
away with an item or two which brought him a pleasant
profit. Antique shops were legion; another one wouldn't
make sense, so he sold mostly to private customers. He
had planned to take Jesse with him on some of his buying
trips, whenever Gladys would let him go, but after the
first week or so, Jesse was nowhere to be found. If he

came with Gladys to dinner, he would either have to go home with her, or he would vanish completely. Paulus was puzzled; he'd looked forward to a friendly companionship with Jesse.

George was puzzled, too, and George was also huffy. "I d'no where he goes now. He used to come around when I first got the boat, but he got, like, sore at something, and ain't been back. Maybe he thinks I'll hunt him up, but I ain't got any time. He'll have to scratch his mad place."

Set-Fire said, "I don't know what to make of it. Jess was always right to George's heels, and George feels it. Once in a while I catch up with Jess over around the pigpens, but if he sees me first he takes off, don't even say 'hi' to me. He's made a pet of that big sow, Janine, and I got a problem there, Polly. Janine's about ready to drop piglets and I got a customer for her, Gene Dunning, he wants her, piglets and all, before she does. Offers a good price and would take her tomorrow, if I said the word."

"Don't sell her," Paulus said. "You must have other sows he could buy."

"Sure. I got Pixie, Janine's sister. They're neck and neck, far's littering's concerned, look just alike, too. Jess says he can tell the difference, but nobody else could except Pixie takes after her pa and Janine don't. They both come from a load that was put aboard of Betsey, my old sow, the night that crazy boar we sold to Joe Preble got loose and busted into her pen. Her and me both was, you might say, took by surprise. I didn't know she'd been to a party till I see signs of it. Now, Pixie's wild-acting, needs a strong pen to keep her in, but she's from a good line. That boar of Joe's is a dandy, got a pedigree and so's Betsey. But Gene wants Janine because she's gentle. Says his wife Fanny does all the feeding and she'd be scairt to death of a wild-acting sow."

Paulus meditated. "Let me go see Gene," he said. "I've got an idea."

He recalled that, some years ago, when he'd been over at Gene's place for one reason or another, he had spotted in the barn a pretty nice old table. It was one of the items of furniture that Gene's grandfather had salvaged out of the *William Carey*, valuable if only for that reason, but it had other points of interest which had put a glint into Paulus's eye. The *William Carey* had been a hundred years old; she had carried the first missionary to India and had been named after him. Some of the furnishings which local people had saved out of her at the time of her loss had borne the name of a famous English cabinet-maker, and Paulus suspected that Gene's table did, too. He drove over to talk with Gene.

"That sow you want, Janine, she's kind of a pet over at our place. Set don't want to sell her and she'd cost you twice what Pixie would."

"Damndest thing," Gene said.

"What is?"

"You name all your sows?"

"Me? No, Set does, some of them, the good ones, and so does young Jesse. He likes pigs. Actually, Janine belongs to him. You can see why—"

"Hell, that boar of Preble's is crazier'n a wildcat. All them piglets going to have that wild blood. I don't want um around."

"Too bad. I was going to try to fix up a swap with you, so Pixie wouldn't cost you any cash at all."

"Young untried sow, first litter, can't tell what she'll do. Go crazy, eat up the young, I've known um to . . . uh, what was't you wanted to swap for?"

"Even-steven for that old table you've got in the barn."

Gene planted his bony stern on a nearby keg. He pulled

out his pipe, filled it, got it going. Paulus was known to be a smart swapper. "That old table, godfrey mighty, it's got sent'mental value to me. Me and my father'n granfather's built lobster traps on it all our lives. That's a pretty good table, too, Polly. It's solid mahogany. Likely it's worth more'n a litterin' sow."

"Could have been, once. Now, the top of it's all pounded into fuzz, looks more like cloth than wood. One of the legs is half off of it, and I'd say your hens been roosting on it for a considerable time. Old Betsey's first litter, she had thirteen, kept it up all the years we've had her."

"Them antique dealers, likely the more fuzz it's got on it, the higher they'll value it."

"Could be. Well, sorry we can't sell you Janine, Gene. See ya around."

"Hey, where you going? I never said I wouldn't swap. Got to be even-steven, though, like you said."

"Fine, it's a deal. Set's gone today, he's upstate looking at some cows and I won't be around this afternoon either. How's about if we deliver Pixie as soon as he gets back?"

Together, they loaded the table into the back of the farm pickup truck. It was a mess, and Gene cackled, looking at it. "Be almost worth it to see one of them antiques nuts scrubbing off hen turd," he said. He felt good. This was quite a swap—on his side.

"Wouldn't it, though." Paulus felt good, too. He had already spotted the cabinetmaker's mark he was looking for.

Deliver nothing, Gene told himself, as Paulus drove away. Dickered with him for a sow, I'll go get it myself. He grinned a little. Don't matter a hell's bean to me if everybody *is* gone. Haying time, likely wouldn't be a hired man on the place.

The two pens were side by side in the long row of pig-pens, Pixie in one, Janine in the other, empty ones on either side. The partitions between were removable gates. Gene had noticed them the other day when he'd been over here arguing with Set-Fire.

"Looks like a lot of trouble for just a batch of fool sows," he'd said to Set.

"Oh, the little fellers keep healthier when they got room to run," Set had told him. "So I just take down a couple of gates and let 'em use the empty pens till they're big enough to go on range."

Handy, Gene thought. He drove cautiously through the farmyard, backed his truck up to Janine's pen. He took down the front gate, laid a couple of planks at an easy angle from the tailgate into the truck, urged Janine up the planks. She went, good-naturedly enough, gave a couple of contented grunts, and settled down in the straw. "Nice and gentle, like he said," Gene told her. "And not you, you cussed loucifee," he told her neighbor next door, for Pixie was already beginning to ravage around at the sight of a stranger.

He put back the gate of the pen, leaned over and opened the gate between, tossed a handful of straw into Pixie's face. She came roaring, mouth wide open, full tilt at him into Janine's pen, and Gene slammed the gate behind her. "So there you are," he said. "And not a hand-ful of difference in looks between the two of you."

He drove home, pleased with himself. Didn't doubt but what Polly'd thought he'd done him on that table, likely it was worth a mint. But not to me, by gorry. All I done, I got my own back. That crazy sow he tried to work off on me would've scairt the bejeezus outa Fanny. Poor old flapdoodle was scairt of all the farm critters, even the rooster. She milked the cows, fed the hens and pig, lugged the firewood and so on, when he was busy, as he always was. Wouldn't want her to git an arm bit off, so's she couldn't.

Paulus had taken his table down to Walter's wood-working shop to refinish it. He had spent part of his time helping Walter work on the house, using Walter's tools, since he hadn't got around to equipping a shop of his own. Walter had a fine set of tools, kept oiled and sharp, as might be expected of him, and Paulus spent contented hours scrubbing, sanding and regluing. The table turned out to be what he had suspected it was—would have been valuable even without the cabinetmaker's mark, which showed up cleanly as layers of filth fell away from it. He was delighted to see how the old wood came to life under his hands.

He was pretty sure he had a customer for the table. Mrs. Bradley, a summer woman whom he had met at auctions, had been on the lookout for items known to be salvaged from the *William Carey*. He phoned her when the table was finished. She came at once to see it and offered him a price which made him blink.

"Oh, that's beautiful!" she said simply, with no dicker-ing whatever. "I must have it, Mr. Scott. I'll send a man over to pick it up right away. And do let me know if you run across anything else as good as this."

He thought briefly of the captain's dresser which had stood in the farmhouse dining room since 1863, of the banisters and stair-rail which his great-grandfather had built out of teak from the *Carey*. Good Lord, no! he told himself firmly. Leave us not get carried away, and grinned a little at his own pun. It was heady stuff, this antiques business. He could see Gran's face now, if he dared to suggest it.

"By the way, Mr. Scott," she said, as she was leaving, "I think my husband would like to see you. He collects antique cars, you know, and restores them. Foss Bailey's been talking to him about you."

"Thanks," Paulus said. "I'd be pleased to go see him." Jobs are schooling, he thought. Ganging up on me. Vacation? Looks like no way.

Foss, who loved antique cars and knew quite a lot about them, had mentioned Jones Bradley's collection. "Got his outbuildings stuffed full of them beautiful old babies. My God, Polly, they'd make ya drool. You ought to go see'm. He's a nice feller, Bradley. Loves to talk about 'm, too."

Certainly got a nice wife, Paulus thought. A little stunned, he stared at the check she had left in his hand. Wow! This would pay Set-Fire what Pixie and her litter would have brought in the market with a handsome sum left over. Would put Set's farm account in order, too. Paulus began to list in his mind the woodworking tools he'd need to buy, when and if he set up a shop of his own. Not fair to wear out Walt's tools; besides, some he needed Walt didn't own.

He had swept up the mess he'd made in the summer kitchen and was putting away Walt's tools, cleaned and oiled, in his box, when Henry raced through the door. He made at once for Paulus's leg and started to climb. "Single-track mind, hey, Little Grundoon?" Paulus said. "Come ahead. Let's see how far you get." He was surprised at the strength in the small hands, as Henry patiently wormed his way up the pants-leg.

For some time he had been aware of Henry outside, being prevented by Suzy from coming in because Uncle Polly was busy. Apparently, they had company for there'd been three sets of squeals and laughter in different keys. Jess, maybe? Could be it's here he comes, now he's given us at the farm the go-by. Paulus scooped Henry off his leg and carried him to the doorway, just in time to see Jesse disappear around the corner of the house. "Hey, Jess!" he called. "Come on back, I want to see you," but Jesse didn't come.

"Jess is a hard man to catch up with," Paulus said, as he deposited Henry on the kitchen floor. "Doesn't seem to like us anymore up at the farm . . . oh. It isn't Suzy, is it?"

The young woman at the sink turned around and smiled at him. "No," she said. "It's Annabelle. Suzy's gone shopping in Machias. I'm baby-sitting. How are you, Polly?"

Annabelle Franklin, he thought. Aaron's girl. At least, she had been with Aaron at Gran's party. He had known her, or known who she was, for years, about the way he had known Suzy before she and Walt got married—she had been a classmate of Aaron. Lord, they all seemed so young, these kids. This one had grown up darned pretty. Lucky guy, Aaron. "I'm fine," he said. "Getting my teeth into settling down at home. Or trying to."

"It's hard to, isn't it?" she said. "I know how I felt. Like the lady who was caught in the cyclone—flying off in all directions at once."

"If you've been away, too, then you know. Where'd you go, Annabelle?"

"Oh, I went to Boston and took nurse's training. Was there three years. Came home and got a job in the Machias hospital. This is my day off. How'd you like some coffee? I was just about to have some."

"Sure. Like to," Paulus said. He sat down, impeded a little by Henry, who had started climbing again.

"Hank, for heaven's sake, quit climbing up your uncle's leg. Look, here's cookies. Go find Jesse and give him one."

Henry said, in a wondering tone, "Chess?" and started for the door. He made it to the bottom of the front steps, before he fell down with a thump and an outraged roar that brought Jesse on the run from wherever he'd gone to.

He said, "That was good, Skipper John. Y'almost made it all the way down without fallin', and next time you won't fall atall, like I told ya. Come on, wipe the dirt off your cookie, and we'll go find old Doctor Pilgarlic and make him show us the hair on his teeth. Shut up, now, you make that noise and he won't come out."

Sounds faded as they moved away somewhere, and Annabelle said, "My soul, what doctor around here has hair on his teeth?"

Paulus laughed. "That's first-hand, right out of one of Gran Scott's old folk-yarns," he said. "Skipper John, he's the hero of it, he goes around with a bottle of squid-ink and blots out all the villains. Lots of villains. There's the Aber-nits that spit on your shoes, and Big Tunk and Little Tunk who live in the pond and go tunk-tunk all night. Doctor Pilgarlic, he's the worst actor of all. He does have hair on his teeth and he lives in a hollow tree."

"That's lovely. Squirt with the squid-ink and whammo! Right?"

"Right. Ralph and I and Amanda grew up on Doctor Pilgarlic and them."

"Does it come in a spray can?"

"Would nowadays, I guess. You could ask at the store."

"Darned if I don't. Darned if a nice big can of black squid-ink wouldn't be handy to have around, right now."

Paulus glanced at her. "You sound pretty sore at someone," he said.

"Oh, not too. I'll live through it. I have, for a number of years. Nothing that some kind of disappearing-juice won't cure, that's for sure. Forget it, Polly."

But she was good and sore, put out with someone—he could tell by the way her eyes had flamed up and snapped. He wondered who. Aaron, maybe? Take more than squid-ink to handle Aaron.

She kept talking. "That little Jesse, he's wonderful with Henry. I spend quite a few of my days off over here with

Suzy—she's my cousin, you know, the only family I have
left now. And those two kids together, it's really nice to
see. What they do, playing. They've got all kinds of little
secret games and stories they act out. Suzy says that
sometimes she could swear there're more than two kids
out there in the yard, the gabble that goes on. But there
never is, and if you go out, everything stops, as if whoever . . . whatever . . . *it* goes away. A little weird-o,
isn't it? Like some poem I read; somewhere once:

"When children are playing alone on the green,
In comes the friend who never is seen."

"It was in some school reader, I think," Paulus said.
"Yes, it was. And it ends up:

"When children are quiet and lonely and good
The friend of the children comes out of the wood."

"I guess I was pretty hard-boiled in the fourth grade
or whatever," Paulus said. "Or Ralph was. I took it from
him, as I recall, that that little ditty was something the
old Holy-Joe who put together the reader stuck in to
tell kids to be quiet and good and not bother the grown-
ups and see what lovely happened. So nothing happened.
Likely who came out of the woods would be old Grampa
Dunning with a bucket of blueberries."

"Seemed like that, didn't it? Kids learn early, after they
wonder a little. These two, now, when I'm here, I can't
help but get interested . . . how they are together.
Hank's a little tartar, into everything; taking care of him
is a full-time job, you better believe. You spend your day
hauling Hank out of things by the seat of the pants. But
with Jesse, he's good as gold. They go off together, gab-
bling as if they were the same age, no trouble to anyone,
unless you butt in. I did, this morning, but only because
I'd made a batch of cookies. Jess is an odd boy—you try

to talk to him and he just oozes away and vanishes, and then there's hell to pay with Henry."

"As if they were the same age," Paulus repeated, thoughtfully. "Maybe that's where I slipped up with Jess. I've been trying to figure out. We've always been pretty good friends, but since I've been home, I can't get to first base with him."

He felt a sudden desire to talk about it. He hadn't; at least he hadn't mentioned to anyone his doubts and his very real concern about his ability to understand kids. As for Gran and Amanda, they both had unlimited faith; he was home at last, he could handle any problem that stuck up, and it was no use to tell them he couldn't.

"I don't know," he began. "It's likely my fault. I told the boys' father when he appointed me their guardian that I knew more about a bagful of monkey wrenches than I did about kids, and I guess I was right." He went on to tell about what he had tried so far: the picnic at the lake, the bikes, George's boat and traps, the interview with the Judge. "And now I'm stumped. What more can I do?"

"Well, you asked me," Annabelle said. "You haven't tried hard enough. You haven't bothered, have you? Suzy says you've been running around happy as a clamdigger, busy with your own affairs, as likely you've had to be, but do you think for a moment Jesse knows how hard you've tried to get him away from that frightful mother of his? Has anyone told him? Have you?"

"I told you," he said, "I'm a duffer at it—"

"Well, don't be. If Hank is old enough to be treated like a . . . a person, instead of a baby, Jesse certainly is. Collar him and back him up against a wall, if you have to, and tell him, man to man, what you've done, how you feel . . . and . . . and as if . . ."

"As if he were my own age," Paulus said. "Like you said." My God, that'll take doing, he thought. "Thirty-eight to twelve, Annabelle?"

"What's it matter, if you can only get through to him? You could try. Oh, Polly, I'm sorry, I've been reading you out like a schoolmarm, and I'm a poor one to do that with . . . with anyone."

"Read me out? You've blown me out of the water, fantail first, is what you've done. Time somebody did, I guess, and you've given me an idea I can try instead of sitting around on my . . . uh, fantail."

"Oh, good. Maybe you'll let me know, if it works. Tell Suzy; she'll call me."

"Tell Suzy? No way. When's your next day off? Let's go somewhere. Do something together. Blueberries are ripe. We might go up the mountain, blueberrying."

She gasped a little, then burst out laughing, he couldn't think why, unless—well, this could be Aaron's girl he was trying to date. And so what? Let Aaron look out, then. "Or maybe you're tied up with someone else that day," he said, waiting.

"I'd love to," she said. "Next Thursday. And I'm not tied up with anyone, that or any day."

Paulus drove home feeling a good deal better about Jesse. He made up his mind to have a man-to-man talk with Jesse as soon as he could corner him. That was a smart girl. Had brains. Pretty, too. Nice eyes. Gold-brown in the center, greenish around the edges. Turned greener, when she lit up and laughed, and what the hell was so funny? Blueberrying? He suddenly remembered, and began, himself, to laugh, though he did feel a little warm around the ears. "Going blueberrying"—local slang for when a young couple lit out into the bushes. Lord, he thought. I've been a long time away.

Out with George in his skiff, that afternoon, he realized that he certainly had been. Most of his boyhood, before he'd joined the Navy, he had gone lobstering in a skiff of his own and had known all the likely places to set traps. He'd planned to help George, show him all the places; he found he couldn't remember any of them. George knew more than he did; George had asked around. He was handy with the skiff, too, and, Paulus thought, sitting uneasily in the bow, he had better be. He had loaded eight ballasted lobster traps aboard, balanced carefully four on a side, and while the skiff was a good stiff boat, still with all that weight she hadn't above three inches of freeboard. No lifebelts, either, unless George had a couple stashed under the stern seat.

"Don't shift your gum, Uncle Polly," George said cheerfully as they shoved off and a couple dollops of cold salt water splashed aboard. "Not likely," Paulus said. But the bay was calm as a lake—no wind and coming up for slack tide. George had picked his weather and his tide with considerable know-how, Paulus could see that. He felt better, however, when the last of the traps splashed overboard and they anchored, on the way home, with handlines over, hoping to catch a haddock or two for chowder for supper.

"Well, that's the last of 'em," George said. "I got twenty traps in the water now."

"You always load her so deep?" Paulus asked. "Eight's a lot for this size skiff, isn't it?"

"Day like this she'll handle eight all right," George said. "Might be a little hefty for her, but jeest, Uncle Polly, I've had to hustle like the devil to git going, if I'm going to make anything before school begins. I plan to tend traps early mornings or after school, that ain't really time enough. Not like take your dinnerpail and be gone all day if you feel like it. School, for gaasake! Waste the best part of the day on stuff that don't mean a gaadamn thing." He left off lamenting his freedom about to be lost, to haul up a good-sized fish and toss it flapping into the boat, and then went on.

Reading he didn't mind too much, if it was stories that made some sense, he liked stories. But writing, wow! His paper always came back out of sight under red marks, he was lucky if he ever got more on that than a D.

" 'Write about something you know,' she'll say. 'Something you saw today.' Well, *take* today. I know about rocky bottom and kelp beds today. And that's it. That's, for chrissake, *all* of it. And what does she want, a hundred words writ down on *paper*! She expect me to make my living that way?"

Paulus chuckled. "Some do," he said. "Make a living that way."

"Not me. Hell, they's a kid in my class copied a part of a piece out of a magazine and got an A on it, only they caught him and had a catfit. One way to get an A, but I d'no's I'd want one that bad. Shoot, I don't want one at all and that's for sure."

"No, I don't guess that's the way," Paulus said. "You'd have to be pretty smart in things like that to get away with it. I know a boy who did—at least, he said he did. Real pleasant young feller I knew in the Navy, name of Wylie Cope. He was a terrible kidder, though, had one of these deadpan faces, so you never knew whether he was ribbing you or not."

Sensing one of Paulus's stories, which he loved, George said, "Go on, Polly, tell about him."

"Well, I don't know as—" Paulus began and stopped. He'd been going to say, "it's the kind of story you'd go for," because it wasn't. It was, in a way, a boy's story, but quite a bit out of George's range; he would have to reach. Or would he? If Hank's old enough to be treated like people, so is Jesse. And so is George. So don't talk down. Okay, man to man. Let's see what George makes of Wylie Cope.

"He was big and solid-built, a darn good boxer, but what he said, he didn't want any part of boxing, he wanted to be a writer. Planned to be, after the War. One of the ratings, young college kid he was, told him that the way he handled his fists, he'd better stay put. He could be champion of the world with a little training. Writing, this college kid said, was one of the toughest fields there was to bust into. Said even if you did write a good book, chances were you couldn't get nobody to read it. Send it in, he said, you were lucky even to get it back, let alone get it printed. He'd tried, he said, and couldn't. He was pretty sour about the whole thing.

"Wylie said he couldn't find a job in town after high school graduation because all the bosses knew he was going to be drafted. He didn't like to hang around doing nothing and he got broke and sick of living on his folks. After a while he recalled a story of his grandfather's about a shipwreck and what took place in it. He hunted up books in the library that told what it was like to be in a shipwreck, what the ocean looked like in a tommycane and so on. He used Joseph Conrad and Homer, even put in a love scene from a nice lady writer named Ethel M. Dell. Didn't write in great slabs of any one of them, just picked good stuff and shuffled it all together to make a full deck. It didn't run as long as a book, so he took the address off of a drugstore magazine and sent the tale to them. Darned if they didn't buy it and look over their shoulders for more. But then Wylie got drafted and hadn't had time to write another one.

"The young college kid was some disgusted. He told Wylie that what he'd done was a crime he could be put in jail for, and Wylie said nobody was going to put a loyal defender of his country in the slammer for letting it be known how noble some of the old classic books were —that stuff being written now couldn't hold a candle to. Besides, some of the defenders before they got through defending might come to think a nice quiet jail would be a pretty good place to be. The next day the ones of us left decided that it might be. The destroyer was lying off Iwo Jima at the time."

He glanced over at George, who was sitting up straight, tense with excitement, zeroed in. He said, "You got something on your line, Uncle Polly."

"So I have," Paulus said. He hauled on the line, which yanked back, hard.

"Hey, could be a halibut," George said. He rooted around under the stern seat, came up with a short stout club, a cosher. "If 't is, you let him know I'm ready for him."

But the fish turned out to be a skate, big as a dining room table, no good for anything and a pest to get off a hook. Paulus struggled with it, finally got the hook out and let the thing go.

"Shoot, Uncle Polly," George said, "you don't never want to let your sinker sag down on bottom. You do, you most always ketch one of them cussid things, if they's one around. You stick with me, I'll show you how to git a halibut. You got a lot to learn. Bet you'll be darn good at it, though, once you know how."

"Right," Paulus said. "First chance we get, we'll try again, and you can show me."

Talk of any kind was impossible on the trip back to the harbor because of the outboard motor. Paulus lounged in the bow, thinking peacefully that he couldn't care less if his trick story had bounced like a lead balloon. First things first, he told himself. He watched with affection George's intent face, his knuckly brown fist skillful on the steering handle, showing off his newfound treasures which he would be pleased to share. If Hank was old enough to be treated like people, so was Jesse; and so was Uncle Polly, seemed. And Uncle Polly had better take a good loud laugh at himself.

"But it's not!" Jesse panted. He was red in the face, breathing hard from running. "I started to go in the pen to give her a good scratching and she come at me so hard she almost knocked the gate down. If I hadn't jumped fast, she'd've bit me. Janine would never do that, and it's not Janine. It's Pixie! I tell you, it's Pixie! Janine's gone!"

"Can't be," Set-Fire said. "Now, look, Jess, it's coming on the time for Janine to drop her piglets, first litter, too, and sows is tittlish-tempered, sometimes, then. Harry says Janine's been hard to git along with for some days now, comes at him when he feeds her. And you got that stink-pretty on your hair today. Maybe she smelt it and didn't realize it was you. Pigs goes a lot by smell."

Jesse stared at him. He had come to dinner today with his mother and he had to go back with her this afternoon. She had been already hollering after him when he had left the pigpens and had raced down the short-cut to Set-Fire's house.

"What would Pixie be doing in Janine's pen, anyhow?" Set-Fire asked.

"I don't know. But old Gene Dunning's got Janine, and he'll kill her. And he's ugly to all his animals. And she's . . . she's . . ."

"Gene's got Pixie, Jess. We sold him Pixie and he come and got her. It's all talked over."

"What'd he come and get her *in?* All he's got is that stake truck, and you think Pixie'd stay in that, stay hauled around in that, for five minutes? You said yourself, I heard you, that when you sold Pixie you'd have to haul her in a horse-box. I heard you."

"That's right, so I did. Have to hogtie and throw her, otherwise. Could be that's what Gene done. I'll go up and check—"

Jesse backed away. He spun on his heel and screamed back over his shoulder, "No, you won't! You won't do nothing! Nobody'll do anything!" He flashed out of sight around the corner of the house and back up the short-cut the way he had come.

Now, that's rough, Set-Fire told himself. Damn rough

on the poor little duffer, Glad-rags is up there hollering like a cat troddled on, and he's got to go back home with her before he finds out for sure.

Set began to think back a little. Gene Dunning. A righteous and holy old skunk, if there ever was one. Wanted Janine in the first place. Janine and Pixie just alike, dead ringers for each other, except for actions. No one could tell the difference, except Jesse, he said he could. I and Polly both gone that day, boys out haying. Stake truck, hanh?

He left the rest of his lunch unfinished and walked up to the big barn, where the three hired men were sitting around having theirs.

"Any you guys happen to notice Gene Dunning the day he come after Pixie?" Set-Fire asked.

Nobody had, face to face. But Harry Flanders spoke up. "I had the hay-baler halfway up Carey's Hill," he said. "I see a truck drive in and go out again. Was that him?"

"Stake truck, was it?"

"Uh huh, I could make out the stakes, all right. Hey, he wouldn't come after Pixie in a stake truck, would he? *Pixie?*"

"He's going to find himself in one hell of a merry mixup if't wasn't Pixie he hauled off," Set-Fire said.

"By the god, that explains it, by the god!" Harry said. "I been puzzlin' my brains baldheaded, wondering what's been wrong with Janine, thought she must be sick. By the god, that's Pixie down there, ain't it! I oughter known!"

Set-Fire walked out of the barn and across the yards to the pigpens, just in time to miss Gladys, who came around the corner purposefully stalking Jesse.

Jesse charged along the woods path, churning. The path was marshy, full of puddles, muddy in some places six inches deep. Sometimes he had to pull his feet, sucking, out of the mud, which rose over the tops of his sneakers and splattered up and down the legs of his jeans. He had on his new sneakers and clean jeans, because where he was supposed to be headed now was back home. Ma would likely kill him if he didn't show up in time for the séance. But this woods path was the shortest cut to Gene Dunning's place. Jesse didn't even wish for George to be along to help him let Janine out. She'd follow him home, Jesse knew she would.

The path let out into a cleared field a hundred yards or so above the shore. There was the Dunning farmhouse: apple orchard, garden, barn. And pigpen. Jesse made his way with caution up through the apple trees, keeping an eye out for Miz Fan Dunning, who might appear at any minute out of the kitchen door and screech at him to get off the place. She hated kids. Just walk by, and you'd think you was a visitor from outer space, the way she carried on. He got down on his hands and knees, crawled the last fifteen feet or so, stuck his head carefully over the fence. There she was. Janine. Lying there asleep in the sun.

Head on one end, tail on the other, four stubby legs. Big fat hams. And covered all down the side that showed with wet and dried mud. And scratches, too, some deep enough so's they'd bled.

Jesse stared in fury and outrage. Never in all her life had one ounce of mud touched her clean white sides. And that cussid old pirate had beat her up, too. Jesse choked and whispered softly, "Hi, Janine."

She didn't move. Couldn't hear him. He didn't dare to raise his voice. Couldn't reach her with his hand, either. He picked up a pebble and tossed it. It bounced off her rump but she only wiggled her tail a little. She was tail-to him; if he could find a stick long enough, he might poke her—not hard, just enough to make her turn around, see him, and know he was there.

He couldn't find any stick, but inside the open barn door was old Gene's bamboo fishpole he used for pickerel up in the pond. Jesse steadied the pole on the top rail of the fence, gave Janine a tentative poke. She only flipped her tail again. "C'mon, Janine. Wake up." He started to try again, but this time Janine did the poking.

She had had a frightful time since she had been in this filthy place. Miz Fan Dunning, who always fed the pig, was terrified of all animals bigger than a mouse—even a mouse could put her on top of a table. Every time she came near the pig yard with her bucket of slops, she used the bamboo pole to poke, prod, and thwack the pig back into the shed, before she dared to lift the bucket over the fence and empty it into the feeding trough. The pole was Janine's enemy. She had, if not as much as Pixie, a certain amount of wild blood, too, and her nerves were in shreds and tatters. She hated the pole; whoever was poking her with it made no difference to her now.

She scrabbled her legs under her, heaved her stern into the air as she got up. She moved so fast that Jesse couldn't yank the pole away in time. The tip of it went right into the little round hole under her tail. She let out such a squall as Jesse'd never heard a pig make, spun around and charged the fence. She slammed her whole weight against it. A whole section of it crashed down.

"Oh, my gorry!" Jesse gasped. He took one look, made for the nearest apple tree and swarmed up. It seemed to him that he used his fingernails like a cat's claws—he had never climbed a tree so fast in his life. Even so, she grabbed at his dangling foot as he tucked it up under him and tore the sneaker right off of it. For a minute, it looked as if she was going to climb the tree after him. And could. Through the leaves and nubbins of green apples, he watched her ravaging around under the tree, still squalling.

My gorry! She was *eating* that sneaker! She couldn't be Janine, she'd got to be Pixie.

But no. There behind her left ear, flapping the way it was, was the little round brown spot that nobody but him knew about so he knew that this was surely Janine. He looked down at her with black sorrow. Set-Fire had said that after Gene Dunning got hold of a pig, it wasn't going to get any love, that was for sure, and any sow treated mean would show up wild blood whether it had any or not.

"C'mon, Janine. It's me, can't you tell?"

But she couldn't, because another female squall cut in, coming from behind him. The two together hurt his ears. Miz Fan Dunning was standing in her kitchen door screeching.

"I seen you, what you done, you little devil! Goosed that pig, poked that fishpole right up her tailhole! Not any cruel mean monster would've done it. You come down here straight to me!"

Jesse wasn't about to do that, not with Janine and her, either one of them or both, down there waiting. He latched on hard to his tree limb, felt the one he was sitting on give a little. He stared around wildly. This was the tree, oh, my godfrey mighty, yes, it was—the one he and George had swiped the apples off of last fall, and George, an old hand, had said always be careful of a Northern Spy tree, because the wood was soft and likely to break off at the crotch.

Well, let it break off. I d'no's I care what I fall down into, right now. Jesse closed his eyes and waited, then opened them again as he realized that Janine, at least, had stopped squalling.

She had spit out his sneaker and was hightailing it down the shore path. Sounded like a galloping horse. Something must've scared her, maybe Miz Dunning's hollering. Anyway, she was leaving the scene. At least, he could get his sneaker back—enough of it to run back through the woods in, say he ever got out of here able to.

Miz Fan Dunning went up on a higher note. A man with a trumpet couldn't have done better. "Gene, Gene! Look out for the pig! She's out and crazy, insane mad! Call the doctor!"

There was old Gene coming up the path with a skunout fish in one hand and his rubber boots on. Jesse stared in horror. Call the doctor was right, if he and Janine met head-on.

It didn't seem possible that a man with rubber boots on could jump so high. Old Gene's fish went up ten feet, his hat flew after it. Janine galloped under him; it looked as if the wind of her had blown him right up into the air. He landed on the path behind her, laid there all sprawled out.

Miz Fan Dunning stood where she was in the doorway. "Gene! Gene? Oh, my Go-ud, are you dead? Oh, I know you're dead, Gene."

Gene sat up. He bawled back. "No, I ain't dead nuther! How'd that chriseless sow git out? Gaadamn it, she'll drop them piglets all over the woodlot!" He scrabbled to his feet and took out after Janine.

Miz Fan Dunning stood screeching on, how it was, waving her arms at Jesse in the apple tree, telling. She ran down, slowly, like a wind-up phonograph, opened her eyes and stared all around. She caught sight of Gene's skun-out fish hanging in an alder bush, came creeping, tiptoe after tiptoe, and shook it down. Then she rushed back with it to the safety of the house.

Jesse wasn't in the tree now. He had grabbed his chance, skinned down, scooped up his mangled sneaker, and put for the woods as fast as he could pelt. It was rough going, over blackberry bushes and tree-roots, with only one sneaker on. He had to stop, put on the other one before he'd gone very far. The sneaker was in terrible shape, all muck and pig-spit. One of his new ones, too. It felt awful, cold and slimy on his foot.

Deep in the woods, he stopped, leaned against a big beech tree, clasping the trunk to hold himself up till he got his breath back. This was going to mean big trouble, and he knew it. It would begin right away, too. At home, and when old Gene got to Set-Fire. And all he could say was, I never meant to. . . . And realized, suddenly, that trouble had already begun. Someone was chasing him, crashing and pounding through the puckerbrush. Old Gene, he thought, and braced himself against the tree, because, no way, he couldn't run anymore.

But it wasn't old Gene. It was Janine. Coming after him and looking as big as a battleship.

Quite a number of people were in the Post Office waiting for the late mail to be sorted when Miz Fan Dunning stormed in and told in a voice everybody could hear what horrid torture Jesse Scott had put to her pig, and what a scandalous, criminal-acting boy he was, and that she and Gene were going to get the law into it and have him sent straight to the reform school, get him off'n the streets so that other people's children and their animals would be safe and maybe they'd learn him better but she doubted it.

Amanda, who was busy sorting mail, said nothing. She knew Miz Fan Dunning well. There had been other crises about young kids hassling her, which, in their time, had caused as much commotion. If Fan didn't like kids and showed it the way she did, she could expect to be hassled, miss stuff out of her garden and apples when they were ripe. What on earth could Jesse have done? She only hoped that George, who had come over to the store to help her out with late rush hour, wouldn't blow up a storm. She could see him, already red to the roots of his hair. But Gladys, who was waiting for her mail, suddenly spoke up in accents of ice.

"I will not stand here and listen to this kind of lying dirt spread on my son," she said. "Jesse is one of the sweetest boys ever lived and there ain't a bird or an animal on God's green earth that he don't love his heart out on."

Well, that's certainly so, Amanda thought. Jesse does love animals, he always has. It did seem strange to hear Gladys standing up for one of her sons, but of course she'd established his reputation as a sweet little cosset lamb at the séances, and must want to keep it so.

Amanda stole a look through the office wicket and stifled a grin. Miz Fan Dunning had huffered up in front of Gladys—their noses weren't six inches apart.

"And if the law is to be called in," Gladys said, not backing up any, "it'll be called by the whole Scott family on *you*, for spreading wicked lies which wouldn't be true if there were more of them."

"You shut up and go home and read your thing." Miz Fan Dunning wasn't backing up, either. "I'll bring you a pigturd and you can hum to it and maybe help us find out where that poor suffren animal is."

Behind Amanda, George snickered. "Jeest," he said in a hoarse whisper. "Ma's lost a good customer right there."

"*Sh-h*, keep quiet, George, do. Skin out the back door and locate Jesse. See if you can find out what happened. Try to keep him out of sight over at the farmhouse till I get home."

"Gene and I been ransackin' the woods this whole afternoon, and we ain't found that poor sow, not no-wheres. Gene says she's either crawled off and died or drownded herself in the ocean to git shed of the turrible pain that boy put her into. If we had any neighbors worthy the name of, they'd be out there helping to find that helpless thing, and you menfolks can put that in your pipe and smoke it! And you can, too." Miz Fan Dunning flashed around on Gladys. "If you got anything at your house as sensible as a pipe, which I good and damn well don't believe you have got."

Neighbors were helpful. Most of the men picked up their mail and went off to help Gene hunt for his sow. The search went on till suppertime and into the evening, covering woods and fields within reason, alongshore, or any known cave which Janine might have crawled into. She was not to be found and neither was Jesse.

In the woods, Jesse clung to his beech tree, watching Janine plow towards him. He was so scared that he didn't even think of ducking around to the other side of the tree, getting its big trunk between them, he just stood there. She wasn't running very fast now, only jog-trotting, and he could hear her breathing as she came closer, quick hoarse grunts. He said in a whisper, "Janine, don't . . ." and flattened himself against the tree. She didn't look at him and didn't stop.

Limp with relief, he watched her go out of sight around a turn in the path. Why, she's tired, he thought. Tired about to death. He moved out into the path, followed her first at a safe distance, then coming nearer as she slowed down. When they came out of the woods and crossed the field towards Set-Fire's pigpens, he had his hand gently moving on the back of her neck. At her own pen, she stopped and stood drooping, nose to the gate. Pixie wasn't in it now—she was nowhere to be seen. Jesse opened the gate and let Janine go in.

Set-Fire came around the corner of a shed and stood, hands in pockets, not surprised, just looking. "How'd you find her?" he asked. "Didn't steal her, did ya?"

Jesse shook his head. "She got out," he said. "And she found me."

"Be dag! Followed ya home. Whole town's out and around looking for her, you know that?"

"No." Jesse was tired out. He had had it, and at the thought of Janine's being carted back to Dunning's, he burst into tears.

"What's bad enough to howl about?" Set-Fire asked. He leaned over the gate and scratched Janine's back. She had nosed up to the fence and stood there, humped up, heaving as if she still couldn't get her breath back.

"Look, she's sick or something. She's all tired out and she's come home because she wants to . . . and you've got to help me fix it. . . ." Jesse stopped and gulped, seeing that Set-Fire was grinning at him.

"First place, you blow your nose, boy. Second, this ain't Janine in here. This is Pixie. You told me it was, didn't ya? And you was right, for all Gene Dunning can tell. We got Janine in the horse-box, and Harry's gone to tell him that his sow's lit down here, and we'll bring her over tomorrow morning as soon's he gits his pigpen fence shored up. And third time round, this girl in here, whatever her name is, ain't going nowhere. She's home here where she belongs, and she's going to pop them piglets any minute now. So you hop it over to the dairy room and fetch a couple buckets of clean hot water. She is dirty"—Set-Fire grinned—"as a pig."

For a moment, Jesse was unable to take in the grandeur of Set's scheme. Then he blew his nose with a great toot, and went racing after the water.

Janine stood good as gold while they scrubbed off the filth from Gene Dunning's pen. Set swore, loud and long, as he saw the scratches on her neat white flanks. "Damned old blood-sucker, I hope Pixie clobbers him. She will, too, if he slams her around like that, and serve him right.

Atta girl, atta good smart girl, knew right where to come, din'ja?"

After a while, he said, "I told ja. I told ja you was one good old smart girl, look at that, Jess, ain't that one gaadamn beautiful sight? She ain't wasting one minute of time."

She wasn't. Jesse watched, awestricken, clutching the top rail of the fence. Suppertime came and went without his knowing. He helped, handing Set-Fire what was needed, horsed bales of straw out of the shed, brought more hot water for Set's final clean-up. When Set finished and came out of the pen, Janine, comfortable in warm straw, was giving their first meal to thirteen piglets.

"There comes Polly," he said. "He looks kind of sober, but I don't b'lieve he's looking for you with a split stick."

Paulus wasn't. He said, "Thank the Lord, Jesse. We've been looking all over for you. Where've you been?"

"Been here with me, mostly," Set-Fire said. "Had a little emergency. Sow pigged ahead of time and I needed help. Jess was here, so I kept him. He's worked like a major, and look what we got for it."

"Thirteen piglets," Jesse said. "And she's got fourteen faucets." He went on fiercely, "So even the runt's got a chance."

"Good for the runt," Paulus said. "I guess you're in some trouble, Jess."

"No, he ain't," Set-Fire said. "Who's in trouble is that damned old sneak, Gene. Rolled in here as big as Billy-be-damned the day we was all off the place, took Janine instead of Pixie, the one he swapped for. Swapped the pens around so's we wouldn't know it. Jesse knew it. He went over and brought Janine home. Seeing she belongs to him, anyway."

"Of course she does. But what—"

"Gene ain't lost his sow, she's in the hoss-box now, and she's Pixie. He can call her Janine or any other name he

wants to, and I wish him joy of the crazy damn thing.
Harry went to tell him we'll deliver her as soon's he gets
his fence shored up, and Harry was so mad about it he
said he didn't give a cuss whether Gene had his fence
fixed up or not, he'd be pleased to haul Pixie over there
and deliver her in person to Miz Fan Dunning in her
kitchen. Had to persuade him not to."

Paulus grinned. "No, better not do that. No sense handing out for free a wild tale that had some truth in it.
She was carrying on quite lively in the Post Office this
afternoon. None of us believed any of it, I guess."

"I take it Jess went to considerable trouble. Had to.
Got Janine over here just in the nick of time. I don't know
what he done, I ain't ast him. He can say if he wants to.
Don't appear to make much difference to me. Had an
emergency and done what he could, is all. You and I
good and well know that if we'd tried to pry Janine out
of Gene, we'd of had one helmonious balls-up with law-
yers and arguments and proof and a court case, take us
weeks. That old devil would sue God for making him
what he is, if he ever realized the skunk he is. Look at
them smart little fellas. Look what they're up to."

The piglets had finished their meal and were looking
for the only warm place they knew about—the one
they had come from, which wasn't available. Janine lay
stretched out sleeping in her straw. They had found the
space between two studs of the shelter wall and were
arranging themselves in the way they remembered—rows
of four, one row on top of another, until all that showed
of them was an upright rectangle of small rosy sterns,
stacked as neatly as a tier of cordwood sticks.

"Now, ain't that some beautiful," Set-Fire said.

"Good managing," Paulus said. "Well, Jess, Cora's keeping supper hot. After you've eaten, I'll walk home with
you."

So far, Jesse had said nothing. Hearing Uncle Polly

and Set talk, he knew now what had really happened. Down at Walt's, he had heard Walt tell Suzy that Uncle Polly had swapped one of Set-Fire's sows for a busted-down old table, and there had been Uncle Polly in the shop working on the table. And when he'd found Janine gone, he'd thought they'd swapped her, didn't care a hoot if she belonged to him and he loved her. He'd been all wet to get so mad and tore out—hated them both. He didn't know how he could explain now without hurting their feelings. Couldn't think of what to say; he was so tired he could hardly stand up, and now he had to go home. The high spirits which had come at the peak of his day hit bottom with a thud he could almost hear.

"You don't have to, Uncle Polly," he said. "Ma'll clobber me anyway. Likely she'll kill me for getting these clothes dirty."

"Don't worry," Paulus said. "We'll clean up that mess over at the house while you have supper."

There was nothing to be done about the sneakers. George was sent on the run down to the store for a new pair. Jesse went into a hot bath; his T-shirt and jeans went into the farmhouse washer and dryer, were pressed smooth by Cora's hot iron.

"Neat's a pin you are now," she told him. "Got that awful stink washed out of your hair, too. These clothes is cleaner than they was in the first place. You can tell your Ma that, if she raises any Cain."

Jesse didn't seem to be comforted. He said thanks to Cora, but that was all, and walked along beside Paulus in glum silence, dragging back a little as they neared Gladys's house.

"I'll go in and talk to your Ma, Jess," Paulus said.

"She'll just wait till you go home." Under his breath, Jesse added, "She'll flip. She likes to."

Blast! Paulus thought. I should have let Set-Fire walk him home. Set would tell her the kid got treed by a wild sow, or anything else he happened to think of to get Jess out of trouble. Maybe *I* will.

But as it happened, neither of them had to worry. Gladys had something else on her mind. A gleaming new Chevrolet was parked in her driveway; the street light sparked up its color and its chrome. The trunk was open and a girl about Jesse's age was struggling to pull a heavy suitcase out of it, having no luck.

"Oh, hey," Paulus said. "That's quite a load, Miss. Let me help you with it." He lifted it out, set it on the sidewalk. "Where are you taking this? Not far, I hope."

A woman's voice came from the front seat of the car. "My God, a man! I didn't expect to find one in this jerkwater town." A car door banged.

Gladys? Sure sounds like her, but what gives? Paulus thought.

The woman came around to the back. Not Gladys, but someone so like her as to make little difference. Light shone on bracelets and bangles, which clicked as she walked.

"We just got here," she said. "And let me tell you, we're pooped. I'm Madame Preston, Gladys's sister, and this is my girl, Frankie. I'll give you a quarter if you help us horse this stuff into the house."

Paulus choked back a roar of laughter. "Show me the quarter," he said soberly.

She stared at him. "Well, of all the . . ." She fumbled in her purse and produced a fifty-cent piece. "Have you got change?"

"Sorry." He leaned, flicked the coin out of her fingers, dropped it in his pocket. "I'll have to owe you," he said.

"For heaven's sake! I always heard you downeast Yankees were some sharp," she said. "You see I get a quarter back, Mister, or—"

But he was already halfway up the front steps with two of her suitcases. They were heavy, and the poor soul surely did need help with them. He bumped one hard against the door, which Gladys opened.

She stared at him and at the suitcases with a sudden gleam in her eye. "Why, Paulus, dear! Come in and welcome."

"Sorry, Gladys. Life has many little surprises. Gives goodies and takes them away. Your sister's come. Where do you want these put?"

The gleam in her eye changed to a glare of fury before she realized what he had said. Then she bumped past him with a flurry of welcoming squawks. The two voices clanged together down beside the car and Frankie dragged wearily up the steps carrying a big wrapped bundle which she dropped and sat on. "Have you had supper yet?" she asked the air in front of her.

Round-eyed, struck dumb, Jesse stared at her.

They looked alike, Paulus saw; not in the face, the girl had a square, tough little mug with a pug-nose, with bangs somewhat too long which hid her eyebrows, but she was bone-thin, as Jesse was, and she had his air of exhaustion—too down-spent even to breathe.

Oh, goddamn it to hell! The kids. They broke your blasted heart. "Haven't you had supper?" Paulus asked her.

"No," she said.

Gladys came up the steps towing her sister. "And there's dear little Frankie!" she said. "You must be tired out, honey, and I expect you'll want to go straight to bed. Jesse, you take Frankie up to your room. She'll have to use George's bed till we get squared around. And good night, Frankie, I'll see you in the morning."

Frankie looked her up and down. "I want some supper," she said.

"Oh, mercy, dear! It's a long ways past suppertime. And I haven't got a thing handy to cook."

"You must have an egg," the girl said. "If you'll show

me where it is I'll cook it. I'm not going to bed without my supper. No way!"

Atta girl! Paulus thought. Stand up to the old besom, time somebody did. The whole situation suddenly struck him as hilariously funny, because Gladys looked as if someone had hit her in the face with a dishmop. He grabbed Frankie by the hand.

"Come on," he said. "The restaurant's still open. You too, Jess. We'll go and feed your cousin some supper." He went, and both children came plunging after him. He heard the sister say as the door closed, "Who's that man? Don't let him leave, he owes me a quarter."

He couldn't think what had got into him. He opened the door of the shining Chevrolet, climbed into the driver's seat. "You're both too tired to walk," he said. "And we'll get there quicker if we use your mother's car."

"I don't think there's much gas," Frankie said.

"Then we'll fill 'er up. And you, too."

He heard a faint shriek behind him as they pulled away, but paid no attention. With glee, he fed Frankie the best the restaurant had to offer, found that Jesse could eat again, and seeing that supper was a ways back, decided that he could, too. They were gone quite a while before he delivered the kids back to the house.

Voices in the kitchen and the smell of fried meat indicated that Gladys had found something Madame Preston could be fed. Frankie looked at Jesse and shrugged and Jesse shrugged back.

"Go on, scoot upstairs to bed, both of you. Which is your suitcase, Frankie? If it's too heavy for Jesse, I'll carry it up myself."

It wasn't. Frankie's possessions, it seemed, like Jesse's, were few.

He fished a quarter out of his pocket, bowed to it politely and left it on the living room table.

VII

Walter had saved up enough money to have a well drilled and the water piped into the house. He planned someday to replace his wood-burning furnace in the cellar with a modern one and a hot-water baseboard heating system; but that would have to wait until another year. This season, he could manage the well.

Suzy said she didn't mind—she rather liked the old wood furnace. It smelled good and its coals were lovely to broil steak over. "If I get too enormous to navigate the cellar stairs," she told him, "we could hire someone to tend it when the cold weather starts. Maybe Jesse."

"Well, better be George," Walter said. "Jesse wouldn't be able to keep anything we paid him, and once we start him on regular wages, Ma'll be down to say it ain't enough. I won't risk getting a dose of her. I'll be damned if I'll have her in the house."

"Hush, now. She's your mother."

"God help me, she is. Poor old Jess, she doesn't need him around now, he says his Aunt Preston has brought gimmicks and gadgets to go click and tunk, and she's the one greets the customers at the door in a white bathrobe with the signs of the Zodiac on it. At least, I gather that's what they are from Jess's description. He says when she greets, she greets."

"Oh, you've seen Jess lately, have you? Henry and I haven't for quite a while and we miss him."

"He's tracking around now with his cousin, Frankie her name is. They're down around the wharf a lot, now Jess has got some free time."

"Oh, good, he's got loose from those awful 'sayonces.' Why doesn't she let him go live at the farm, if she doesn't want him?"

"No way. She's hanging onto him to blackmail Polly into giving her part of the farm, blast her. Well, she ain't welcome here, and if she comes anytime, you tell her I said so."

Gladys didn't wait to be made welcome. She spotted the well-driller's outfit at Walter's house—another sign of his prosperity. She didn't send Jesse down this time, she came herself on the day after it arrived, choosing a time when she had seen the *Sarah* heading off down-harbor. She appeared on the dot of lunchtime, to find Suzy feeding Henry a poached egg on toast. There was no sign of a meal otherwise, not even a smell. Perhaps Suzy hadn't started her own yet. Gladys sat down.

"Walter not home?" she asked. "Oh, dear, I did so want to see him. I've got something very nice, good news, that I want to tell him."

"I'm sorry," Suzy said. "He and Aaron went out today. Perhaps you could telephone, sometime when he's home."

"No," Gladys said. "I come here to bury the hatchet with him. My control has told me that families ought to love each other."

Suzy, at a loss for something to say to that, said nothing. Fundamentally a nice person, she couldn't think of how to tell Gladys to get the hell out, the way Walter had told her to.

"And there's my dear little Henry!" Gladys said. "Ain't he a booful 'ittle widgums-wadjums. My only grandson, Suzy, dear. I do miss the young voices around the house, now my own kids have got older. Do let me hold him a minute when he gits through his dinner. My arms is just aching to, and I can see to him whilst you git your own."

Dear little Henry was a hearty, if messy, feeder and a splendid sleeper. He sagged over in his high-chair before he had finished his egg, his eyelids drooping.

"You'll have to excuse me a minute," Suzy said. "It's time for his nap." With a damp washcloth she mopped off egg which was widespread over Henry and lifted him out of his chair.

Gladys gave a great gasp. "Suzy! Oh, dear girl! You mustn't lift that heavy baby and you pregment!"

"It doesn't bother me." Suzy took Henry to the small bedroom off the living room, where he had his naps, tucked him in. Coming back, she was in time to hear a stealthy click of her icebox door and a quick scamper of feet. Nice person or not, Suzy had a temper. I *will not*, she told herself, put up with this.

Gladys was sitting where she had been. "I guess you wonder how I know you're expectin'," she said. "My control told me. He tells me all things."

"He must be a regular mailbag," Suzy said. "Does he fly nights?" She picked up Henry's dish to take it to the sink and saw that the scraps he had left were gone, completely cleaned out.

"I guess you notice that I've finished Henry's lunch," Gladys said. "I'm so hungry I feel faint all over. The doctor's told me not to git to feel so, or I'll go the way my poor mother did. Just dropped. Passed away from it. My control's told me that, too. He watches over me for my poor mother, you know."

"That's nice of him."

"He watches over my family, too. So you see, he watches over Walter. But of course he won't do that anymore, if Walter is mean to me."

This was so preposterous that Suzy lost the rest of her temper. She had planned not to eat her own lunch until after Gladys left, but now she went to the icebox and took out her egg salad. The old snoop knows it's there anyway, she might as well see me eat it.

"Oh, egg salad! I do love it so! Thank you, dear, it's just what I've been looking forward to."

"I wasn't expecting company. I've only made enough for one. All I can offer you is a glass of water."

"I can't drink water, dear. Not when I'm empty. If I do, I can jump up and down and hear it splashing around my heart."

"Then if I were you, I wouldn't jump up and down."

Gladys got up. "Well, dear, I guess you haven't been in the family long enough to know that there ain't none of us lets anyone leave our house hungry. Oh, I see you're going to have a well drilled. Ain't that very costly?"

"I expect so. You'll have to ask Walter."

Gladys laughed her high, silvery laugh, waved a hand gaily and left. The sound of her heels clicked down the walk and faded out of hearing.

Oh, Lord! Suzy thought. I hope I haven't made any trouble for Walt. Well, if I have, he'll settle her hash, the old hagfish.

She found, to her surprise, that she was—well, not exactly scared, but uneasy. Of course, all Walt's mother was interested in was getting money out of him, and she wasn't about to do that, no way. You might think she was an old flub-dub, but she was more than that. She gave off something—whatever it was—that you couldn't put your finger on, only it made you feel creepy and it was still in the room after she'd left. Maybe it was because the look in her eyes, a kind of glitter, didn't match up with all those lovey-dovey dears and darlings.

After a while, Suzy decided she wouldn't say anything to Walt about it—he'd fly into the air and tackle Gladys about it and that wouldn't do any good, either.

August was always blueberry picnic time on Black Mountain, whose clearings in a good year were lush with blue—the color of borage and delphinium, of the blue-jay and the indigo bunting, of parts of the sky on a northwest day. The steep slopes of the mountain were still wilderness, unchanged since Sarah Thomas's time, but lumbermen had cut down the virgin growth in the foothills and as high as they could go without themselves and their gear tumbling down the mountainside. They had made clearings where the waste wood of the big trees had been burned, the ashes left to combine with an acid loam which nourished one of the earth's loveliest creations. With modest small leaves, unnoticeable for most of the year, the blueberry plant in summer, wherever the sun could get at it, carpeted the high clearings with color so luminous and pure that it might seem like patches of blue fire without flame or heat, burning in the wilderness.

Whole families drove up the mountain road, mostly on Sundays when the menfolks were free for a picnic, and spent the day gathering in the bounty which meant blueberry pies and puddings; blueberry muffins; pancakes for breakfast on the bleak mornings of winter to come. Housewives, sometimes, on a weekday when the men were busy and the children obstreperous, would think of jars and freezer boxes to fill and would take the kids in the car and go. In August, in blueberry time, the high silences on Black Mountain were alive with voices.

Paulus, on the day of his date with Annabelle Franklin, had decided that he *would*, by gum, take her blueberrying up Black Mountain. He had a new car which he wanted to try out—that is, it was new to him, but older than most—the result of what he'd considered the swap of his lifetime with the summer man, Jones Bradley— three days a week of his time for an ancient town car, a deal which satisfied him to the depths of his soul. He had gone to see Bradley, as invited, and Bradley had offered him a job overhauling and restoring antique cars, putting them in shape to run, if it could be done.

"I've got some valuable models stowed away in these outbuildings," he'd said. "No room for any more and I can't resist buying the things when I run across one. I'd like to find out which ones to get rid of, which ones are worth keeping. Usually I bring a Boston mechanic down here for the summer, but his wife got sick and he's had to leave me high and dry. Foss Bailey's helped me out some, but he doesn't have much time. He says you could bring a dead elephant back to life, given time to tinker with it. How about coming to work for me?"

"I'd certainly like to," Paulus said. But he had to hesitate, remembering that he'd offered Walter another week or so work on his house. He explained this and Bradley grinned.

"I see you could be tempted," he said.

"I sure could." Paulus glanced along the double row of old-timers, parked side by side by side in the long building.

"My wife says you're a swapper of considerable reputation," Bradley said. "How'll you trade three days a week of your time for that old heap there on the end of the line?"

Paulus stared and caught his breath. "You know what that is?" he asked.

"Certainly. I'm willing to pay value for value. She's had work done on her—engine taken apart and put together again, some parts replaced, and she'll run, but Chet had to leave before he finished her, and she's not right by a long shot. You drive her home and see what you can do. I'll trade you. Three days a week for now, full time when you can, and we decide about regular wages later on."

The Packard, Paulus judged, dated from the late '20's or early '30's. The glass screen behind the front seat was intact and could be opened and closed. Vases for fresh flowers still hung between the rear windows. In spite of chipped paint and rust, brasswork dulled with verdigris, this lady had kept her dignity—the affluent dignity of a bygone day. "It's a deal," he said.

Foss Bailey, who dropped around a few evenings later, properly envious because he, too, loved antique cars and knew a good deal about them, stood in the farmhouse backyard listening to the big old engine, which was whispering so silently that a passenger in the back seat with the glass screen closed could barely hear it, said, deadpan, "Polly, it looks to me as if you'll make a mechanic, someday."

"I was lucky to get broke in on this engine," Paulus said. "She's one of the greatest ever built and they don't make any like that now, Foss. By the god, listen to her! You couldn't kill her with a maul."

It was a beautiful day on Black Mountain. Paulus drove up high, because the higher clearings, the more difficult ones to climb to, were likely to be unpicked. Lower down, he could already spot quite a number of his neighbors busy with rakes and pails. Among them, to his surprise, he saw Cora and Gran Matilda, who waved to him as he drove by. I hope she doesn't get too tired, he thought. Try and make her think she's not as tough as she used to be. But Cora would make her be careful.

Someone, he couldn't make out who, yelled at him as he went by. "Hey, Polly! Where you going in Queen Mary's royal bathtub?"

He grinned at Annabelle. "I guess I expected to take some kidding," he said.

She laughed. "You good and well know you wouldn't call the queen your cousin," she said. "I love it, Polly! I'm so used to driving something that sounds like a mad eggbeater, that if I drove this . . . this kitten, I'd probably go to sleep at the wheel."

"She'll look better when I get her cleaned up and painted," he said. "And not gold for Queen Mary's bathtub, either."

"Of course not. Black. A nice, dignified glossy black. Very glossy," she said. "I'd love to help. I'm a whizz with sandpaper and brass polish."

"Good! You'd be welcome, any time." He stopped the car at a place he remembered, where the narrow road widened enough for a parking place. "You sure you like to climb?" he asked. "I thought I'd head for a place where Ralph and I used to go when we were kids. But it's pretty steep and rocky. Nobody else goes there."

"I love climbing. I came up here last summer vacation, but it wasn't a good year. This one is, though."

"Right you are. It's a dandy."

They went along. The climb was a stiff one. Not by any stretch of the imagination could it be called a trail. You made your own decision, simply, as to which boulder to go around or climb over. She was as expert a climber as he was, he saw, and after a while he let her get ahead of him for the pleasure of watching her trim, limber figure moving neatly and with precision up the rugged track.

The first clearing which opened out was a small one, but it was paved with blue, clusters of big round berries so thick that scarcely a green leaf showed.

"With Ralph and me," he said, "it was always a case of last-one-up's-a-rotten-egg, and whoever found a good spot was entitled to pick it without anyone's cotton-picking fingers snatching in. You want to pick this spot by yourself? You saw it first."

"No, I'd like company, and there's plenty for two."

They picked a while in silence, but it was a companionable silence and you didn't talk much, anyway, when you were picking blueberries. It was the way to, he remembered. The sun hot on your back, the quiet in the clearing—not even a birdsong at this time of day—only a small, secret sound of water dripping somewhere among the stones. There was no quiet anywhere in the world like the quiet on Black Mountain. As if, he thought, it spoke to you through its silence.

His hand, reaching for a fat cluster of berries, closed over hers, reaching for the same one. He stared, astonished, at the blueberry juice squeezed out between their fingers.

That had been a reflex he hadn't expected or planned.

"Look at what you've done!" she said. "Those were lovely big ones, too."

"Just being grabby," he said. "It's always a temptation to snatch for the big ones. I remember Ralph and I used to do just that, and once when I got there first, he let me have it right across the nose with a whole handful of blueberry juice."

She laughed. "Brings out the worst in me, too, but I guess I won't do that. Blueberry stains wash off hard, remember? Besides, I'm having too good a time to start any kind of an argument."

"Likewise, I'm sure."

"It's so peaceful. And isn't it quiet!"

"Yes. Seems as if the higher up you go, the quieter it gets. As if silence lived here," Paulus said.

"Suzy was telling me that Black Mountain's haunted. Says some people are scared to come up this high. That silence gets under their skins."

"There was an old superstition that Sarah Thomas comes back to visit, once in a while. Gran Matilda says it started when some smart old cookie claimed to have met her wandering around in these clearings. What with this funny silence, it worked quite well. Scared the bejazus out of a lot of berry-pickers, so for years he had all the good spots to himself. Walt told me once that his mother uses that old ghost story in her séances, so even now, you and I don't have as much competition up here as we might—*what is it?*"

She had clutched his hand, hard. This time, it was she

who squashed the handful of berries. She was staring past him at something in the next clearing, her eyes wide and darkened. "Ssh, Polly, look!" she managed, in a strangled whisper.

The next clearing was through some straggled-out puckerbrush and clefts between boulders, but parts of it could be seen; as he looked, a good-sized black bear crossed between two clefts, and following her, two half-grown cubs.

"Wow!" he said, under his breath. "Don't move fast. Just ooze out of sight as quiet as you can. I don't think that old gal has seen us yet."

He sat where he was, watching. Annabelle went, slowly and carefully—he didn't even hear her go. When she was out of sight, he went, too, carrying both berry buckets. She had left hers behind.

Likely there's no danger, he told himself, feeling the sweat come out on his upper lip. If a bear sees you, you don't see the bear. They always make off out of sight before you even know they're around. But a she-bear with cubs was something else again. If you got too close. If you surprised her, when she didn't see you first.

So take it easy. And don't run, damn you, he told his legs which seemed to want to. And don't look back.

But at the edge of the clearing, before he started down, he couldn't resist looking back. And she'd seen him, all right. She had risen on her hind legs, as tall as a man, her forelegs spread wide, the yellowish claws dangling. A piece of Sarah Thomas's old wilderness, massive and wild and beautiful. And he fled as fast and as silently as he could down the side of her mountain.

Halfway down, he found Annabelle waiting, leaning against a boulder. "Thank goodness!" she said. "Am I glad to see you!"

"All in one piece, too." He managed a grin. "That was really something, wasn't it?"

"This far away from it, I'm able to say I'm glad I saw it." She reached for her own bucket of berries, went off with it down the slope. "Golly, was I scared!" she said, over her shoulder.

"Me, too. Why don't you let me carry that bucket?"

"Oh, I'm all right now. Still a few goose-prickles playing hopscotch up and down my spine, but I've got my breath back." She went out of sight behind a tall boulder and got down to the car a little before he did. She was sitting in the front seat, looking somewhat white around the mouth, when he climbed in beside her.

"All right, now?" he asked.

"Moderately," she said. "My legs still feel a little bit limber."

"Don't think yours are the only ones," he said. "Look, I did plan to drive up to the peak, thought we might eat lunch up there. But seeing what's happened, would you rather go somewhere else?"

"Of course not. It's beautiful up there. I'd love to."

The highway, which had been blasted out of the mountainside, plunged steeply upward in parallel S-curves, so that anyone, looking down, could see where, a moment before, he had been. Somebody almost always said, "Meet yourself coming back," but Annabelle didn't say even that. She sat beside him, silent, leaning back relaxed, he hoped, against Queen Mary's bathtub's comfortable front seat.

Today, there was no one else on the flattened-out peak of the mountain. Paulus drove up and stopped beside the cut-stone parapet which the road builders had set on the edge of the dropoff. From here, they could see the city of Machias, made small by distance, the built-up countryside, the houses, the sunny farmlands. Nearer, down below, was their own quiet town, the harbor full of water traffic; Cooper's Inlet; the swale of the marshes, piercing green with summer; Paine's Pond; the State Highway snaking out of sight to avoid the foothills. But in spite of the neat rectangles of the stone parapet, one of which was crowned, giddily, with a lone empty beer can, a feeling of wilderness still blew with the cold air over Sarah's mountain, as if no human foot had walked here since her time; and down under the steep granite outcrop, big trees hid the savage and secret places into which no one could see, where no one would want to go, where a climber's foot could seldom find hold enough to keep him from pitching backwards down.

Paulus got out to reach Cora's lunch basket from the back seat. She had been delighted at the idea of his taking out a girl. "At last!" she'd said. "I've put in all the things you like and you let me know if she likes um, too."

"*Br-r*," he said, handing Annabelle the basket and climbing in after it. "Quite a patch of the real old wild left around in these places. Makes it chilly. Let's eat in the car. I don't believe there's a ghost on the mountain, but if there is, up here is where it would be."

"And not down below, where some piggish old grampop set up a bogus one, because he wanted all the best berries for himself," she said. "If it had been a ghost that came walking out into the clearing today—"

"You wouldn't have been scared of it?"

"Well, I wouldn't be such a fool as to say it wouldn't have taken a jump out of me, if I could've been sure that was what it was. Suppose it had been Sarah Thomas walking? There must be half a dozen women, old or young, living around here, direct descendants of hers, and I don't know what she looked like anyway."

Paulus laughed. "And likely you'd have said, 'Hi, come and help us pick this spot—there's plenty for everybody.'"

"Likely I would. My, what's in this sandwich, Polly? It's heaven."

"Lord, I don't know. Sandwiches are Cora's thing. Good, isn't it?"

"Lovely." After a moment, she went on, soberly. "But what we did see was real. An honest-to-God direct descendant of what Sarah Thomas met up with on top of this mountain. I won't say I thought of that, just then, only now, when you said that if the ghost walked anywhere it would be here. . . . What I did think was, oh, look, it's a bear, and it'll make off as soon as it sees us, and isn't it a beautiful, once-in-a-lifetime thing to see. I was taken aback when I saw the cubs, it was pure panic. Because a she-bear with cubs . . ."

"Right," he said. "We were both considerably taken aback. In the old days, they had stout fellas who'd face up to anything, with only an ax, but the modern hero goes running down the mountain like a rabbit lugging two buckets of blueberries."

She smiled at him. "But you didn't have an ax, Polly."

"Didn't want one. All I thought about was making like an eel out of there before the old lady saw me. And she did see me. She stood up tall, snout pointed my way, and gave me a look, just before I ducked out of sight."

"As if she was wondering whether you'd taste better than a blueberry?"

"No. Just saying don't tread on me, bud. I'm no hunter, but I don't talk bear and I couldn't holler over and tell her so."

"Or make it clear that you and I are the kind of irresponsible citizens who aren't going to tell a soul we saw bears on Black Mountain?"

"Well," he said, a little doubtfully. "I wouldn't like to think of anyone running into that family, unawares. Still, so far as I know, Ralph and I were the only ones who knew about those good spots up there, but that was a long time ago and there might be other youngsters—"

"Who'd be up there, tomorrow, would be half a dozen eager beavers with high-powered rifles," she said. "Or bows and arrows. Some think it's very, very sportsmanlike to hunt with a bow. Like Aaron. The only bear I ever saw, before, was a dead one. He got it with an arrow somewhere up-country. I got sick of hearing him brag about what a wonderful shot it was. He even showed me the arrow—a great deadly thing with a point sharp as a needle. All I could think of was how much it must have hurt when it hit. Also, he made me go look at the bear. The poor thing looked defenseless enough, hanging from a tree down in front of the Falls house, like a dirty black fur mat. Like the rug he had made out of it for his bedroom. That was the day, last fall, when he asked me to marry him, and I said no, he'd be better off with a girl who could step on his bedroom rug without throwing up. He was put out with me. Called me a sentimental bitch."

"I can see why," Paulus said. "Hunting, to hunters, is one of the untouchable and sacred rights of man. In some ways, it's almost like a kind of religion, has the earmarks of one. Look at the tools they have to do it with, the way they talk about their guns as if they were saying their prayers. And the hunting season—just as sincere about that as if they were going walking into Heaven. You're quite a gal, Annabelle. It takes guts to throw mud on an altar. I expect Aaron would be quite positive on the subject."

Paulus was feeling good, a little surprised at how pleased he was to find out how she felt about Aaron. She was pleased, too; he could tell from the way she looked at him.

"This has come busting out of me like a waterfall, seems," she said. "Because I don't want the bears hurt; I couldn't stand it. And being here, in this place where we are, it's all a part of the same thing. It hasn't anything to do with the sacred and untouchable rights of the slob who left his beer can on the wall out there—I can hear him now—"

Paulus laughed. "'Nobody's going to tell *me* where I

can throw my own trash,'" he quoted. "I know what you mean, Annabelle. You're talking about the sacred and untouchable rights of mountain."

"Yes, I am. That's just what I'm talking about."

"This old granite slab's been here a long time," he said. "Its roots go down, solid and deep. It's outlasted the great-grandfathers of the slob that dumped his beer can here. It'll outlast him. It'll be here when the beer can's rusted out and gone. Some of it's still untouchable, can't be got to, can't be made use of, whether it's big old trees that'll never be lumber, or a stone outcrop too steep to make a house lot. And the life on it, down in there, stays a secret, to itself. Doesn't belong to anybody. You can't get there from here. Or from anywhere else. And that silence you can almost hear says, don't try. I seem to've been carrying on considerable about this. I told you I couldn't talk bear, but I've been trying to and that was as close as I could come."

"You can talk mountain," she said. "I hope the old granite heard you. And I expect if a bear could understand human, she'd know what you meant, that's for sure. You're good to talk to, Polly. You listen. You get the point."

"Not hard to," he said. "Seeing we see eye-to-eye on bears and hunters. About not letting one lot know about the others."

"Yes. You've just told me."

"Let's go down and see how Queen Mary's bathtub likes the State Highway," he said. "You like to?"

"I'd love to. Get down off the mountain while the road's still there. Who knows—she might get tired of that road any time."

"Give a shrug, you mean? I expect she could if she wanted to bother. She doesn't, you know."

Queen Mary's royal bathtub whispered pleasantly along the State Highway, getting an occasional catcall or comment from passing traffic; but most people, after they'd glanced once, turned around to look again, before they went on.

"Jealous, that's what they are," Annabelle said. "None of them have got anything like this lovely old bird."

After a while, sensing something more than plain interest and love of riding, Paulus said, "Want to take over and see how she drives?"

She gasped. "Oh, Polly! If you'd ever let me! I could, you know. Aaron says I can't drive a cow into the barn, but I can drive almost anything with a standard shift."

"Go ahead, then," he said.

They changed seats. Some ten miles along, he said, "Nuts to Aaron. He's got to be loony. I'd forget all that hoo-ha, if I were you."

She flashed him a quick smile. "I already have," she said. "I can't get there from here. No way."

They went for miles up into the back-country, occasionally turning off on a by-road for the simple pleasure of seeing where it led to, usually some small quiet village, dreaming in the hot August afternoon. The sun was setting when, on the way home, they came up on the old road that led in to Paine's Pond.

"Cora'll flip if I take any of that lunch back with me," Paulus said. "She'll say if a girl can't eat, she's the wrong one for me and I'd better make a change. Let's go in to the pond and have supper in there. We've got food left to patch hell a mile."

"Oh, but we'd better walk in, hadn't we? I haven't been in there for a long time, and I don't know what the road's like."

"Bumpy," Paulus said. "But the guys who built this old lady had the sense to set her high enough off the road so she wouldn't leave her crankcase on the first rock she comes to. She'll do it all right."

She did. They came out on the bank, just above the

sand beach, where he had been with George and Jesse in June.

"I was here a couple months ago with the kids," he said as they climbed down the bank. "We had a fine time in swimming. They used to hang out here quite a lot then. Used to cook whatever they could raise to eat on that old fireplace there. I don't suppose they come anymore, now that George is working his head off, and Jess is spending his time now with his new cousin."

"Yes, I heard. Suzy was saying that nobody sees Jesse anymore, now that his mother's turned him loose from the séances. Seems, it's being talked around town how she and her sister, Madame Something-or-other, are renovating all getout out of the séance business—new drapes and new furnishings, new ghosts, for all I know. The Madame's got Jesse's job—some ladies don't like it, Suzy says. They liked Jesse. Some of the new professionalism gets their goats. Anyway, Jesse's free of it, he's on his own, which is probably a good thing, but he's practically vanished. You haven't seen him, have you?"

"It isn't because I haven't tried. I can't catch up with him. Set-Fire can't, either. He and his cousin, Frankie, her name is, must go somewhere."

"Maybe they come here," she said. "That fireplace was used not too long ago."

It had been. The ashes were fresh and mounded into a fairly good-sized pile. But there were no other signs to be seen, only a faint track on the bank of a bicycle tire, which could have been anybody's.

"Jess is likely having a swell time being on his own," Paulus said, "not being hollered at and chased after. I expect George knows what he's up to, and I'll find out sooner or later."

"Or he'll come hunting you up. Suzy says you're a regular Pied Piper—"

"Well, now. Kids are fine. I like 'em all right. But a

grown man, times, would be glad to see an interesting woman. Is that a date, your next day off? We don't have to spend it on Queen Mary's paint job, you know."

"Might be fun to," she said. "What time, Polly?"

That night Gran Scott seemed tired and listless and in the morning was so poorly that Amanda, worried, called the doctor.

"Oh, shoot, Duggie," Gran told him. "You go home with your pills and stuff. You know perfectly well what ails me. Blueberry stomachache."

"That's right," he said. "And got tired to death as well, hightailing it around on Black Mountain. You can get over it on your own if you want to, but if you'll drink a couple of swigs out of this bottle once in a while, it won't take you so long. She'll be all right, Amanda, but make her rest. If you can."

"Oh, I'll rest," Gran said. "As much as anybody with a blueberry stomach can be expected to."

She let Cora tuck her up under a blanket on the porch couch-hammock, where she lay reading the morning paper when Gladys came hurrying up the walk.

"Oh, my Go-ud!" Cora said. "Here comes Glad-rags. Good thing breakfast is et and cleared away."

But Gladys, for once, wasn't after a meal. She spotted Gran in the hammock, pulled up a porch chair and collapsed into it with a face of tragedy.

"Oh, Gran! My dearest Gran!" she gasped. "Are you all right?"

"I'm well enough to read the paper, as you can see," Gran said. "I see where Aaron knocked young Rod Colcraft spizzle-end-up down on the wharf day before yesterday. Father's suing him for assault 'n' batt'ry. Wonder why he done that. You know?"

Gladys seemed not to hear. She breathed hard once or

twice. "Oh!" she said. "My control! Oh, Gran, my control!"

"He dead?" Gran said. "Well, don't bring him here."

"He came to me in the night and brought me the most terrible news about you! He said you were awful sick, might be dying. He never lies to me, you know. He said in two days you'd be dead, and I thought—"

Amanda had gone off to the store, but Cora stood in the porch doorway, stony-faced with wrath. "Gladys Scott!" she said. "You pick up your slinky ass and haul it off'n this piazza, or I'll dump a kittle of bilin' water over you! That is one ugly, nasty story to put to an old lady ninety years old who ain't feelin' well. You make tracks, heels t'wads the house!"

Gladys glittered a smile at her. "Listen, dear. I rightfully own part of this house and you ain't nothing but a hired girl here, so I could well be the one to tell *you* to git. I have got business with Gran. You kindly take your nose out of it. That's all, dear, for now."

"My teakittle," Cora said, "is full."

"Wait, Code," Gran said. "Let's see what Gladys's business with me is. Now, Gladys, go on. I can't think what it could be."

"Well, Gran, dear, you know my control comes straight to me from the Sacred Powers. He knows—"

"All right. So he knows. What's your business?"

"I know you, dear. You wouldn't leave this earth for your eternal home without doing justice where it belongs. If you knew beforehand, you'd deed me legally Ralph's share of—"

"I see. You say you see ghosts that common people don't, it's time you got this one laid. Ralph's share of the farm was legally paid before his disappearance. It's in the bank, in trust for his children. You can't touch a cent of it. Will you get that through your head once and for all?"

Gladys sat still where she was. The only indication of her feelings was her hands, tightly clenched in her lap. "Ralph's deadly hatred follows me. From the grave," she said. "Now I find he's left me destitute, without a cent to—"

"If Ralph hated you, and he did, you've got only yourself to blame. You made his life a misery from the day you married him. And don't try to put out to me that you're destitute. You had three quarters of his money all his life and squirreled it away, or put it on your back. Don't think he didn't know how you let his children run ragged and hungry. And you know they did, in spite of what we up here tried to do to help them."

"And you was in on it, too, wasn't you, dear?" Gladys said.

"I could've been, but it was Ralph's choice. He wouldn't take a cent for himself, only a trust fund for the children. He asked us not to tell you about it, afraid you'd take it out on them after he was gone. I'm sorry he did. I think you ought to've known right from the beginning, but I had nothing to do with Ralph's decision."

"And he's fryin' in hell for it, right now!"

"If it comforts you to think so. The only reason I tell you now is because you've tried to scare me into dying before my time and that I won't put up with. You're not such a fool as you think I must be to swallow such a dirty trick. You've got the brains to take in that when I do go, you'll get a big piece of nothing, and always would have."

Gladys got up. "There must be some income from that trust fund. You must know, dear, that if it belongs to my children, I'm entitled to it till they're of age."

"You give up about as easy as a tick, don't you? All right. Here's the rest of it. Walter's of age. He gets his share of the interest. You won't get any of it out of him. He spends it as fast as it comes in on his house and his boat. The rest of it is held in trust until the other two are twenty-one. And that's all."

"So it ain't a bit surprisin', is it, dear, that you and Polly have tried, times again, to get me to sign my boys away from me by legal adoption? My goodness, how often I've wondered what on earth you wanted them for."

"Oh, Lord," Gran said. "No, Gladys, it ain't a bit surprising. And I think you'd be better off if you go away before I lose a-holt of Cora."

Why her sister Peg—who preferred to be called Madame Preston—had come, unannounced, to live with her, Gladys didn't know, and Peg didn't say. Of course there had been her husband's trouble with the law in California—perhaps Peg had been in the same kind of trouble, had had to put-foot because of it. Gladys was dying to know. She didn't ask—it would all come out someday, maybe when Peg was rested. She had been tired to death—had driven a long ways all in one jump, so she'd said. But not from California; she'd been living in Michigan since Gladys had heard from her last.

"I got your letter about Ralph just about the time I was starting to move east," she'd explained. "I'd heard of a fine chance to set up shop in Grand Rapids, and I tried living there, but it didn't work out. So I got to thinking about you being all alone now, Ralph dead, and I wondered if we might not throw in together."

Actually, though Madame Preston hadn't said so, she had come because of the letter. In it, Gladys had told about the farm which she was heir to. She had bragged about the farm. "One of the richest in the State," she'd written, wanting to impress Peg, who had always tried to impress her. "I'll be sitting in a buttertub as soon as Ralph's estate's settled."

Then, when Peg had arrived, bag and baggage, Gladys

had wished she hadn't written that. Peg had always been funny about money—had nosed it out wherever she'd thought some might be in their own family. Why, look at the way she'd done with old Uncle Amos—went to housekeep for him before she'd been married and finagled him into leaving her every cent he had, and him with a bushel of other relatives, too! That had been how she'd got her start.

And not one penny for me, Gladys thought, remembering that bitter time long ago.

It was all right with Gladys if Peg stayed, at least for a while. From the looks of her clothes and her new car, she wasn't by any means poor, and it was time somebody else brought some cash into the house.

But she needn't think she's going to take over my business here, Gladys told herself. Peg had always been pushy, even when they'd been growing up together at home. She'd always been their mother's favorite, too. Ma learnt her a lot more about sayonces and second-sight than she did me. Told me I didn't have any and Peg did, was all. Well, this is my house, even if she has got the money.

It was going to be embarrassing if Peg found out she hadn't got her share of the farm after all these months. Gladys set her teeth. That was when she'd made up her mind that she'd go up and have it out once and for all with old Gran Scott.

Madame Preston had, at once, let Gladys know that she thought little of the way the séances were run. "Now, Gladdie, dear, you got to be professional in this business, or people think you're a fake. You should see what I had at home, stars-in-heaven wallpaper on midnight blue. Lights that would swell out bright and fade away, give a real feeling of the Great Beyond. Atmosphere, dear, is what loads the customers in."

"For heaven sake, I've got plenty of that," Gladys almost snapped. "And all the customers I can handle, too. This room will scarcely hold more."

"It will, dearie, it will. You wait and see what happens when we get rolling. People'll come just to see the lovely surroundings. We'll fix this dingy back room up for now. I'll send right away for the wallpaper and we'll get an electrician in. If we have to, we'll build on."

"It'll cost a mint. I can't afford—"

"Can't afford to double, thribble, the receets? Why, honey, and you with all that money coming in from your farm!"

Well, there it is, Gladys thought glumly. If she'd had misgivings, she'd been perfectly right to. "I ain't got it yet," she said aloud. "That stingy old devil, Ralph's mother, is holding up the probate, or something."

Peg gave her a look. "After all this time? We'll have to see about that."

"*I* will see about it."

"Sure-lee, dear. Of course you will. Now, remember, you was always a stick-in-the-mud about changes. One reason I come here is, this place is lousy with summer people, that's where the money is. *They* won't go for anything that ain't a real show place, with some spiritool meaning to it. I don't guess you get much summer trade, do you?"

"Of course I do. I get a lot."

"Well, we'll do more than skim the top off. Anybody that knows what's what ain't going to come in here just to see you wrapped up in a sheet, that's for sure. Why, I had a real medium's cubicle with all my gadgets right to hand, built in, and I had some beauts, believe you me. I've brought most of them with me."

"Simple is best, Peg."

"Yes, but what you're doing, you might as well use one of them Fourth of July spin-rattles. What I've got ain't a gawky teenager thumping and scratching on the wall. That boy of yours has got to go. He ain't right for the atmosphere—he looks sulky, and what we need is to give out joy and rest-in-peace at the very door. That damfool control of yours has got to go, too."

"Now, you look here, Miss Peg—"

"Madame Preston, *if* you please. I've got a nationwide reputation—"

"You ain't said what it is, have you?"

"—to keep up, and your control's old stuff."

"You ain't going to come here and take over. Once and for all, this is my house and—"

"Oh, shoot, dearie, of course it is. What I come here, first and forever, is to see *you*, make up for all the years we was apart, foolish, wasn't it? I'm just suggesting how we could double your take. I've been around, you know. I could've doubled it years ago if Ralph had been willing to let me have your Jesse when he was a baby. Hank Preston was just the same kind of a fool over Frankie. Four thousand dollars apiece I could've got for each one of them, even then, and the price is double, more than that, now. Too late, though. Market's low for gawky teenagers."

"I thought you had to get out of that business."

Madame Preston smiled. "Hank did," she said. "But I've still got some addresses. Too bad you ain't got any babies to spare in your family, dear."

Gladys brought up with a round turn. "Well," she said before she could stop herself. "There's Henry."

Set-Fire had found out where Jesse spent his time, at least some of it. Set had had a couple of the men clear the blowdowns out of the path that led down to his old fish-house on the cove shore, and one of them, Harry Flanders, had said, "I think someone's hanging out in your building down there, Set. We didn't get time to check it out, but there's a couple of bicycle tracks going down t'wads there."

"Kids, probably," Set-Fire said. The first chance he got, he went down to check, not that kids could do any harm to that old wreck of a building. They were welcome, just so they didn't tear it down.

He found there unmistakable signs of occupancy, as if somebody had cleaned the building and had set up house-keeping. Be dag, he thought. Neat's a pin. The place had an old cast-iron stove in it, put there when Walter had used it as a workshop to build his traps in. Someone had cleaned the rust off of it with grease. Split wood and kindling were stacked in a box nearby. An ax, practically new, leaned in a corner, along with a new bucksaw. A frying pan, a coffee pot, and a kettle hung on nails driven into the wall. They were battered, obviously salvaged from somewhere, but scrubbed shiny. Two cots, rough frames built of driftwood boards and filled with hay, each with its neatly folded quilt. Looking more closely, he identified them as his own, the ones which had been on Jesse's cot up at the house. And on Walter's old work-table was an unmistakable sign of Jesse—a pocket com-pass, one of the presents Walter had brought him from town, a treasure which Set-Fire had seen before.

Delighted, Set glanced around the neatly kept place. Jess wasn't living here alone, that was for sure. George didn't come here anymore, now he'd got his traps done— he didn't even keep his boat in the cove now. He'd moved her around into the harbor, where she was on a haul-off, somewhat inshore from the *Sarah's* mooring; it was more convenient for him there, and, besides, the cove wasn't safe for a boat in any kind of an easterly. So it wasn't George who was in on this. No, it had got to be that smart little girl cousin of his—what was her name? Frankie.

Set smiled a little to himself, but at the same time he

couldn't help feeling sad. This was where two troddled-on and pawed-over kids had made themselves a place to be decent and private in, and by the god, they'd done a good job of it, but both of them deserved better. They ain't pigging it, they've made the room clean and cozy. Only thing they ain't washed is the window, and that likely's because they don't want anyone outside to notice they're here. Goddamn and set-fire! If I ain't gettin' myself all choked up.

He pulled a pencil out of his pocket and looked around for something to write on. There wasn't a scrap of paper in the place, but in the kids' kindling box was the end of a new, smooth-finished pine board.

"Dear Jess," he wrote on it. "You got to have something to eat on."

He didn't sign the note because there wasn't any need to. He left the board on the table with a ten-dollar bill on it, anchored down by Jess's compass. Then he blew his nose with a powerful toot and went quietly away.

Frankie was the only friend of his own age Jesse had ever made. George was older, and Henry too young, and he loved them both, dearly; but Frankie was twelve, as he was; their birthdays were only a week apart. There was something *to* that, he found. He'd liked Frankie from the night she'd come. She'd been around, had seen the whole United States, could tell him what driving fast across it was like. She wasn't scared of anybody or anything, not her mother or even Ma. She stood up to them and got away with it. She even stood up to George.

From the first, George had hated Frankie and she'd turned up her nose at him. Jesse had mourned over this. He'd dearly wanted her to have a ride in George's skiff, but no way. George wouldn't hear of it. "You can come if you want to," he'd said. "But she can set her shirttail afire and go flying to hell."

"Pooh on the nosy old butt-in," Frankie'd said. Butt-in because, at first, George had come hunting Jesse. "He's jealous, that's all ails him, and every time he chase-tails us he spoils our good time."

Jesse had to be convinced that George could be jealous of anything that had to do with him. But Frankie was right; whenever George caught up with them, he sure spoilt the good time. And they were good and well having one. They were having a ball.

Since Gladys no longer needed Jesse to help out with her séances, she didn't want him around, and Aunt Preston never bothered with Frankie anyway. So they could go where they wanted to; nobody checked up on what time they got home. If it was three in the morning, nobody cared. If they appeared at a meal, Gladys raved because they ate too much, but Madame Preston put her foot down about that. She liked to eat almost as much as Gladys did; she could cook, too, and did, and she cooked plenty.

"Now, Gladdie," she'd said, "as long as I'm buying the groceries, which I am, I ain't having my kid go flapping around town telling she's hungry. If you don't know it's rotten publicity, you ought to."

"Yah," Frankie'd said. "We can always go to the icebox and pick over your leftovers, can't we, Ma?"

Which Gladys had taken amiss, but which Madame Preston, for some reason, had not. She'd said simply, "Why not?"

"I'd tan that fresh brat if she was mine," Gladys had said.

"Well, she ain't. And if you lay a hand on her, you'll see the last of me for keeps."

So there was always something to eat in the refrigerator, or to be taken out and cooked, and for the same reason, whatever it might be, Aunt Preston saw to it that once in a while Frankie got a little spending money, which Frankie carefully saved in the toe of her sneaker—the one she always wore to bed because of Aunt Gladys.

Frankie's reason for saving her money was made clear to Jesse when they were getting together the things they needed for their room in Set-Fire's building. He had pointed out to her that it would be a lot easier to lift new stuff out of the hardware store, instead of rummaging through the town dump for beat-up old cooking dishes. "We could bust in some night and get 'em there, and an ax and saw to cut wood with," he'd told her. "I know an awful easy way to get in, George and I used to—"

Frankie turned white in the face. In fact, she turned almost green. She was good and mad, he could see. "Yah, you do, do you? I don't care one damn what you and old buttinsky George used to do. You track around with me, you gotta quit being wet behind the ears."

She went down to the hardware store, marched in and took off her sneaker. "I want a ax and a saw to cut wood with. How much?"

The clerk was amused and showed it. "You going to cut pulpwood, you need a chain-saw," he said. "You got enough money for one?"

"I want a plain ax and a plain saw. If you got any to sell, you can stop drooling down your chin and say how much. Like I ast you."

The clerk, who was elderly, and getting used to a new set of lowers, was taken aback. He wiped away the evidence of it hastily, produced the goods and took her money. "Lord almighty," he said to his next customer, "that brat of Miz Preston's is some old gristly tough, you know it?"

Frankie took the tools out to Jesse, who was lingering nervously in front of the store, and handed him the ax. The bucksaw she carried herself, fair was fair. "Once and forever you keep your cottin-pickin' fingers off somebody else's things," she told him.

Jesse, appalled at the idea of being seen with a brand-new ax in full daylight in front of the hardware store, took off at a gallop down the narrow alley between it and the bakery. The alley let out into a cluttered yard backed by a line of unused sheds, past which he and George had cleared a path for night escapes; from there he could make it into a thicket of alders on the edge of one of the farm woodlots. The way from there to the cove was roundabout and took time. He arrived there breathless and sweating to find Frankie sitting on the doorstep with the bucksaw beside her.

"I walked home," she said coldly. "I din't have to run."

Jesse was desperate. She was his friend; he couldn't lose her now. "Frankie, most of what George and I stole was stuff to eat when we got awful hungry and Ma didn't . . . didn't . . ."

"All right, I know what *she's* like; I'll buy that. Okay. Seddown. You ain't ever seen the inside of a jail, have you? Well, I have. My Pa was in one. If I ever wanted to see him, I had to go there. And I wanted to. I wanted to see him something awful. It was a mean, ugly place and he died in it."

The way she talked hadn't changed, but Jesse could see she wasn't mad anymore. He said carefully, "What . . . why was he . . . what did he do, Frankie?"

"What you don't know won't bust your head open," she said.

There was a long silence.

Then she said, "I'm talkin' tough to you because I got to. I *am* tough. I been tough since I was nine. That was when Pa took so sick and he told me he guessed he wouldn't be able to take care of me anymore, I'd have to grow up tough and take care of myself. And he said don't I ever do anything the cops can come after me for, so I ain't, and you ain't, either, because you're my friend. See?"

Jesse nodded. "Jeest, yes," he said, under his breath. He saw, all right. What she'd had, it must've been an awful bad time. For a minute, he couldn't say any more. Then he burst out, "I won't, I won't ever, Frankie! I thought you wasn't my friend anymore."

She grinned at him. "Well, I am. But you watch it, bud."

The town dump at the edge of town was a good place to find things—it was surprising, the things people threw away, stuff that could be cleaned up, some of it good as new. But the dump was a long ways to walk to; by the time you got there and did your hunting around, you were too beat-out to carry very much away. Then, one day Jesse remembered his bicycle and wondered if Foss Bailey had still kept it around.

Frankie said, "You got one? You *own* it?"

He explained about the bicycles—how Uncle Polly had bought them and what Gladys had done.

"Huh! A real doll, ain't she?. Let's go see."

Foss not only had kept the bicycles, he wanted very much to get rid of them. "Paid for, and I can't sell 'em, what d'you think, Jess? Clutterin' up the shop. Take 'em both."

"Just mine," Jesse said. He glanced uneasily at Frankie. "Mine's all I want."

"Shoot, you can ride a bike, can't you?" Foss said to Frankie. "Ride George's home to him, why don't you?"

"Okay," Frankie said. "I'll take yours, Jess, and you ride old Georgie's." She rode it expertly all the way down to the cove, leaned it against the side of the shed. "There, you've lent me yours and you've borrowed George's. It's here if he wants it."

So we ain't took a thing we hadn't ought to, Jesse thought, marveling at how smart she was. George couldn't care less about a bicycle now—he was too busy. Besides, he could have his when and if he did.

They could go anywhere now, bring home almost anything they wanted to. After a while, they didn't even need to go to the dump anymore. They could ride out to Paine's Pond, catch fish and cook them on the fireplace there; and then, if they felt like it, go skinny-dipping in the pond. Frankie didn't care if Jesse saw her all over; he got so he didn't mind if she saw him. After a while, neither of them thought anything about that.

If they went to the farm or to Set-Fire's, they didn't ride the bikes there, in case of running into George. They walked, usually up to the pigpens to see Janine and her piglets, once in a while running into Set-Fire, who always invited them to eat a meal with him if they wanted to. As for the other grown-ups at the farm, when Jesse didn't appear so often, they all thought he was being kept home by his mother; Gladys and Aunt Preston supposed they were staying up at the farm or down at Set-Fire's house. It all worked out very well. Frankie said, "What they don't know won't bust their heads open," which she liked to say about almost everybody.

Every so often a ten-dollar bill appeared on the table under the compass, and Set always left something good to eat, too—a cake, some ham slices, a pot of baked beans, a stew. So living was easy and peaceful; Set was the only one who knew where they were and he didn't nose in, only left the stuff. They were careful when and where they rode the bikes, usually following back streets out to the highway, then over towards Machias. And they did a lot of their riding at night.

VIII

For Walter and Aaron, late August turned out to be a time of vacation, which they had not foreseen. One night, for no reason anyone could find out, the *Sarah* came loose from her mooring. She drifted out of the harbor on an ebbing tide and across the bay, where she went aground on the reef at the north end of the Three Brothers Islands. By good fortune, the weather had been calm, with scarcely any wind, but the fall and rise of the tide had chafed the boat's bottom on the reef's sharp-edged underwater ledge. She was holed and leaking. The Coast Guard helicopter spotted her before she could sink and the boys were able to get aboard in time to patch the stove-in plank, pump out the water, so that she could be towed back into the harbor. Nothing could be done about her engine, which was full of salt water.

Aaron raged. The *Sarah*, his dear love, his home and his castle, was up on the ways at Moses Allen's marina, her immaculate paint scarred and scraped, her bottom stove, her engine ruined. The air around the marina turned blue with his cussing.

"It was them hoodlums of kids that hang around the harbor," he howled. "That damned Colcraft kid. By God, I laid him out flat once for raising hell with my punt. This time, I catch up with him I'll tear his head off his neck!"

Aaron already had had to pay Rod Colcraft's father a fat sum for knocking his boy around. He referred to this now with some blistering adjectives that fairly curled Walter's hair.

"I'd be sure it was him before I beat him up again," Walter said. "You hurt him pretty bad and what I hear, he's still wearing a cast on his ankle where you kicked it. For chrissake, Aaron, he's only a kid."

"Kid, nothing! You oughta know what he is. Him and your brother was always devils on wheels, still is, if you ask me."

"Oh, come on, cool off," Walter said. "George's doing all right now." He'd come to be pretty proud of George.

"Where was you the other day, when George had young Rod and two-three of them other half-assed little skunks out in his skiff, blasting to hell around the harbor in her? Seeing what she'd do?"

"I don't know where I was. I didn't see him."

"Well, I did. I was aboard the *Sarah* at the time. Don't try to tell me George ain't tracking around with that gang anymore. I wouldn't put it past him to cast us loose himself, take it out on me for giving his pal a good bust on the nose."

"Oh, stuff it!" Walter snapped. "You get a-hold of your goddamned tongue before it flies loose and sets something afire."

Usually when Aaron flew up in the air about something, which happened fairly often aboard the boat, Walter was able to hold his own temper, knowing that Aaron would blow everything out of his mouth and then cool down. But this time, the situation was different. Walter himself was appalled and shaken, furious at the damage which somebody's ill-will—or kid foolishness?—had caused. He had let go. Said exactly the wrong thing.

Aaron glared at him. "All right, stand up for the useless little bastards," he said. "We ain't feuding with anybody, and who else is there? Unless you just hooked the chain over the bow cleat and forgot to make it fast last Thursday night."

This *was* unreasonable. Because Aaron himself had moored the *Sarah* the last day they had had her out, Thursday, and Aaron must know it.

"Maybe one of us does need to be told how to do it," Walter said. "But it ain't me. You fix the chain, sure, take hitches around the bow cleat with the rope. Coil up the rope. If *I'd* done it Thursday night, that's how. If you're blaming me, you can damn well take her and run her alone."

"She never had a mark on her, not one goddamn scratch, when I was running her alone."

"Okay, if that's the way you feel. I'm fed up. I'd just as soon go shares with a bear with a bug up its arse."

Aaron's reply was another blast, which rang out over the harbor like a bell ringing changes.

A towheaded youngster, rowing by in a punt, yelled, "Wow!" And then, "Scott-ed that one up, din't ya, Aaron?"

Which didn't help.

Walter moved away, out of the gust of it. Let him cuss. We've both got reason to cuss somebody. Whoever it was. Had to be somebody with a grudge. But who? Not George, that was for sure. Give a dog a bad name and hang him, he thought, thinking of George.

He walked around the far side of the *Sarah's* scarred hull, stood looking along the smears and scratches in her glossy white paint. He and Aaron had gone over the boat earlier on, looking for clues, and hadn't found any. Still, no harm in looking again.

By gum, there was something. High up, under the gunnel, where the bow of a dinghy might have rubbed, was a small, clear smudge of royal-blue paint.

Well, the joker had had to row out to her in something. Could be that some punt or dinghy around might be painted that shade of blue. Offhand, he couldn't think of any—most of the tenders in the harbor were white or drab punkin-yellow.

Shoot, that daub might have got on there at any time —somebody came up alongside, maybe, or blue paint on something in and around the wharf. Still, if it had been there long, Aaron would have noticed it, and anything that got on the boat's white paint got scrubbed or sanded off in a hurry. Aaron would have seen it today, if it hadn't been in the middle of a lot of other scrubs and scratches. No sense leaving it around for him to find, though—the wild mad way he was feeling right now, he'd likely go raving around and beat hell out of some poor guy who didn't have anything but a blue dinner bucket.

Walter got out his jackknife and scraped the daub off, carefully catching the blue scrapings in his handkerchief. Find out who had a blue rowboat and compare color. George might know. . . .

George, he thought, with a sudden sinking feeling. George's skiff was white, but it had a darkish-colored gunnel. Walter had never really noticed it, hadn't bothered to look. But hadn't that skiff's gunnel been blue?

But, for the Lord's sake, George had been doing so well. Why would he want to go back to raising hell nights, now? Sure, he and young Colcraft had raised plenty, caused a lot of trouble. And according to Aaron, he was still tracking around with Rod. A stinking trick like this, though—set somebody's boat adrift . . . Walter didn't believe it. He walked out of the marina and went off along the shore road to see if he could locate George.

George, too, had found trouble when he had gone down to his skiff that day. He saw as he walked down the shore path that the boat wasn't on the haul-off. She was gone. Someone had taken her. Furious, he broke into a run, jumped down the bank to the beach and stared wildly this way and that. The first thing he saw was his outboard motor, which had been taken off the stern and dumped on the beach. The incoming tide was just beginning to lap up to it. He went tearing down to haul it up before salt water got into it. As he was horsing it up the beach, he located his skiff. She was a ways down the shore, afloat, bumping lightly against the pebbles as the flood tide butted her in. He raced down, put his hands on her bow, held her still while he got his breath back.

She was all right. Whoever had taken her hadn't even bothered to drop the anchor over when he got back. Hadn't give a damn whether she went adrift or not. The oars he always carried in case his motor ever conked out had been hauled from under the thwarts and chucked down all-anyhow. The rowlocks had been left in their sockets. The guy must've dumped the outboard on the beach and used oars, likely because he didn't want anyone to hear the motor start up, and of course the skiff rowed awful hard with the outboard weighing down her stern.

Who? He closed his eyes and saw against his eyelids what he'd do to any louse who'd fool around with a guy's boat like this. He was so mad that he didn't even see the smudges of white paint on the clean blue of the skiff's gunnel. He didn't notice them until early afternoon, when he had got back from selling his lobsters at the fish-wharf and had his skiff on the beach by the haul-off, washing the slime from the day's hauling off of her. By that time, he had seen the *Sarah* towed home, had heard Aaron cussing down at Mo Allen's and had listened to the talk over around the wharf about how some bugger had set her adrift in the night.

Appalled, George stared at the white smudges, which hadn't been there yesterday. Jeest, I bet that guy used my boat last night. It's the closest one to the *Sarah*'s mooring. Jeest, what if somebody over at the wharf noticed them smudges! The way everybody thinks about me, they'd sure put it on me. Things I done already, helling around town with Rod, they ain't nobody wouldn't blame me.

He rubbed frantically at the white smears. Most came off, but there was one, dented in, that wouldn't budge. Panic-stricken, he dropped the anchor over, left the skiff where she was and took off for the farm workshop as fast as he could pelt. He found the can of blue paint he'd used, but he'd forgotten to soak the brush in turpentine. It had dried stiff. Still, he guessed he could worry enough paint out of the can with it to cover that white spot. Wet with sweat and breathless, he jumped down the bank by the haul-off and saw that he was too late. Standing by the skiff and looking down at her gunnel was his brother Walter.

"You're in kind of a hurry to get that gunnel painted over, ain't you?" Walter said.

George tried to say, "Who's in a hurry?" but he had no wind left behind the words and they came out a croak.

"You know anybody else in the harbor got this shade of blue on his boat?" Walter asked.

George shook his head. He put the paint can down on a flat rock, flopped down beside it and panted. "So what?"

"There's a smooch this shade of blue on the *Sarah*'s hull." Walter showed his handkerchief. "I want to know how it got there."

"How'd I know? Could be some of that blue smoke Aaron was putting out, splattered and stuck."

Walter blew up. "Look, you smart-ass, don't you get funny with me about this. Not right now. You got a white paint smooch, the *Sarah*'s got a blue one. How'd it happen? You tell me what you know or I'll slap you bow-legged, along with the rest of that gang you run with."

Here it was again. "Oh, cool it," George said drearily. "Somebody swiped my boat last night. Chucked my out-board out on the beach in the tide's way, where I found it this morning. Left the skiff to grind on the beach, not even the anchor over. That's what happened, and that's all I know. Go ahead, call me a liar if you want to, I don't give a good gaadamn whether you or anyone else believes me."

Walter pursed his lips in a soundless whistle. He stood

looking down at George, but George didn't look back. He sat with his elbows on his knees, staring down at the beachrocks.

"Aaron says you and Rod Colcraft was making waves in your skiff around the harbor the other day."

"Only one, going out. Rod wanted to see what she'd do."

"Aaron was wondering how sore Rod felt about him."

"Rod's sore, all right. Me and a couple of the fellers had to help him get aboard the skiff. He can still hardly walk, let alone set a boat adrift, if that's what you and Aaron thinks."

"Okay. You get any water in your outboard?"

"What's it to you?" George rose suddenly to his feet, towering over Walter, whose build was considerably less husky than his. "Anything stinkin' that happens round town, who gets the blame for it? Rod Colcraft and me. Sure I stole stuff to eat when Jess and me was so damn near starved we had to grab whatever we could find. You ought to remember how it was, livin' with Ma. Okay with me, if you've forgot it."

"I ain't forgot it," Walter said soberly. He recalled also that Ralph's looks weren't the only things George had inherited. He had some, at least, of his father's temper. "Let's you and I talk this over sensible."

"Sensible, nothing! You ain't able to make any sense. Why in the name of the jumpin' old god would you think I'd cut your boat adrift or help anyone else to? I . . . I always been all for you, tried to show you I was. I ain't like Ma, hates your guts because you been makin' money and she can't git her hands on any of it. I've felt good, you've been doing so well. I been trying. . . . Sure, I used to raise hell with Rod, screeching tires and hollering at the tourists. But I ain't, not since I got my boat and traps. And you want to remember that whoever let loose the *Sarah* tried to clobber my boat and engine, too." He stopped, staring at Walter's face, which was expressionless. "Oh, hell, think what you want to. I don't care. But if you try slappin' me bowlegged, you'll find out like Ma did that I'm a little mite too big to lick."

"I wouldn't want to find that out," Walter said. "No way, bubba." He leaned over, picked up the paint can, started to stir it up with the dried-out brush. "Godsake, this is a hell of a way to treat a good paintbrush. You run out of turpentine up at the farm?"

He turned and, with a few neat strokes, painted out the white dent on the skiff's gunnel. "There. There'll be no more questions asked about that, and no need for any. What you'n I have got to do now is nose around, see if we can find out who it is has got it in for both of us." He climbed up the bank, stood for a moment, looking down. "You better overhaul your motor, make sure she didn't take in any salt water. You need any help, give me a holler." He went off along the shore road, headed towards the marina, where he had parked his car.

George, suddenly and to his own amazement, burst into tears. He cried for quite a while, sitting on his boulder, alone in the shade of the trees along the bank above him.

The fishermen began to keep a more careful watch over their boats. Anyone caught rowing around the harbor at night had to have a good reason for doing it. Joe Falls had notified the County Sheriff's Department and the State Police. The law tightened up on the so-called wild kids and arrested one or two of them for stealing tires.

"Oh, stuff it!" Joe Falls told his son. "This town makes me tired. Anything happens out of the way, folks dump it onto the kids. It warn't any kids frigged with your mooring, Aaron, and you can't make me believe it was. They're wild, all right, but not that wild, and young Colcraft's still laying around getting over the pounding you give him. So it warn't him."

Aaron grunted. "His gang was running loose. And the kid's goddamn father ain't any particular friend of mine."

"Jason Colcraft was in Machias to a Lodge meeting that night. Didn't get home till nigh morning. In a nice way, we've checked on him and we know where he went after the meeting."

"You and your pals in uniform are too damned nice," Aaron said. "Me, I'd ha' blasted the town wide open."

"I just bet you would. What you want to be such a cussid fire-eatin' kag of gunpowder for? There's more'n a likely chance that somebody was sore at me and took it out on you. You thought of that?"

"Well, find out who," Aaron said. "Whole damn Police Department settin' on its arse, all I can say."

"I wish to God it was all you could say," Joe said. "I'm sick of hearin' my ears ring and so's your Ma hers. Why don't you cool off, go have some fun somewhere. Hunt up Annabelle. Her day off, ain't it? Maybe she's over to Suzy's."

"I've got other fish to fry. Right now."

"You fry too long, Polly'll beat your time."

"*Polly?* You nuts? He's old enough to be her father."

"Been taking her out some, I hear. And she's been helping him paint that old car he got from Jones Bradley. Quite a bus, that is. You seen it?"

"No, I ain't seen it. Up to now, I've been too busy trying to earn a living. *Polly*, for gaasake, Pa. You think Annabelle's going to let that Good-time Charley beat *my* time?" He went off, chuckling to himself, and after a while Joe saw him leave the house, all dressed up, and take off somewhere in his car.

"Well," Joe told his wife, "I guess I've took his mind

off raving around town looking for a fight. I think he's
gone to hunt up Annabelle."

"I wish they'd make up their minds," Sarah said. "They
been going together, off and on, ever since she got home
from Boston."

"Mostly off," Joe said. "Le's see what happens this
time."

What happened was, Aaron found Paulus sitting in
Queen Mary's royal bathtub in Walter's driveway, waiting for Annabelle. They had planned a picnic and were
going off for the day. Paulus grinned and waved. "Hi,
Aaron. How's it going?"

Aaron leaned out the window of his this-year's-model
Buick and let go with a guffaw. "Gawd Almighty, Polly!
What town dump did you haul that old clunker home
off of?"

The town car had had her undercoat of paint; her
brass had been cleaned and polished, mostly by Annabelle, who had spent last week's day off helping Paulus.
They were both proud of the job they'd done and the
way the old car looked, so far. But Paulus didn't lose his
grin; he was used to Aaron's kidding. He had just opened
a bottle of ginger ale. He said, gesturing with it, "Have
one?"

"Kee-riced!" Aaron said. "Flowers, you got! Sweet
peas and pansies in little nipped-up vases, oh, my God,
ain't that gay, though. Sweet petunia, Polly, I'm beginning to wonder about you. Or are you planning to run
a hearse for the undertaker?" He rocked back and forth,
shouting laughter.

Annabelle had picked the flowers and filled the Queen's
vases. "To celebrate the first paint job," she'd said. She
was coming down the porch steps now, dressed in slacks
and sweater for the picnic. "Hello, Aaron," she said.

"Hi, Annabee! You look like hell. Go get some decent
duds on; you'n I's going sporting."

"I'm sorry," she said. "If you'd bothered to call me, I could have told you I was busy. Saved you the trouble of coming by."

"Busy, hell! With Good-time Charley, here? Go on, get fixed up. I ain't waiting around."

"Good idea," she said. "Don't."

Aaron turned red. He got out of his car and slammed the door. He grabbed her by the shoulders, spun her around, gave her a shove towards the house. "You hop it. You're going with me."

"Hey, Aaron, take it easy," Paulus said. "What in the world's that in aid of?" He got out of the car and laid a hand on Aaron's sleeve.

Aaron shook it off. "I'll show you what it's in aid of if you don't crawl back into that goddamned oil-tanker and haul ass out of here," he said furiously. "That's my girl you're frigging around with."

"Oh, come on! Calm down. Whose girl she is depends on how *she* feels. Be your age, boy, we're just going on a picnic."

He saw the fist coming, inclined his head sideways, felt the wind of it as it whizzed past his ear. He stepped back, limberly, out of range, not that that helped—Aaron was still coming.

Annabelle screamed, "Run, Polly! He'll hurt you!" She caught Aaron's jacket behind and tried to hold him back, not that that helped, either; but it gave Polly time to give the opened bottle of ginger ale, which he still held in his hand, a hard shaking-up. He clapped his thumb over the nozzle and took aim. The stream of stinging white froth took Aaron fairly between the eyes.

Aaron yelled; he backed up. His heel caught and he sat down hard on the ground, both hands clapped to his face.

"Don't rub your eyes hard," Paulus said. "Makes it worse. Annabelle, would you get a pan of cold water?"

He pulled out a clean handkerchief, slipped it between Aaron's frantic fingers and his face. "That was a damn dirty trick, Aaron," he said. "But no worse than trying to clobber a man who's ten years older than you are and about half your size. I wasn't about to let you ruin me. And you'd better know, here and now, that nobody's been frigging around and I haven't been trying to beat your time. Annabelle told me a while ago that you and she were through for keeps, and I think she understood you were. Here's a bucket of water. Dunk your face into it, it'll help the sting. You'll be all right."

"I'm sorry about that, Annabelle," Paulus said, as they drove away. "I wouldn't have had that happen if I could have stopped it any other way."

"Why be sorry? It wasn't your fault. You know as well as I do that nobody's ever beaten Aaron in a fist-fight. That's what ails him. He lets fly at anyone he gets sore at and right now he's sore at the world, Walt says."

"Runs in the family, in a way," Paulus said. "Ralph had that kind of a temper, but he had better control. He didn't lose it often, but when he did, you made tracks fast." He chuckled. "I saw Amanda cool him off once, that same way, with a bottle of soda pop. When we were kids. Doesn't do any permanent damage, I'm glad to know. I can't say I blame Aaron for being sore at the world."

"Of course not. But it's little-boy stuff to take it out on his friends. Even Walt. Walt says he's right between Moses Allen's boys down at the boatyard, and the repair work they're doing—has to inspect everything, make sure it's right. Drives them up the wall. Oh, I'm glad we're going fishing. I feel as if I'd been sandpapered."

"Well, in the process of," Paulus said. "I do, too. Sandpapered and sorry. But it'll be nice out on the pond today." He had borrowed Foss Bailey's boat, which Foss kept at his camp, somewhat farther up the pond from the usual sand beach. Foss, with his peace and privacy in mind, had made only a narrow path in from the road. He worked on the theory that trespassers, if they couldn't ride the last hundred yards or so in to his place on the shore, certainly wouldn't make the effort to get out of the car and walk there, and he was mostly right. Fishermen in boats could land at his small dock, and sometimes did, but his privacy today was uninvaded, except for an out-size bullfrog, who, hearing footsteps behind him, took a header into the water and landed with a small *chunk!* sound and scarcely a ripple.

"You dive nice, old man," Paulus told him. "We'll be gone in a minute and you can come back." He stowed the fishing tackle and lunch basket aboard the boat, steadied it for Annabelle to get in. "Foss said we could use his outboard. But this is a slick-rowing skiff, balanced just right. You want motor- or manpower?"

"It's so peaceful," she said. "Let's not make any more noise than we have to. I'll help row if you get tired."

"Good. Want to sit in the stern and troll a line?"

"Not much use to, is there? Not while the sun's so bright and there isn't a wrinkle on the water. Really, I'd just as soon trail my fingers."

"Tell you what. Let's row up to the north end of the pond, find a nice place to eat and wait for a salmon rip-ple. Be a breeze this afternoon, looks like. Ought to be northwest, too. We can drift back, troll lines. Fish lazy if we want to. It's a lazy day."

The skiff slid quietly along over the still water, her wake scarcely troubling the reflections of trees, which rippled a little with her passage, settled back into their undisturbed perfection. Paulus's oars made no sound except a slight metal-clink of rowlocks. He's good at that, Annabelle thought, watching the expert feathering, the effortless, smooth rhythm of the oars. And he likes the way we're doing, not roaring up the pond, with an outboard wide open. "Just to see what she'd do." He doesn't need to know, almost seems like.

Strange to be out with a man who didn't need to brag, to show off, to make known that what he had, what he owned, what he *was*—his fist, his muscles—were better, stronger, more priceless; even the arrows from his bow were sharper and deadlier than other people's. A quiet man. But don't anyone think he isn't able—make the same mistake Aaron did.

She trailed her fingers in the water, and her nerves which had been jangled up into knots began to unwind.

I like the way his hands are, on the oars, she thought. And the funny quirk he has of talking to things—like telling the bullfrog what a good dive that was. . . . Who else do I know who ever paid a compliment to a bullfrog? She smiled a little to herself. Absurd, maybe, being respectful to a bullfrog, as if it was as important, as valuable, as anybody, had the same right to be there. Not like the types who'd yell, "Hey, there's a frog! Gimme a rock." And *whammo!*·

I'll settle for the compliment, she told herself. It's so . . . so peaceable.

Paulus stopped rowing and leaned on the oars. He was not looking at her, but studying something on the shore. They had been rounding the end of a small promontory which had a pocket-sized sand beach shaded by some kind of leafy, shrub-like trees. "Look at the elderberries," he said. "Scads of 'em. There's a glorious batch of wine, all ready to go, if only we'd brought something to pick into."

"We could eat here," she said. "And fill up the lunch basket."

He shook his head. "Won't hold enough. Takes a real slug to make a serious batch of wine. Too bad. Those ought to be just about prime."

"There's the minnow bucket," she said, tentatively.

"We could let the minnows go and rinse out the bucket and each have a pail to pick in. Only I expect you'd rather fish, hadn't you?"

"To tell you the truth, no. I wouldn't. I'd do what my Grandfather Dennis would do. If he came across this kind of a treasure in the woods, which wouldn't be quite so much of a treasure later on as it is today, he'd say the fish'll be there tomorrow. He'd tie up the neck of his shirt, make a bag out of it." He backed water, swung the skiff around and headed for the sand beach. "What was holding me back was you. I thought you wanted to fish."

"I'm no great hand at it," she said, smiling. "I don't care."

"Good. Gramp wouldn't even have had a minnow bucket along. He wouldn't be caught dead fishing with live bait. He learned his trick in a lumber camp, up in the Moosehead region. The camp cook would make two holes in a shiny tin pie plate, hitch it onto his line with a sinker and a hook, troll it deep enough, and catch all the salmon the camp needed for supper in an hour or so. Besides, Gramp said, he never could stand the flutteration against his hand when he reached into a minnow bucket. All he could think was, Who's next?" He shipped one oar, picked up the minnow bucket. "Let'er go?" he asked.

She nodded. "And glad to see the last of them," she said, watching the terrified little fish scoot out of sight in the clear water. "You take after your grandfather, don't you?" she said.

"Gran Matilda says I do. Want to eat yet?"

"Well, I could nibble. Breakfast seems a long time ago."

They had filled all the containers they had—the emptied-out lunch basket, both halves of the minnow pail, the makeshift bags created out of Paulus's shirt and Annabelle's old windbreaker—when they became aware that the pond shore was inhabited by someone besides themselves. The first sound was a clear silvery laugh, not very far away, followed by light splashings.

Annabelle jumped a little. "What was that? It wasn't a loon, was it?"

Paulus was peering out through the elderberry trees. He chuckled. "No. Come and look, Annabelle."

Two swimmers, youngsters, were heading up along-shore; as they came abreast, the one behind called out, "That's far enough, Jess. And you beat me fair and square this time. Good for you!"

Jess and Frankie, Paulus thought. I'll be darned. Jess has learned how to swim. Good at it, too. I'll have to tell George.

The kids came plowing out of the water into the shade of the trees that grew along the bank. The sunlight and shadow speckled their brown skins; neither one had anything on and they were laughing.

Beside him, Annabelle caught her breath. "Oh, Polly, aren't they beautiful!"

They were. Jess had lost his downspent, sick-chicken look; he had filled out, and his arms and legs which had been skinny as sticks showed the beginnings, at least, of healthy muscles. They seemed more alike now than when Paulus had first seen them together. Frankie's light hair was sun-bleached almost lemon-color, her compact little mug as pug-nosed as ever. They were both tanned Indian-brown from head to foot, but the resemblance wasn't entirely that either, Paulus thought, watching and listening.

"I beat you this once, swimming," Jesse said. "I might not be able to do it again."

"Yes, you would, you got longer arms and legs. You keep on, you'll beat old Georgy, someday."

"I'd have to get a lot bigger," Jesse said. "He's awful strong."

"Well, you will be, too. You've got almost an inch

taller, remember, just since we been swimming a lot and riding the bikes. And he's got a lot more hunk to haul through the water than you have. You wait. You'll see. I just can't wait for the sight of old Georgy's face the day you do." Frankie kicked at the soft sand, sending a fan of it all over both of them.

"Oh, come on," Jesse said. "You promised you'd try to be friends with him."

"Sure, and I will. Like I said. Even if I do feel like telling him to go fry his bellybutton, okay. I'll go along with that. But I still think you ought to tell Set-Fire or somebody about your Ma."

"No, I ain't going to," Jesse said, and Paulus was surprised to see him so positive about something. "You said that was up to me and it is, Frankie. That's over and done with and nobody got hurt. I ain't going to get mixed up in it. No way."

"Okay."

"What people don't know won't bust their heads open," Jesse said. "Le's swim back easy, so as not to scare the fish. Might be a big trout around, and we still got to fish up some lunch."

That alikeness, Paulus thought. It's in the way they are together, their manner to each other. As if Jesse had traded some of his gentleness to Frankie and she had passed back to him the tough-minded confidence he'd needed. Well, whatever it was, Paulus felt like putting back his head and shouting with delight at the change in Jess. And in Frankie, too, bless her tough little heart.

He touched Annabelle's hand and motioned to her. They moved quietly away without saying anything.

"Yes," she said, as she began helping him to load their things aboard the skiff. "If anybody finds anybody, it's better if they find us first. Otherwise, we're a pair of nosy old sods."

"Right," Paulus said. They waited until the sounds of

"easy" swimming had died away along the shore before they launched the skiff. "Bikes, they've got," Paulus said, thoughtfully. "Explains how they've managed to get this far away from home. Jess must have picked his up at Foss's. Could be it's that, Gladys has kicked up a row about. She blew up a whacker of a row when the boys first got their bikes. Made them take 'em back to Foss and tried to get the money for them."

"Walter told me. Whatever she's kicked up, it's probably something horrible. Walt says she's always had a genius for making kids miserable. These two seem to have survived pretty well, though, haven't they?"

"I don't know how, in that household," Paulus said. "Unless it's Madame Preston, holding the old girl back, and *she's* no kind of a sweet motherly soul, either, from what Ralph told me. But somebody's been feeding those kids and they're happy as a clambake. I've tried, but I haven't been able to catch up with Jess, he doesn't eat at the farm anymore. Set-Fire says they visit the pigpens every so often to check up on Jess's pet sow, and he's told them they're both welcome to eat at his house or ours whenever they want to. I don't know. It's a monkey puzzle."

"Seems to me they're managing all right by themselves," she said. "And, maybe, better left that way. But we've got a lot of lunch left we won't use, because we've got to go home and take care of these elderberries before they mush up and spoil, so why don't we make believe we were just rowing by and spotted the kids, and go in and leave the lunch with them, before we—"

"Annabelle," Paulus said firmly, "every time I go out with you I find myself lugging around buckets or bags of berries of one kind and another, or all wovelled up with a bunch of kids."

She grinned at him. "They like you," she said wickedly.

"All right, they do. But the question in my mind right

now is, when's a man going to get time to do his courting?
And the answer is, he doesn't get any. So I give up. I'm
not going to do any, I'm going to grab this God-given one
minute and ask you. Will you marry me?"

"You don't need to do any. All I had to do was get to
know you. Yes, I will, darling. I'd love to."

What Jess and Frankie knew about Gladys had nothing
to do with bicycles. It was what they had watched her
do on the night when the boats had gone adrift. They
had been out at the pond and were riding home late—
how late, they had no idea, except it was long after
dark. Lights were out in most houses; there was almost
no traffic. They'd decided to ride down through town,
which was the shortest way back to Set-Fire's shed; nobody would be up to see them.

Supper was a long time ago, and there hadn't been
much of it. They'd split a hotdog and two slices of bread
between them, fished until they couldn't see their bobbers,
and not a bite. As they passed Gladys's house, Frankie
braked and got off her bike.

"I'm roaring, flapping hungry," she said. "Ma's always
got something in the icebox. I'm going in and see what's
there."

"Oh, my gee, Frankie." Jesse started to protest, but she
had already started wheeling her bike towards the kitchen
side of the house, where the unlocked window was, the
one he and George had always sneaked in by, times
Ma had got mad and locked them out. This wasn't the
first time, either, that he and Frankie had used it. And
Aunt Preston didn't give a hoot if they raided the icebox,
so long as they didn't bother her. Besides, he was starving, too.

They parked their bikes out of sight behind the steps
and slid quietly in through the window. In the refrigera-

tor, they found half a stuffed roast chicken, a panful of
bread pudding, and a pint of cream.

"Whee! That's an old whacker of a pudding," Frankie
whispered. "Le's take all of it, it's so good. We can use
the pan it's in, too. Ma won't care, she's got lots of pans
around."

"It'll be tough to carry on the handlebars," Jesse said.
"That big pan. Wouldn't want to drop it. Wait! I know.
Paper bag." He rummaged cautiously in a kitchen drawer
and came up with, not paper bags, but two ample plastic
ones and a ball of string. "Put everything in these and
tie 'em with loops to hang on the—"

"Ss-h," Frankie hissed. "Listen. Someone's coming. Duck
under the table, Jess."

But it was too late to move without being seen. Because
whoever it was was carrying a flashlight and its circle of
light was already bobbing on the floor by the door which
led in from the dining room. For a panicky moment, Jesse
thought it must be a burglar; his mother or Aunt Preston,
of course, would have turned on the switch by the door.
But it was his mother, he saw from the reflected glow,
and she was stalking through the kitchen not looking one
way or the other. She unlocked the back door and went
out, leaving it ajar behind her.

The kids had stood paralyzed, waiting to be discovered.
Then Frankie moved. "Wow! Was that funny! Didn't even
see us." She tiptoed over to the window and peered out.

"Which way'd she go?" Jesse said, shakily.

"Off along the street. She's just turned off the light.
C'mon, le's tie up this stuff and hop it out of here before
she comes back."

"Leave it," Jesse said. "C'mon, hurry. She never goes
out nights like that, she'll—"

"*Leave* it? Chicken and that lovely pudding! I thought
we'd awready lost the works. You know how she comes

down and mugs-up, cleans out everything. Here!" She thrust the ball of string at him. "Tie loops!"

Jesse tied loops, good strong ones. They set off down the street, each with a plastic bag dangling from the handlebars.

"We better go by the shore road," he said. "She wouldn't have any reason to go down there."

"Oh, she's likely headed for the graveyard to raise up the hants," Frankie said. But she turned into the shore road, all the same.

Frankie was wrong. Gladys wasn't headed for any graveyard, and she did have some reason for going down the shore road. Some ways ahead of them, they saw her light suddenly come on and turn down the path to the small cove where George kept his boat now. As they came abreast, they could see her dark figure against the harbor water, which was white and still. They heard splashings as she hauled George's skiff in from the haul-off, and a *thunk* as if she had thrown something heavy from the boat onto the beach.

"She's taken George's skiff," Jesse said fiercely. "And I think that was his outboard motor she throwed out onto the flats. If the tide comes up over it, salt water'll ruin it." He laid his bike carefully down and stepped away from it, staring at the gleam of bright metal down below on the beach. They could hear cautious clinks and splashes as Gladys got out rowlocks and oars. Then the boat slid away, a pale shadow vanishing out into the harbor.

"C'mon!" Jesse tore down the beach, trying as best he could not to let the sound of his running rattle the beach-rocks.

The gleam of metal was certainly the outboard left on the flats, and there was no doubt whatever that the flood tide would come up over it. The ebb tide, already under way, had sucked water out of the shallow cove so that a few feet of flats were uncovered; farther out, the mud would be a foot deep, but near the beach it was only up over the tops of sneakers. But, Jesse thought, as he felt the ice-cold slimy stuff deepen on his ankles, even a little mud could ruin a motor. Despairing, he felt around it and found with relief that it had landed on a thick patch of eel grass and hadn't sunk in the way he had.

"That was one dirty old mean trick," Frankie said, beside him. "What's she got against George?"

"A lot." Jesse laid hold of the outboard and tried to lift it, but it was heavy and he had no underpinning. He only slipped and slid and sank deeper. The motor rolled a little but didn't lift.

"Here, wait," Frankie said. "Le'me latch on to the other end."

They managed, but it was rough going. Frankie kept her end of the outboard dry, even when she skidded and sat down, by holding it high on her lap. The few feet to the hard, dry part of the shore took time, because they had to be so careful. They were soaked and shivering and had to rest several times, before they got the awkward thing almost to the top of the beach. They tried not to rest too long, because no knowing when Gladys might come back.

"I . . . guess this . . . is far . . . enough," Jesse panted. It was too dark to see where high-water mark was, but he could hear some dry seaweed crunch under his feet.

"It'll *have* to be," Frankie said. "Listen."

There it was. The sound of oars and rowlocks.

"She'll see it . . . she'll fall over it . . . if we leave . . . it here."

They horsed the motor as far along the beach as they could—as far as they dared take time to—away from the cleared place where the path let onto the bank. Then they fled on their bikes back to the only place they knew where they could sleep safely and where tonight's harm—

whatever it was—could not find them—Set-Fire's old shed
down by the back cove's water.

Gladys did not go anywhere near the motor, or the shore
path either, when she came back from setting the *Sarah*
adrift. She had had enough of flats-mud when she had
launched the skiff—had gone almost to the tops of her nice
new Russian boots when she had had to shove so hard.
She certainly wouldn't want to get them muddy inside.
What was on them now was bad enough.

She hadn't counted on flats-mud when she'd made up
her mind to hand Walter a good one, right where he lived
—in his pocketbook. Damn him and blast him, he was getting the income from Ralph's share of the farm, which belonged to her. He'd find out where *that* got him, doing
down his own mother. But that mud! For a moment, she'd
thought she wasn't going to be able to shove the skiff
through it. In the coast village where she and Peg had
been brought up, in and out of rowboats all the time, the
shoreline had been mostly cliffs, the only harbor there was
man-made, out of concrete piers, so that boats were afloat
whenever you needed one. Not remembering about that
mud, she'd almost spoiled her whole plan. Then she'd had
the brains to heave the motor overboard, which was all to
the good. That took care of George, too.

Coming back, she rowed to the south end of the cove
which made out into a rocky point where the water was
deep enough to land without getting her feet wet, stepped
ashore, and gave the skiff a shove. Then she washed off her
boots, carefully, in a tide pool and walked home through
the woods.

At the house, everything was dark, the way she'd left
it, the back door still ajar. Nobody would know she'd even
been out of bed, let alone gone, doing what she'd done.
She made straight for the refrigerator, hungry, she thought,
as she'd ever been in her whole life. There'd be the rest

of the chicken and that wonderful, great bread pudding Peg'd made—she felt her tongue splash in her mouth. But when the refrigerator light came on, there was nothing. Nothing! Her hands shook as she rummaged, and found only a jar of peanut butter.

Had Peg hid that food somewhere, too lazy to cook anything new for tomorrow? She'd threatened to, once or twice, if Gladys didn't stop raiding the icebox nights.

I got a good mind to go straight up and face her with it; that ain't no way for people to live—hiding away the food!

But no, better not. Peg, waked up, would be flame-fire mad. And, Gladys knew from past experience, Peg could get an awful lot madder than she could. No guessing who'd be the one to knuckle under. Besides, Peg was on a short string these days. She was sore because in spite of the new gadgets and the stars-of-heaven wallpaper, the séances weren't doing well at all. Not much money was coming in. Regular customers were dropping off; one of them had even come right out and said that the ladies liked the old way better, they couldn't get used to everything's being so different, made them feel uncomfortable. And Peg had really spit fire about that. She'd said that the people in this jerkwater town were so ignorant and so far behind the times that it was a wonder the womenfolks didn't all wear hoopskirts and bustles. She'd told Gladys that she'd have done better if she'd gone back to Nova Scotia, to Uncle Amos's old house which she still owned, and set up her business there.

No, better not poke up Peg, right now. Because if she was to take it into her head to leave before all the bills on the house renovations were paid, my soul and body, Gladys thought, I just don't know what I'd do.

She settled for bread and peanut butter, which she ate out of the jar with a spoon. She thought, suddenly, of the pint of cream which Peg had laid in for the pudding—she could drink that; but on looking in the icebox, she found that was gone, too. So, as an expression of a hungry woman's ire, and a reminder, she left the heel of the loaf of bread and the empty jar on the table, and went up to bed.

Walter relaxed and rested through the long days of late summer weather. It was wonderful to have time to be at home as much as he wanted to, instead of a few rushed-up hours between fishing trips. Another baby was on the way, due in December, and Walter marveled.

"How'd we manage that?" he asked Suzy. "Seemed like all I could do last spring was make a grab at you once in a while."

"Darn good grabs, if you ask me," Suzy said. "The way this one's booting my insides around, he's going to be an old whacker, like Henry."

At first, Walter had made daily trips down to the boatyard to see how the repair work on the *Sarah* was coming along and to offer his help, if needed. But each time he went, the visit had ended up in a spat with Aaron, which could easily have grown into a roaring row if Walter hadn't backed down. Early last spring, they had talked over having a new engine put into the boat, and Aaron had been all for buying a diesel. Now, when Walter mentioned it, he went up in the air.

"Okay, okay," Walter said. "I didn't know you'd changed your mind."

"For godsake, when did I say I'd run the *Sarah* on a diesel? Look, you need a vacation, go on and take one. Let me handle this myself."

Walter started to say what was on the tip of his tongue— that he owned equal shares in the *Sarah* now and might be expected to have some say. He didn't. He said, simply, "All right, go ahead. I can use the time. Just let me know when you're ready to roll."

He did use the time, working on his house. He and Suzy helped Paulus and Annabelle make elderberry wine, following Grampa Dennis's formula, which as usual produced "a masterpiece."

"At least," Paulus said, "looks all right. Along about next spring, we'll know for sure."

He and Annabelle hadn't announced their engagement yet, but most of the family knew about it and were delighted. Walter, himself, was pleased, but he also wondered if the engagement didn't have something to do with Aaron's temper.

Mo Allen said, "The boys is gettin' damn sick of havin' to walk around him, down here at the boatyard. We'll all be some glad to git him outa here and that cussid *Sarah* down off'n the ways."

On the day when Walter glanced out into the harbor and saw the *Sarah* on her mooring, looking like a million dollars in her coat of glistening white paint, he still hadn't heard a word from Aaron, so he hunted up Joe Falls.

"Let me tell you, his mother'n me is some teed-off with him," Joe said. "Times, I could kick that boy's arse all the way from here to the boatyard. Know what he's done now? He's moved aboard the *Sarah*, sleeps there in the cuddy. Gets me to row him out there after dark and bring the punt ashore, so's nobody'll know he's there. Says if any bastard sneaks aboard at night now, he'll run into something he can't handle. All I can say is, I hope to God he don't find out who set the *Sarah* adrift, or there'll be trouble none of us can handle. That's what's on his mind, Walt. Nothin' to do with Annabelle."

"I wasn't sure. I haven't seen him."

"Shoot, Aaron's always played the field, I don't think he ever cared two hoots about any one girl. Brags about having several he's asked to marry him and then backed off, tells them just be there when he comes around, and some are. Annabelle's the only one ever turned him down flat and that itched him. Being on a short string anyway, he lit into Paulus." Joe grinned. "Wish I'd seen it."

"I don't know, Joe. The *Sarah's* ready, and I haven't heard a word from him. And I'd just as soon touch a red-hot stove."

"Look, Walt. Aaron's like a machine, no use to himself or anyone else unless he's working. He'll get over what's chewing him pretty soon and be around after you. The trouble right now is, he can't stand being crossed up. Been like that ever since he could walk. His mother'n I's used to it. Never seemed to be much we could do but let him be, never done a bit of good to lick him. He'd sull around awhile, and then come back and ask us where we all was. You take all the vacation you can git. You and him's been going it, lickety-tilt, for God knows how long."

"I was pretty pooped out," Walter said. "But I've got my half of a damn good boat paid for and some cash put away. Let me tell you, I couldn't have done that without Aaron. I don't owe him money, Joe, but I owe him al-mightily, other ways."

"Put it he owes you, too. Ain't another man he can find around who could, or would want to, keep up with him. About the *Sarah*, though, there's one thing you can be pretty sure of, maybe you'll want to keep it in mind. As soon as Aaron gits a little bit farther ahead, he's going to want to sell her."

"He is! Why? She's a swell boat. He thinks a lot of her."

"Not anymore. It's the way he is. Anything he owns has got to be the best, and it's got to be bright, shiny, and not a mark on it. His guns, his tools, his clothes, they git a scratch or a stain and they ain't no good to him anymore. He sells them or gives them away, buys new. You recall that jacket he got the frosting on, at Gran Scott's party? Code Willis cleaned that sleeve off so's you'd never know a spot was there. God knows what he done with it, but he ain't wore it since. The *Sarah*, now, she's had a plank stove in. She's got gouges, sealed up and painted over so's they don't show, but he knows they're there. She's second-hand to him. She ain't a living doll. Not no more. You take notice of it. You'll see."

Walter saw. In early September, when Aaron came after him and they went back to work again, things seemed much the same as they had been. Aaron drove as hard as ever, never missing a possible fishing day, and insisted on going farther offshore for better catches. But from the short-tempered, almost slapdash way he handled the *Sarah*, Walter could tell. She wasn't his living doll any longer. Not anymore.

September meant school, the end of the good times of summer. Everybody had to go. Set-Fire came down to the cove one day to say that school would begin on Tuesday. "Kids has to go to school," he told them, expecting grouses and grumbles. To his surprise, there weren't any. The kids, it seemed, had been expecting that; it was all talked over. September had always meant school; they would have felt uncomfortable not going. There were other problems, however.

"We can wash out these old jeans, like we've done all summer," Frankie said, "but they've had it. Ma won't bother to buy me any school clothes, but she'll hand out some money for some and I can split it with Jess."

"And we ain't going back down there to live," Jesse said.

"No way," Frankie said. She scowled at Set-Fire and her underlip stuck out.

"Well, now. No need to go off half-cocked. Some things has been tended to, up to the farmhouse. Code and Amanda's fixed you each a room, all yours. Any clothes you'll need for school there'll be plenty of, don't worry about that." He fumbled in his pocket, produced a padlock and two keys, which he dropped on the table. "These is yours," he said. "Don't make sense, you trying to live down here in the cold weather. Git a couple of good snow-storms, the way'd be snow up to your middles, and you couldn't load enough wood int' that little stove to keep you warm." He glanced around the neat little room. "This is your summer cottage, I been real tickled at how you've fixed it up, clean and nice. You'll need to lock it up when you ain't here, keep some nose-almighty from fooling around with your things. You each got a key, so's you won't have to come hunting me, any time you want to come down."

"What about . . . about anyone wants to yank us around?" Jesse said.

"Your mothers think you've been living up at the farm anyway, where they ain't seen you around all summer. They ain't raised any dust about it. Polly says they ain't likely to. Polly had a talk with them, seems. Your Ma started to yak, but Marm Preston clapped her foot hard down, said don't be a fool, Gladys, the kids' expenses'll be took care of all winter. So there we are, home free, looks like. You going to go along with us?"

"There's George," Frankie said. "He lives up there at the farm and he don't like me much."

"George is so huffy about going back to school himself that he ain't likely to have much grief to spare for you or anyone else. He'll be glad to see Jess. And I wouldn't be surprised if you could make up with him, if you was to try."

"Well," she said doubtfully, "I could tell him I'm sorry I thought he ought to go fry his bellybutton."

There was a short silence. The kids looked at each other. What passed between them Set couldn't say, but Jesse leaned over and picked up the padlock.

"We'll have to get hold of some screws and a steel strap to hook this onto the door, Frankie," he said.

"We can buy some," she said. She sat down and began to take off her sneakers.

* * *

George sat humped at his deck in the sophomore room at the high school, dividing his attention between the loose-leaf notebook in front of him and the blue October world outside his window. He had managed to get the seat next the one that overlooked the harbor, from which he could see the wharves and the water traffic—the fishing boats going out and coming in. He could see the *Sarah's* mooring, and, not far from it, his haul-off where his own boat was waiting, idle.

It was afternoon, only a half-hour before school would let out, but before he could go he had his essay to write and the notebook page was still blank, except for three words: *What I seen. . . .*

They left it to you to write about what that was, where it was, and what you thought about it.

Jeest! Don't make it fancy, just write about the real thing.

He stared glumly at the paper, crossed out *seen*, substituted *saw*.

Made a swell beginning. Catch the old boober's eye the first thing. Okay, what did I saw? That don't sound right. But, hell, anything that didn't sound right most likely was.

After some thought, he added three more words: *out the winder*. So what was out the winder? He turned to look, and presently began to write:

Out the winder I seen the sky. It is blue. Got two clouds on it. I think it looks nice. I seen a yellow maple tree, leafs fall offa it. I think it is pretty. I seen ole Gene Dunnin goin down the road. He has got pants and a coat and a hat on. I think he is a ole skunk. I seen Nels Wokker light out with a load of traps on. His boat is red. He has a deezle enging. It makes a hell of a noise without no muffler on it. I think he is settin traps. I think he is goin to set traps all round anyone traps that he thinks is catchin any lobsters. I seen the Sayra comin in early. She is some damn deep in the water. Ain't hardly any freeboard showin. I think walt and aron has had a good trip. I think if aron keeps on loadin her so heavy he will sink her to hell in the tiderip someday.

George stopped, astonished to find that he had seen so much to write about.

Jeest, must be a hundred words, but just in case, he added a few:

what I wisht I coulda seen out'n the winder is a feller name of Whyly Cope. I think he could of be some help to me.

He closed the notebook, sat waiting for the bell that would let him out of prison. Three minutes to go. Set here and wait, he fumed. If I was to go now, nobody'd miss me.

Afternoons between three and suppertime were so short now. They'd be shorter when the clocks got set back an hour, which would be pretty soon. He wouldn't begin to get all his traps hauled before dark. The law said he had to stick school till he was sixteen, and that would be on the tenth of December, when his birthday was.

And then! And then, I quit. And then, he told himself, using a phrase he'd heard from Gran Matilda, I'll be neither to hold or bind.

He heard the click that meant the bell was going to ring and beat the sound of it to the door.

IX

At 2:00 A.M. on the first day of December, the temperature was six degrees above zero, the sky cloudless, with no wind. Not a breath rippled the harbor. The full moon, westering, made no track on the polished surface, only gave back its own reflection. A trail of evenly spaced blobs followed the punt, where Aaron's oars had disturbed the water.

"Some calm," he said. "Too calm. Something tells me that old moon don't mean what she says."

"One thing she says is damn cold." Walter shivered inside his sheepskin-lined coat. "*Br-rr!* Goes right through you."

"This kind always does. Dampness in it. Feel it inside the house with the heat turned on, morning like this." He eyed the layer of ice which had formed in the night around the *Sarah's* waterline. "We won't be going anywhere till we get that cussid stuff howked off of her. I'll do it whilst you warm up the engine."

"I'd just as soon help," Walter said. Knocking off ice was a mean job and a cold one.

"Hell, no. Crawl down in the cuddy, warm yourself up, too. Cold don't bother me the way it does you," Aaron said, and in the moonlight Walter caught the brief whiteness of his grin. "Growed up on hotdogs and candy bars. Never et right when you was a kid."

"That's right," Walter said. He almost said, All the same, I don't need a nurse, bud, but thought better of it. At this time in the morning, and cold as he was, he wasn't about to listen to a lot of whys and wherefores from Aaron.

Joe had been right about Aaron. In October, Aaron had left the boat idle on her mooring for three weeks while he went off somewhere in his car. He hadn't said where he was going, and nobody knew. Then, one day, when Walter was on the roof of his house reinforcing the flashings around his main chimney, Aaron appeared at the top of the ladder, his head stuck up over the eaves.

"For godsake, Walt, ain't you had enough vacation? Where in hell have you been?"

"I didn't need as much as I got," Walter said. "So where in hell have *you* been?"

"Down-coast. Looking over boatyards. Having a new dragger built. She'll be ready by spring. How about that?"

"I don't know how about that. You doing it on your own, or am I supposed to be in on it, unbeknownst to myself? How about the *Sarah?*"

"No need to get huffy. Same deal's we've always had, and the *Sarah'll* be turned in on the cost of the new boat. You wait'll you see that one. I tried out one just like her the same yard built, and you talk about a dream-baby! Oh, we'll go in the *Sarah* till April, if I can bring myself to set foot aboard the goddamned stove-up thing, but we sure got to hump ourselves this winter, make up the extra cash we'll need. How about going out tomorrow? We already lost part of the fall fishing."

For a moment, Walter considered hauling his tar-bucket down over Aaron's head, which was all he could see of him. Instead, he said quietly, "How much extra cost?"

"I got all the estimates, I'll show you. Come on, don't look so fish-faced. You and me is high-liners, remember. We make more dough together than either one of us could alone, and we'll tear up the sea bottom from here to the hundred fathom drop-off this winter, earn the extra cost. See ya tomorrow, kid." His head withdrew. The ladder creaked as he went down it and landed with a husky thump on the ground. "A damsite more than the extra cost," he bawled back, and went off.

Of all the goddamn gall! Walter thought. He could make a million peddling it. So what else does he think I can do, if I don't go along with him?

Since then, Walter had had plenty of time to think things over. Through late October and November they had worked with scarcely a break, only the worst weather —one November storm, which turned out to be a near-hurricane—keeping them idle, ashore. Two-, sometimes three-day trips, one following another, wore Walter down and damaged the gear. Aaron cussed a new hole in the dragnet every time they had to patch up an old one. Aaron himself showed no signs of wear, only, Walter thought, shivering in the cuddy while the engine warmed up, he's still on a damned short string.

He could hear Aaron's temper start to boil up as, outside, he pounded off the ice—the cussing, the exasperated thump-thumps, regardless of the *Sarah*'s new paint job. Wow! Sounded as if he was busting right through her hull, poor old girl. She was a damn good boat. Didn't deserve to be racked around on account of a lot of cussed-fool superstitions about jinxes.

Still, salt water ice . . . he didn't know as he blamed Aaron. It was awful stuff, any blue-smoke name you wanted to call it. Walk out across it in some cove that looked to be solid all the way to bottom—if you were fool enough to try it—and a mushy spot would let you down into icewater, quick and easy, like falling through a bank of corn snow. Didn't even crack or buckle under your feet, no warning to say, "This'll kill you, bud," just a *sloosh* and there you were, half-dead to begin with. Three minutes, and you were all dead. If it froze onto a boat, though, from the spray flying, there weren't any soft spots in it. By the god, there weren't. It was hard as glass and slippery, and you chopped at it hour after hour, because if you had to let it build up, the boat got topheavy and over she went, or down, or both. Same kind of *sloosh*, only louder. Same three minutes.

Walter had half-hoped this morning up at the house, when he'd read his thermometer, that Aaron would call off the trip outside today, knowing Aaron wouldn't. Sea dead-calm, and the only forecast of bad weather some kind of a dust-up off the Carolina capes that couldn't get here for a couple of days. He wondered briefly if Aaron really had doubts about the weather—what he'd said about it being too calm and the moon not meaning what she said. Naturally, Aaron wouldn't go by any weather forecast, only by his sense of—whatever it was—smell, probably. Change of the moon might mean a change in the weather, nothing unusual about that. If he'd had doubts, he didn't have them now; he was casting off.

The boat circled away from the mooring and roared out of the harbor. They passed over the place where the drowned submarine lay, gave a wide berth to the reef on the north end of the Three Brothers, and splashed over the drag miles out into a glassy sea on which nothing was moving but slow-swinging ocean swells. All morning the sun shone, the sky was as baby-blue as it might have been on a warm spring day. But there was nothing warm about this morning.

"This ain't going to last," Aaron said. His nostrils worked in and out as he sniffed the air. "Weather breeder. You can smell it."

"Maybe that no'theaster the weather boys forecast is toddling up from Carolina faster than they thought it would," Walter said.

Aaron snorted. "You and them clamheads! More like it's a freak storm they don't know nothing about. We'll give her till two o'clock, see what she does."

By noon, a thin mist that seemed to come from nowhere began to spread across the sky, turning it to whitish-blue; then, as it thickened, to no color at all—a pale mask that blurred the edges of the sun. The swells were higher; there was no wind except a light breath from the northeast, strong enough at times to wrinkle their glassy tops.

"Hell, I told ya. Something's up out there," Aaron said.

"Think we ought to call it a day?" Walter was eating his lunch while Aaron steered, and was nearly finished. When he was through, he'd take over the steering, while Aaron had his. "Look at that sun. Swimming in it."

"Let 'er swim. Kee-riced, what's the matter with you? Still froze to death? Still trying to fight off them raw hotdogs and candy bars? By God, I'm going to get a day's work out of this if I have to dive down there and grab them half-eyeball critters one by one."

"Go ahead. Might be the only way we'd get any today. Likely, the way the weather looks, they've all lit out for as far away as possible."

"Look, bud, if you're scairt of the weather, you can be the one to jump overboard," Aaron said.

"All right." Walter clapped his lunch bucket shut and changed places with Aaron. "Remind me to, if this next tow turns out to be as lousy as the last ones."

Aaron tore into his lunch, still sputtering. "Ain't one cussid thing to bother us, not yet, and you laying down the law to me we ought t' quit, before we got enough haul to put pea soup on the table, let alone steak. Don't you want to make a day's pay? Well, do ya or don't ya?"

"Yes," Walter said, and clamped his mouth shut. Blast him, let him rave, he thought. I've kept up with him so far and he knows it.

He glanced towards the west where the mainland was nothing more than a vague gray shadow on the horizon and the Three Brothers still showed the remnants of land-loom, as if their ends had tilted up far enough to show whitish sky between them and the water. All morning the islands had been completely undercut, mere black pencil marks blurred on the sky. Now there was very little mirage left; it was vanishing fast.

Cold as this, with any spray flying, we'll ice up like the devil, he thought, but he didn't say so. They both knew it, so why talk about it? This wouldn't be the first time they'd had to chop ice off the *Sarah*. Made it in, too, with a full hold, the old girl steering like a wet mattress and iced-up like a wedding cake. Sure didn't look as though they'd have a full hold today, though. Which might be all to the good.

They dumped the last tow at three, when the first

scattered snowflakes began to fall. It was another poor haul. Aaron told the mess of squirming fish what he thought of them, cocked back his head and took a long look at the sky, deep gray all over now, the sun gone. The Three Brothers and the pale line of mainland behind them were lost in a gathering mist of snow. "T' hell with it," he said. "Them buggers got word ahead of time. You gas up and we'll lash down and head in. Be dark, anyway, before you can spit."

The reserve gas was kept in cans on a rack under the washboard, with a wooden batten to hold them from bouncing out when the vessel hit a heavy sea. Walter removed the batten, reached for the first can, felt his heart jump and start to pound. The can was empty. So were all the others, except the last one, which sloshed. From the heft of it, it was about half full.

Walter stood up and tried to find his voice. "Aaron! The gas . . . it's gone!"

Aaron, back-to him at the wheel, said, "What's trouble?" Walter's yell, which had been scarcely more than a husky croak, had reached him, but it took him a moment to realize what had been said, and the sight of Walter's face, with the empty cans clinking together on the deck, to make him believe it.

"Christ, we had them cans filled up last night," he began, low-voiced, wondering. "I handed them down off the wharf to you and you stowed 'em—" Then it hit him. His face flamed red, his big fists closed on the wheel. "The bastard! The dirty, half-assed bastard! Sneaked aboard in the night and swiped enough gas to fill up his own goddamned tank! By the god, I catch that beauty I'll drownd him so deep he'll"—the wind went out of him suddenly—"never come up," he finished, under his breath.

He steadied himself at the wheel, reached a hand to the throttle, slowed the *Sarah* to half-speed. "All right,

damn ya," he said to her, in a half-whisper. "I oughta
knowed better'n to trust you again. Turned into a hard-
luck boat on me, didn't ya. Okay, you work your jinx.
I'll git you back in if I have to row ya, fill up the god-
damned tank with my blood." Walter, he saw, had the
last can tilted into the funnel over the gas tank. "How
much left, Walt?"

"Can's about half gone."

"The tank can't be dreened too dry. What's the mea-
sure-stick say? . . . Hell, that's more'n I thought there'd
be."

The *Sarah* plodded along at half-speed—Aaron was saving gas in the only way he could. Later, when the wind
and sea built up, any steerage-way would be better than
drifting.

Walter stared ahead through the thickening snow. Not
snow, he realized, but tiny ice crystals, already beginning to blow light as down along the *Sarah's* platform.
The wind, more than williwaws now, was strong enough
to make the crystals sting when they hit his bare cheek.
His work gloves, soaked from handling wet gear, had
stiffened with the cold; he saw that Aaron's had, too, and
were slippery on the wheel. Walter ducked below,
brought up two pairs of dry ones from the boxful in the
cuddy. He dropped one pair by Aaron's elbow, turned
and climbed up on the bow to check on the ice build-up.
"Not bad yet," he reported to Aaron. "No worse than a
skating rink."

"It will be," Aaron said. "By Jesus, it will be. You watch
it, up there, bud."

The storm, when it finally decided to move, came on
fast. Wind ripped the ocean swells into chop, turned the
chop into crested rollers. It brought darkness with it and
blasts of snow that thickened and dulled the running
light into soft blurs of red and green. Navigation, now,
was by compass and timing, and, Walter thought grimly,

Aaron's sense of smell. He had, or said he had, another instinct—if it could be called that—which he'd always bragged about, which had never been proved wrong. Or right, either, so far as Walter could see. He knew as well as Aaron did the varying depths of water as it shallowed in towards the coastline. Forty to fifty fathoms west of the fishing grounds. Ten where the Ridges thrust up west of that. Down to thirty, then thirty-five. Twenty, fifteen. Then sloping quickly up to four off the northern end of the Three Brothers Islands reef. If Aaron had a map in his mind, so did he—the contour of the sea bottom between the offshore grounds and the lee behind the Three Brothers, where, with the good luck which didn't seem to be theirs any longer, they could anchor and ride out the storm—if they could make it on what little gas they had, and could keep enough ice chopped off of the *Sarah*. Depths varied, of course, depending on the tides.

Any man who had dragged nets along this coast as constantly as he and Aaron had would know all that by heart. But to insist, as Aaron did, that he could tell exactly where he was at any time, day or night, storm or calm, by the pull of the tide against the *Sarah*, the feel of her steering wheel, and his own know-how, had always seemed like damned foolishness to Walter. He had said so and hadn't backed down the time he'd tried to get Aaron to equip the boat with a depth-sounder, and had had to listen for half an hour to the reasons why Aaron didn't need one.

I wonder, Walter thought, if he don't think we need one now.

In the pilot shelter there was no light except for the small shaded bulb which threw dim light on the compass dial. Walter nudged Aaron's elbow to let him know that he was back from up for'rad where he had been pounding off ice, that it was Aaron's turn now. The ice was building up too fast for one man to keep up with it without a breather. Walter had already been up there twice, and no break, which Aaron must know. But he didn't turn his head or move; he stood braced where he was, as if his hands had frozen to the wheel.

Could be they are, Walter thought. He said, "Hey, wake up!" and nudged again, but it was like nudging a man asleep. Or zeroed in, Walter thought. Could be that, too. Hell . . . no time . . . fool around. From somewhere, he'd have to haul up enough energy to crawl back up for'rad himself.

Coffee. Hot coffee. Thank God they always carried a lot of it in the extra big jug.

He staggered into the cuddy, resisted an impulse to throw himself face-down on one of the bunks, hide his head. The ice was thick now, not only on the platform, but on top rigging too high to reach, too slippery to climb. There was always a point where a beat-out man could commit suicide by trying, with handholds coated too thick for a hand to hang on to and nothing underfoot but a slick glare slanted one way only—straight overboard. Trying to drink his coffee out of the jug—useless to pour into a cup—Walter could feel the sluggish, topheavy way the boat was pitching. Down in a trough as if she had to stay there, then the slow, stubborn heave and rise, as, this time, she made it. At the end of each plunge, he found his own body jerking, forward, back, up. Helping. And a hell of a lot of good that did. It was as if the terrible weight had built up around his own feet; as if his boots were frozen into an impossible slab of ice. He found the hot coffee helped. He could do it again. He could get back up there all right now.

He managed, spilling some, to get a mugful of coffee poured out. By sealing it with his gloved hand, he got most of it across the icy platform to Aaron, thrust the warm mug into his hand.

Aaron did say something this time. Walter couldn't

make it out. He shouted, "What? It's hot coffee," before he realized that Aaron was talking to the *Sarah*.

". . . and sure I know you're tired, you don't have to tell me . . . it's this goddamn following sea lousing us up, slats your tail around and that hurts, don't it . . . but you ain't ever broached-to on me yet and I ain't going to let you do it this time. . . ."

Oh, Christ! Walter thought. The· poor bugger. The poor superstitious damn fool!

Staggering and sliding, his chopper in one hand, clutching with the other at whatever handhold he could find free, Walter made his way again up onto the *Sarah's* plunging bow.

Aaron didn't hear the coffee mug slide away from his hand, fall and smash—he hadn't even known it had been there.

"I'm here, by God, takin' care of you . . . you ain't had only but a couple of squeakers yet and one to go, and that's when we go round the end of Three Brothers reef. You git us by that reef, baby, you ain't no jinx . . . you'll be my *Sarah* girl and I'll never mistrust ya again. . . ."

It was as if the steady vibration of the vessel's engine answered him. He could feel it under his feet and in his hands on the wheel. She was still his good old gal, she wasn't going to let him down. She'd get him in around the end of the reef, into the lee of the Third Brother's high, tree-crowned hill, where he could anchor, be safe, ride out the storm.

What she didn't tell him was that her life-blood was almost gone, burnt away; that she had five minutes to go before her carburetor would be dry as a bone.

Unbelieving, he felt as if through his whole body the engine's first skip, the slowly lessening vibrations. The gas . . . the gas. . . . Gone? He'd counted on it; told himself they had enough to get in, so it had to be so, couldn't be gone.

"Come on, git with it," he roared. "What the hell!" And reached for the throttle, shoved it full-speed-ahead as far as it could go. The engine tried once, thrust the *Sarah* forward with a wrenching jerk, gave up and died.

The sudden jerk tore Walter loose from his handhold; his ice-chopper went spinning as he threw it away and made a futile grab with his other hand. The *Sarah's* deadly roll, as she swung sideways to the wind and dropped into the trough of the next big wave coming up behind her, slid him overboard. He had time to cry out once.

Aaron did not hear the cry. He did not feel the whacking thump when Walter's ice-chopper slid over the edge of the pilot shelter and struck him on the shoulder. He stood, his hands still glued to the wheel, howling his rage and desperation into the darkness around him and the wind-blasted sea.

"I could ha' beat you. I could ha' come out on top of you, damn you," he told the storm. "But I can't beat the bastards . . . the bastards . . . the bastards. . . ."

The rogue storm went as quickly as it had come; it had left its sign in the heavy rollers thundering on the reef and on the eastern side of the Three Brothers; but the morning was calm, almost warm, with the temperature above freezing and a bright sun in a high blue sky. A local lobsterman, out to check on his traps, spotted the hulk of the *Sarah*, high and dry on the steep ledges of the Third Brother. She had, apparently, washed ashore there on the high tide, shoved by the breakers and the wind. What was left of her was a boat of ice, pure white and sparkling against the Third Brother's tall black spruces. But the ice was beginning to drop away in the sun, and the man could read the name on her stern. *Sarah.*

Aboard her, there was no sign of life. The fisherman didn't see how there could be, but he went as close as he dared to the breakers and shouted. No use of that, he told himself. He backed off, switched on his radio telephone and notified the Coast Guard. Then he opened his throttle wide and drove top-speed back to carry the news to the harbor.

Suzy had heard the wind in the night. As she always did in stormy weather when the *Sarah* was offshore, she had worried and had tried not to because it was bad for the baby. Worrying did no good, anyway—only made you feel worse. It wouldn't bring Walter home any sooner. She lay for a while, listening. It didn't seem to be a really bad storm—if anything out of the ordinary were blowing up, it surely would have been forecast.

Hearing the wind, she thought, They've been out in worse than this and got home all right. Anyway, she'd left the door unlocked, in case Walter got home in the night. But she couldn't seem to get to sleep.

Oh, shoot! she told herself after a while. This is crazy. I'm going to get up and bake an old rauncher of an apple pie. She put on a warm robe and went down to the kitchen. Walt'll call me the fool of the world, but if he gets home tonight and finds a nice warm apple pie waiting, he won't growl about it.

She put together the pie and baked it. Somehow the smell of the good Northern Spy apples, slowly merging with sugar and cinnamon in the oven, made her feel better. She felt the tense strings of her nerves let go, little by little, and almost fell asleep waiting for the pie to be done.

There's a lot to be said for a good apple pie, she thought, as she took it out of the oven and set it on the counter to cool. The smell of it was all through the house; she went back to bed and fell asleep, breathing it.

She woke to a fine morning, almost warm, with the snow melting and the sunshine bright and yellow on the kitchen table. She was almost sorry to see that the weather had cleared off so beautifully—that meant that the boys wouldn't be back before tonight; unless they'd had specially good luck yesterday, they'd finish out their two-day trip.

She was surprised to find she'd slept later than usual. Henry was already astir, beginning to holler for breakfast. She put his cereal and her own coffee on the stove before she went down-cellar to start up the furnace fire, which she had banked last night.

Won't need too much of a fire, warm as it is, she thought, as she poked over the coals. A little kindling and a few hardwood sticks would do the job for now. She'd come down later on, make sure the fire didn't go out.

Back upstairs, she put the apple pie in the icebox before she went to fetch Henry. Let him catch a sight of that, there'd be the divvle to pay if he didn't get a piece of pie instead of his good breakfast. Henry loved apple pie.

She washed and dressed him, fed him his cereal and turned him loose on the kitchen floor while she ate her own. While she washed the dishes and tidied up the kitchen, she planned her day. Walt would get home starving—he always did. She'd better drive around to the store and pick up a good big roasting chicken. That would take care of him tonight.

As she came downstairs from making her bed and Henry's crib, she felt the house cooling down around her. Oh, Lord, the furnace fire. She'd completely forgotten it. This old house! she told herself. I love it dearly, but it's got a darned draft blowing out of every corner.

The fire was low, but not out. A few kindling sticks started it going. She piled on wood, waited till it caught, and closed the draft. Humming a little to herself, she started back upstairs. She was halfway up when she heard the kitchen door clap to and steps crossing the room above her. Oh, good! Walter. Here now. Thank God.

"Hi, honey," she called. "Am I glad to—"

A piercing shriek cut her short, stopped her cold in her tracks. It wasn't Walter.

Gladys stood at the head of the stairs, screaming out words between choking sobs, so that for a moment Suzy couldn't make anything out of the muddled, howling sounds. Then she did, and stood frozen, feeling her blood turn to ice and her knees start to give under her.

"Walter . . . Walter's dead . . . drownded . . . the boat's ashore out on the Three Brothers, all smashed up . . . Jack Carney see it . . . he called the Coast Guard . . . we heard it on Peg's radio. . . ."

This was what Gladys was screaming. These were the words between her shrill, gasping cries. Suzy heard them through a roaring sound, as if a great wind with whistling gusts to torment a chimney had driven them into her shock-deafened ears. She lost her grip on the handrail, fell backwards, rolled crashing to the bottom of the cellar stairs.

Gladys stopped her noise at once. Calmly she leaned over and looked. She couldn't see anything but a dark, huddled form because the cellar light was off, but there wasn't a movement or a sound. Behind her, Henry started to scream and scrabbled out of her way as she strode past him to the telephone.

Gladys called the doctor, told him to hurry, that most likely he'd need the ambulance service. She called the farmhouse and got Cora, whom she greeted with sobs and distressful cries.

"Oh, Code! Code, dear! Walter and Aaron . . . it's so terrible . . . I can't stand it. Have you heard. . . ?"

"Yes," Cora said quietly. "We've heard. We can't stand it, either."

"Oh, God, Code, there's worse . . . awful . . . awful. . . ."

"Gladys," Cora said. "You get a-holt of yourself. What is there on God's earth that could be worse?"

"Oo-h, I'm down to Walter's house. Peg'n I drove right over soon's we heard, to be with Suzy, see'f there's anything we could do for her."

"Screechin' and howlin' like that, you think that'll help her any?"

"Code, you mustn't be coldhearted to me now. Nothin' on earth can help Suzy. I found her laying at the bottom of the suller stairs. I think she's dead. I've called the doctor and the ambulance, and where's Polly?"

There was a moment's silence. That's hit her right where she lives, Gladys told herself. Maybe this time she'll show it. She said, "I found poor dear little Henry crawling around, alone, in the kitchen. Peg'n I's taking him over to my house. He mustn't see his mother when they bring her up-suller."

Cora said, "Paulus and Amanda'll be there any minute, Gladys. They're on the way now." She hung up the phone with a quiet click.

If them two's headed down here, she told herself, I ain't got a minute to lose.

She scooped up Henry, snatched his snow-suit from the rack by the door, raced him out to Peg, waiting in the car. "You take him up to the house, Peg. Shut him up if you can. His mother's had an accident. I'll tell you later."

Henry wasn't about to be shut up. He yelled, kicked, and flailed Madame Preston with his fists. He bit her thumb till it bled. An old hand with other women's babies, she muffled him with his snow-suit hood turned back to front, pushed him down into the floor-space beside her, and drove away.

Inside the house, Gladys waited. There was no sound from the cellar; she didn't look to see if there were any movement. Others would be here right away. What could she do if she went down there?

It was foreordained, she told herself. It was just that their time had come. *It wasn't what I did, at all.* The spirits moved against them. That was what it was. Wherever Walter was now, they would let him know what they could do to the enemy of one of their chosen people, tell him what his duty was to his mother.

She had been careful to pick a quiet night to row out and empty their gas-cans overboard. Why, there hadn't been a ripple on the water. And that full moon! The harbor had been so beautiful and still, she had really enjoyed the row. No mud this time because she'd ridden around the harbor in Peg's car and borrowed a punt that had been tied up at the fishwharf float. A moonlight row, like what she and Peg had used to do when they'd been girls at home. Cold, of course. But she hadn't felt it—she'd wrapped up warm.

Mercy, all she'd thought would happen was that they'd lose their day's haul, maybe bobble around awhile on the ocean out there and be uncomfortable, till another boat saw them and towed them in. And she'd left them a half-can of gas, in case they needed it.

No, it was foreordained. The spirits had done it. Who could have looked ahead and seen that storm? Well, the spirits had paid off Ralph, what he deserved, for her, and now they had paid off Walter. And if all went well, Peg would place Henry in a rich home somewhere away, and they would get a fortune of money for him. It all evened up in the end, didn't it?

There! Thank God, there was the doctor. She had better start crying again before she let him in.

X

Walter's second son, named Dennis after his great-great-grandfather, was born in the Machias hospital on the night after his father's death. Suzy had never recovered consciousness. She had died very quickly after the doctors had saved her baby.

"It was almost as if she were just waiting for him to be born," Annabelle told Paulus. "There was only one thing she said that I could make any sense out of and that was, 'I'm so tired now I wish I could die.' I tried to let her know that she'd had a boy, but she went too fast, Polly."

"She was awful bad hurt," Paulus said.

"Yes, it's a living wonder that they saved the baby. They had to take him, you know."

"Yes. I know. We'll get him home with us as soon as he's able to come."

There was no doubt in either of their minds as to where Walter's children were going to live and be taken care of. They had had no time to plan; they were both too stricken by loss to think ahead. Now, driving home from Machias, they spoke about their wedding—they had planned it originally for Christmas Day, but after what had happened, they both agreed on a quiet wedding as soon as possible.

"Because Walter and Suzy's poor little mites are going to need us," Annabelle had said. "And when our own come along, they'll have two brothers, ready made."

She had cried softly with her cheek against his sleeve, for a little while. Then she had straightened up and had wiped away her tears.

Amanda, who had been sitting silently in the back seat, said suddenly, "I think we ought to pick up Henry tonight, Polly."

This morning, while they had waited at Walter's house for the ambulance, Cora had telephoned to let them know where Henry was. Amanda, who had gone upstairs at once to see if he were asleep in his crib, and had not found him, had come racing down, terrified that he, too, might have fallen on the cellar stairs. But Cora's call had stopped her as she crossed the living room.

"I'd go get him myself, right now," Cora said. "But I don't think I'd better leave Gran. She's . . . she's awful hard hit. . . ."

"Yes. All right. I know. Polly and I'll pick him up when we get back from the hospital. . . . . No, she isn't, dear, but she's terribly hurt. The ambulance is here now; we'll let you know."

Later in the day, when Amanda phoned her what little news there was, Cora said that George and Set-Fire had been down to get Henry, but Gladys had locked the doors and refused to let them in the house.

Tonight, Gladys's house was dark, not a light showing. Paulus stopped the car and got out. He had rung the bell twice and had banged hard on the door before he noticed that Madame Preston's car, usually kept in Gladys's side yard, was gone.

His heart turned over. He had kept to himself the reason why any baby shouldn't be left too long in Madame Preston's hands, and Gladys herself was a dim hope, when any marketable product was concerned. Could those two possibly have been coldhearted enough to take Henry away to . . . to where? To whatever place Madame Preston carried on her business? Today? When we were all knocked flat, no time to think of anything but Suzy and Walter? Yet, knowing Gladys, he wondered if there was anything she might not do—if she hated enough, if she benefited, if there was money in it. In her time, she had tried to talk Ralph into selling Jesse. So what price, to her, of a small grandson?

If I can't find them, if they've already left town, it's got to be a matter for the law. Just in case, I'd better get on to the phone for the State Police.

He walked around to the backyard to see if, by any chance, Madame Preston's car had been parked there. It had not, but from there, he could look down the length of the harbor. Walter's house on the point stood out in the moonlight and it was lit up like a circus tent, lights showing even in the second-story windows.

"Thank God! That's where they are. That's where Gladys would be. Going over the house to see what there is, I bet."

"Yes," Amanda said, as he climbed back into the car and backed it around. "That's exactly what's she's doing. And doing it at night, when she knows we're all gone." She and Annabelle were out of the car almost before it stopped in Walter's driveway. Madame Preston's car was there, parked unobtrusively in the backyard. The moonlight shone full on it and Paulus could make out the knobbly shapes of some kind of a load of bulky objects, piled high on the back seat. He opened a rear door and looked in. Suitcases, cartons, bags, small objects loosely thrown in. Moonlight picked out the giddy design of Zodiac patterns on a set of folded window drapes. A pet-carrier, large enough for a medium-sized dog. With air holes, he saw, and felt himself turn cold. He reached for it and lifted it gently, thinking, My God, they don't have a dog; but whatever was in it was heavy and rattled woodenly—it was nothing living; it wasn't Henry.

He stood for a moment feeling the cold sweat form under the edges of his cap and run down. Relief, yes, of course, but mostly rage, a frozen-in-ice anger, such as he had never felt before in his life. Who I need now is Ralph, he thought. To go in there and kill them both. For a moment he wondered if he was going to make it up the back steps to the kitchen door.

Blindly he walked along the hall towards the living room. The clang of Gladys's voice penetrated to him; he stopped outside the doorway, trying to bring himself to his senses.

"I know what you want Walter's children for," Gladys was saying. "You git them, you'll think every stick he owned b'longs to you. Walter was my own son, and this house and everything in it is mine."

"Gladys," Amanda said quietly. "In this house? To-night? Children are to be loved and taken care of. There's nothing for us here but Henry. Where is he?"

"He's up at the farm, where Peg and I took him today, left him with Code. If that's all you want, you might's well go home."

Annabelle said, "If he is, Gladys, he'll need some things—clothes, maybe some playthings. If you'll let me by, I'll go get them. I know where they are."

"You will not take one thing out of this house tonight," Gladys said. "You want Henry, you know where he is, and I'll just ask you to—" She stopped, with a gasp. Her face turned bone-white; she put both hands out, as if to ward off something. Her gaze was riveted on a spot behind Amanda, and both she and Annabelle, startled, turned to look.

The white face, outlined against the darkness in the hall, was, of course, Paulus's. But the living room lamp was shaded; the light which reached him showed him haggard and gaunt, with eyesockets deep in shadow. The tall slimness, the dark hair, were Polly's, too, but they were also Walter's. The resemblance faded as Polly stepped into the room.

Gladys recovered quickly. "For godsake, what's the idea, sneaking up on people, scaring them to death!"

Madame Preston suddenly came to life. So far, she had sat watching and listening, her head turning slowly from one speaker to another. "Glad!" she said. "Come off it and shut your trap. You've made a bad mistake."

"Yes, you have," Paulus said. "Walter left a will, Gladys. Everything here in the house belongs to his children, if this is any time to think about that." He had managed to pull himself together somewhat; at least he could keep his voice down. It hadn't helped any to see the outsized suitcase open on the table, filled with Walter's and Suzy's possessions, but he went on, quietly. "It's no time, anyway, for families to fight. So you go home and get a night's sleep. We'll talk things over tomorrow."

Madame Preston said, "The baby was miserable with us. He cried all day for his mother. We tried hard, we even took some of his playthings with us, but he wouldn't look at them, or at us. So we brought him back here, thought he might go to sleep in his own crib. He wouldn't, and we took him up to Code at the farm. Gladys ain't lying to you, Polly."

Her voice sounded reasonable, even sympathetic, but Paulus went to the phone and dialed the farm. Behind him, he heard her say, "Glad, enough is enough. The way you're acting ain't decent. You get your coat on. Now. We're leaving."

It sounded like a warning, and Gladys, apparently, heard it. In silence, she put on her coat and the two left the house.

At the farm, the phone rang and rang. Well, it was late. They would be tired out, Code asleep upstairs in Gran's room with her. Outside, Madame Preston's car started, drove away. Paulus thought, in panic, Oh, my God, what if they've got him in the trunk . . . I didn't look in the trunk. But then the receiver clicked and Code said, "Hello?"

"Code, is Henry there with you?"

"Yes, he is, dear. And that ain't all. You wait till you

see what we got here. I guess you'll find out that there've been other eyes than ours watchin' from the pucker-brush."

The eyes in the puckerbrush had been watching Gladys's house ever since Set-Fire and George had come back from there and reported that she wouldn't let them in.

"We got to get Henry away from Ma," Frankie told Jesse, and in a few terse words she told him what her mother's business had been in California. "Stealing babies and selling them. She was in it with Pa. He got the jail and she had to leave town. I had to promise Pa not to tell on her. But if she gets away from here with Henry, we'll never see him again. It's going to be hard for us to get him, but we got to."

Horror-struck, Jesse listened. "If they go in her car, we can't catch 'em on the bikes," he said. "We got to have help, Frankie, and everybody's gone."

Paulus and Amanda weren't back from the hospital. All the fishing boats from the harbor had gone out searching the shores and the waters around the Three Brothers Islands for any possible signs of Walter and Aaron; Set-Fire and the men from the farm had gone with them.

"There's George," Jesse said.

Frankie hesitated. Then she said, "All right. There's George." She and George had made a truce, but they were by no means friends.

"Your goddamn mother," George said. "That's one hell of a mess to have for a mother."

"No worse'n yours, is she?" Frankie said. "Look, George, we need somebody strong. Somebody with muscles. Them two is both awful strong, and they got Henry."

"Jeest!" George said, getting it. He stood for a minute, thinking. "What I'd like to do is go down there with a baseball bat, stave in the door, haul old Henry out of there. Can't do that. Git the cops down on us. Ma's his gra'mother, likely she might have legal rights to keep him, like she does us, Jess. No. You two hustle down there and watch the house. I'll bring one of the farm jeeps. If they take off before we can nab Henry somehow, we'll chase 'em. They'll have to stop somewhere, and by that time the folks'll be back and we can phone 'em."

Recognizing that here was a pretty good mind at work and that George might even be smart, Frankie nodded. "Good. We'll watch which way they go. You hurry, George."

The "puckerbrush" turned out to be the lattice under the porch of a vacant house, a few doors down, across the street from Gladys's. Through it, Jess and Frankie could see very well what was going on in Gladys's yard, and a good deal was.

The car was backed up to the side door. Gladys and Madame Preston were loading it, bringing out suitcases and boxes of stuff.

"They're going away, all right," Frankie whispered. "Look, there's them awful curtains all covered with crabs and stuff they use for the séances. They wouldn't take them, if they weren't going off for good. And there's Ma's old black dog-carrier she uses for the babies. She's putting it in the back seat. That's where Henry'll be."

Jesse gasped. "Hank? In that? But he'd cry! Why ain't he crying?"

Frankie said, between her teeth, "He's got his mouth taped up. That's what she always does, if they cry. Don't you, Jess. George's coming. I can hear the jeep."

Jesse dashed away tears with the back of his hand. He didn't know how she'd guessed he was crying, he hadn't made a sound. But Hank was in that awful black box and he'd be scared to death and couldn't cry. And it was already getting dark—they might not be able to catch

Aunt Preston's car, if George didn't hurry.

Frankie grasped his hand. "There's good air holes in that," she said. "And he'll be wrapped up good an warm. He's worth too much money to Ma for her to let him be hurt or sick. He'll be all right, Jess."

The jeep came roaring down past Gladys's house, turned into a side street, a few houses down. They could hear George backing and turning, could see the nose of the jeep, as he parked on the corner and killed his headlights. "Ain't gone, yet, I see," he said calmly, as they piled into the seat beside him. He had, after all, brought his baseball bat—Frankie sat on it, hard, which hurt, but she shoved it over without saying anything. Nothing was worth complaining about now. His hand clutched the handle of it fiercely, and he swore terribly, under his breath, when they told him where Henry was.

"You keep your cool," Frankie said.

But instead of snapping back at her, the way he always did, he said, "I am, Frankie. I got to drive."

He was an excellent driver now, very good with the farm jeeps, which he had practiced on, helping Set-Fire with hauling jobs, but he wasn't quite old enough to get his license yet. That must be what he's thinking about, Frankie thought, and was a little ashamed of herself.

They waited.

If we could only go and grab him now, Jesse thought. But the side door of the house was open, light streaming out; street lamps were on now. They could see Gladys and Aunt Preston bobbing back and forth, loading up the trunk.

Then, at last, the door banged shut, headlights came on, the car's engine started. Aunt Preston didn't swing out into the State Highway. She turned down the west side harbor road to the Point and into Walter's driveway. The jeep followed at a safe distance. George drove on

by, turned and parked on the upside of the driveway en-
trance on the shoulder of the road.

Grabbing Henry was simple—no trouble at all. Lights
were already on in Walter's house; both women had gone
in, plainly to be seen in the living room. They hadn't
taken the black pet-carrier in with them; it was still on
the back seat of the car. Moonlight shone on it, shone
also on Henry's most hated plaything—the big, red,
wooden lobster, whose clacking had put him in a panic
the night Walter had brought it home. It lay on the floor
of the car in front of the back seat.

George stood by with his baseball bat while Jesse
ripped open the straps, pulled Henry out of the box,
and ran with him for the jeep. Frankie said, in a husky
whisper, "Look what the darned old fools brought for
him to play with, he's scared to death of it."

She scooped it up, thrust it into the pet-carrier, fastened
the straps, and followed George, who was doing his best
to run down the driveway without making any noise.

Paulus, as he drove into the farmhouse driveway, noticed one of Set-Fire's jeeps parked by the side of the
house. The front rooms were lighted. Cora opened the
door. "*Ssh*," she whispered. "All asleep but me. Come
and look in your bedroom, Polly."

The big double bed in Polly's room was full to over-
flowing.

"I guess I catnapped some," Cora said. "I didn't hear
them come in earlier on, but later I heard George snoring and looked in here. They was all asleep, so I left
them to rest as they was."

George lay on the edge of the bed, fully dressed, with
his boots on. He had had a blanket over him, but had
thrown it off. From under him, the handle of a baseball
bat stuck out—he had apparently gone to sleep clutching

it, but his hand, limp, had fallen away. His wild mop of red-orange hair was all over his pillow. Next to him, Jesse's black curls touched his; Jesse, too, had his day clothes on. His arm was around Henry, whose head was nestled close under his chin. Henry's yellow hair was damp and draggled; his face was dirty, with dark, sticky-looking marks around his mouth.

The three slept; but Frankie, backed against the wall, in her T-shirt and jeans, lifted her tough, pug-nosed face turtle-wise, as the light came on. "That baby," she said crossly, "has got an awful hot bottom. He pushes it against you all over the bed."

Annabelle slipped her hand under Paulus's arm. "Oh, Polly," she said. "You . . . you Pied Piper. I've always said so."

Gladys and Madame Preston had not gone far. They had waited down the street until they saw the lights go off in Walter's house and Paulus drive away. By the time his car was out of sight, Madame's car was again parked in Walter's driveway, but this time out of sight, hidden by the barberry bushes along the side of the summer kitchen.

Paulus had locked up the house, but Gladys wasn't one to be kept out by mere locks and bolts. She had well in mind how she was going to get back in. She went up the front steps, produced a flashlight from her handbag, counted the narrow glass lights which framed the door. "That'll be the one," she said. Glass fell with a small tinkle as she jammed her handbag through it. She reached in, unbolted the door, swung it open. "Now!" she said. "They's some other things here that's going in that suitcase."

"You can't turn on a light. Somebody's sure to see it."

"I can find what I want. They's room in that suitcase

for Suzy's 'lectric blender and them pretty party plates of hers. *Brr-r!* this house is some cold. Furnace fire's gone out." She brought the blender and the plates, stuffed them into the suitcase. But never in her life had she gone past a refrigerator without looking in to see what was there. As its inside light came on, she gasped with delight. "Oh, my God, Peg, look! A whole pie!"

"Take it with you, for godsake, Glad. They find out that kid ain't up to the farm, they'll be down on us like a ton of bricks."

Gladys didn't even hear that. She had stuck one finger in the air-vent of the piecrust and was tasting. "Apple! Icy-cold though. I ain't going to start out for Nova Scotia, cold as I am, with a bellyful of cold apple pie. I'm going to hot it up, and what's more, I'm going to make me a warm place, nice and homey, to eat it in." She took the pie in one hand, her flashlight in the other, and headed along the hall, passing Peg as if she weren't there at all.

Oh, blast and damn! Peg thought. This was something she hadn't counted on, though she might have known. Gladys, tonight, confronted by a whole houseful of stuff she could rip off, had been crazy as a bedbug, the sight of a lifetime. Confronted by food when she was hungry, she'd really gone over the edge. Poor fool had always been unbalanced about eating. Nothing to do about it, either, until she got fed.

But, my God, I've got to howk her out of here fast or she'll gum things up for keeps. She's no more of a medium than I am, but maybe some sign of a real ghost'll start her moving.

The living room was dark except for some shadowed light from a street lamp which filtered through the windows. Peg found her way to the table where the suitcase was, felt around until she located a round box of bath powder. She remembered Gladys looting it from the bathroom, tucking it in with the rest of Suzy's things.

Damned old magpie! Risk upwards of five thousand dollars for stuff like this and a cold apple pie!

She opened the box, grasped a handful of powder, groped her way along the hall to the door through which she could see Gladys's flashlight beam.

Gladys had just finished filling the summer kitchen stove with kindling and sticks from Walter's supply of furnace firewood. She was in the act of pouring a generous dollop of kerosene from a can in which he had been soaking some rusty tools. The place reeked of kerosene.

Fat lot of good my little trick's going to do, with that stink going, Peg thought. But, oh, Lord, try anything. She tossed her handful of powder into the air and waited.

M'm, smelt quite good. A nice quality powder. Blush Rose, if I'm not mistaken.

Gladys, a smoker, of course would have matches. She produced a paper-book from somewhere, tore off a match, dropped it, lighted, into the stove. Nothing happened. "Oh, shit!" she said. "Them paper matches ain't no good, never was." This time she lit a corner of the matchbook, got it well flaming, dropped it into the stove.

The resulting explosion lifted the stove covers and dropped them with a series of clanks, but the fire caught and went thundering up the chimney.

" 'N there!" Gladys said. "That'll warm up that oven in no time. We can start warm and full of pie. You know my asthma, if I set in a cold, damp place. *What's that*?"

Good and well I know your asthma, Peg thought. What you always got, to make someone do something when we were kids at home. "What's what?" she asked placidly.

"That smell!"

Evidently the stove draft had started a circulation of air. "What smell? I don't smell anything."

"You do, too, you must! It's Suzy's Blush Rose powder!"

"You get whackier by the minute. There's no smell of anything here. Or maybe it's Grammy, letting you know how much money we'll lose, if we don't get out of here fast."

No fake about Grammy, she thought. She could do things that curdled your blood. Whether or not the ghosts of the dead came back was never a question to her. She'd left them both with the conviction that there must be *something* to it.

"I'm going out and start up the car, turn the heater on," Peg said. "We can't let that kid get cold."

"Peg, don't you leave me alone in here. . . ."

"Suit yourself. Come with me, or stay. I don't care."

She went, closing the door firmly behind her.

Outside, the moonlight was bright, making sharp black shadows of trees, of everything. She could see the length of the harbor, the white boats motionless, all heading the same way; and across there, on the other side, she could make out the white walls of the farmhouse—dark, not a light showing. Could they have all gone to bed without checking to see whether or not that kid was there? Didn't seem possible. Still, they were tired to death, worn out, looked to be. Or could be that Paulus was on the way down here now. And he was one she wouldn't care to tangle with tonight.

She waited, sitting in the front seat while the interior of the car warmed up. It seemed to take a long time.

For two cents, I'd light out without her, take a chance on getting stopped. But if I do, it's a kidnapping charge but with her along, she's the kid's grandmother. Makes it legal.

As she went back into the summer kitchen, she heard, from somewhere, a slight scratching sound. She started a little, in spite of herself. It could only be the barberry bushes brushing against the window, but a séance sound, happening so pat, like that, was scary. Maybe I shouldn't have mentioned Grammy. Not in this house. Tonight. Peg shivered.

Gladys said, "Aagh!" and huddled closer to the stove. She picked up the flashlight, swept its beam around the room.

"Gladys, if you're scared here, you good and well know you've got plenty of reason to be. Come on, let's clear out. Right now."

"Nossir!" Gladys said. "The last time I was here I wasn't made welcome. Miss young Suzy et a whole egg salad without offerin' me one bite. I ain't leavin' this house hungry. Not again."

"All right. First things first. I hope your goddamn hot pie gives you one hell of a dreamy bellyache, and asthma on top of it, is all I can say."

There seemed to be nothing more *to* say. They waited.

The fire burned. Heat seeped into the chimney behind the stove, through the cracks and crumbling brickwork of the Dutch oven, which gave forth now no sweet, remembered smell of browning bread, loaves of cake, pots of baked beans, but only a pale stink of aged lime mortar and mold, like the slow heating up of a gone time.

There were no more scary noises. Gladys got herself pulled together somewhat; she was thinking of the triumph of eating, at last, in Walter's house. And going out of here with Suzy's pretty party plates, which that stingy girl should have served her on, that one day she came. She was going to enjoy this pie.

"Cold or no cold," she said. "My tongue's splashing in my mouth. I'm going to cut that pie, right—"

Something went off with a muffled pop. They both jumped.

"What was that? Did you hear—" Gladys began, but she was drowned out by a series of pops, like firecrackers under a pillow, and a muffled thump, as if someone had knocked on the wall with a gloved fist.

Gladys shrieked. "Oh, my God in Heaven, they've come back!" She rose with a swoop that upset her chair behind her.

A lively hubbub began, louder, with more authority. Claps of sound, jangles like breaking glass, ending with a hollow boom which dropped a brick on the floor with a thud. Something started dripping—drip . . . drop . . . drip. . . .

"Blood!" Gladys gasped. On trembling legs she ran for the front door. The hard heels of her winter boots clacked along the walk; behind her, Madame Preston's fashionable footgear clacked in equal headlong flight.

The lights of a car, slowing down to turn in, made hilarious mimicry of their shadows as they ran, but they did not stop, even when the driver called out, "What's wrong, Gladys? What's the matter?" Their car doors slammed, its engine started. Madame Preston's Chevrolet swerved past Set-Fire's jeep, spinning gravel and narrowly missing him. He stared after them in astonishment as they roared away up the highway.

What in hell? he said to himself. Looks like something's scairt the bejeezus out of them.

Walter's death had hit hard; grief for him had made Set-Fire lie awake, unable to sleep. He had walked about the house, staying carefully away from the room that had belonged to the boy; then he had gone outside to look at the weather, hoping that the sight of familiar stars might ease his mind. The moon was bright, the sky clear to the horizon; what little wind there was was cold—signs showed it would be colder before morning. He thought suddenly of the water pipes in Walter's house—ten to one, nobody had thought to turn off the water. Furnace fire would be out—stood to reason those pipes would freeze up without any heat in the house. Do no harm to go down and check, and a jeep ride, right now, would be welcome.

Those two besoms had been inside Walter's house; the front door was wide open, swinging on the hinges. Maybe they'd run into someone who hadn't any right to be there. Something sure'd put Glad-rags and her sister to flight. He noticed in his flashlight beam, as he went up the front steps, the smashed glass light beside the door. Somebody'd broke in, all right.

He found the switch in the front hall, snapped it on. Nobody in the living room, but an open suitcase on the table crammed with things to lug off showed that someone had been here. On it, as if set carelessly down, was an open handbag—Gladys's, he saw, from the initials on it—and it, too, had some of Suzy's stuff in it. Her blue beads she often wore for dress-up; a leather case full of tiny silver spoons, one of her most prized possessions.

Gladys, herself, he thought. What other hoodlum was there coldhearted enough to break in here tonight and make off with Walter's and Suzy's things? By the god! I hope that whatever scairt her was something pretty damned special, he thought. If it'd been me, it would've been.

There was a queer stink in the house—a burnt smell, mixed up with something boozy . . . yeasty . . . had they been drinking beer in here? He followed it, sniffing, along the hall. It seemed stronger out towards the summer kitchen. He found the switch beside the door, snapped it on.

For a moment, he stood staring at the mess. Fire in the stove, oven door open, pie in there, already burnt black around its edges. Two chairs kicked over backwards, not a bottle of booze but a bottle of milk spread all over the floor.

Why, them two bitches had come down here in the

middle of the night to rummage the house and brought a picnic. Must've been setting here about to mug-up, when the whole side of that Dutch oven blowed out. And no God's living wonder it had. What I wouldn't of give to seen them two take off when them bricks hit the floor!

He flashed his light beam into the inside of the Dutch oven. The sight sobered him. The smashed bottles, the glittering heaps of broken glass mixed with pieces of brick and lime mortar; the rich color of the stains on the floor behind the stove, still dripping down, puddled into sawdust and sweepings.

There goes, he told himself sadly, the dagnabbledest, most beautiful batch of homemade wine this side of Heaven.

Gaadamn women. Worse'n minks.

Walter had kept his home brew in the Dutch oven because the temperature there had been just right for wine —wouldn't heat up in summer or cool off in winter. Only you had to be sure not to build a fire in the cookstove. Last year's batch, particularly the raspberry, had been potent; he'd taken a bottle over to Set-Fire for him to try. A good thing they'd been in the barn, because when Set had uncapped it, the whole bottleful skited sky high, all over the front of the haymow. Walter had roared at the sight of Set's astounded face.

Set, who had tried to clap his thumb over the bottle-nose in time to let the stuff fizz off easy, had laughed, too. "Set-fire, Walt! That's quite a bomb you've got there. Like to tore my thumb off my hand. You must've took some directions from Polly."

"I did," Walter'd said, grinning.

"Never mind. The cows'll get a boot out of it."

Later, Walt had brought another bottle over, and it had been the greatest.

* * *

In the empty kitchen, Walter's wine dripped away, soaked down through the splintery pine floor and was gone, leaving its own distinctive smell among the assorted others already there. The fruity, yeasty perfume of his last harvest—the elderberry, blackberry, apple, dandelion, raspberry—would remain longer than the burnt piecrust stink, or the taint, still hanging in the air, of Blush Rose bath power. It would be there for a long time, so that strangers who rented the house, coming in, might sniff and say, "What did they do in here—run a brewery?"

But others who had known Walter well, might smile a little at a pleasant and affectionate memory they had of him.

"Old Walt," one might say. "He made lovely wine."

At the New Brunswick border, the customs inspector stopped Madame Preston, with an eagle eye on the pet-carrier in the back seat of her car. "Have you got a dog in there?" he asked.

Gladys was sound asleep, snoring with her mouth open, and Peg was, for a moment, put to it for an answer. "Why, no, sir," she said at last. "That's my little boy in there. He sleeps that way on long trips. He loves it. Please don't wake him up."

"Sorry, lady. You people over there have had a few cases of rabies, you know."

Madame Preston produced her gentlest coo. "Oh, please, officer. If you stir him up, he'll make us miserable all the way to St. John."

"I'll be careful." He'd better be, he thought. He always was, opening any kind of a pet-carrier. Of course it was a dog . . . and dogs were known to bite. Some people would try anything—not that he'd ever known this particular gimmick before. Lady looked whacky as hell. Probably was.

He unfastened one strap, held the other ready to pull

taut, while he spread an end of the case wide enough to get his flashlight beam in there. What he saw first was a big, ugly, red claw sticking up. He jumped and pulled back. "Great balls of fire, ma'am!" he said. "If that's your little boy, I'd sure like to get a look at your husband." Annoyed, he refastened both straps. "Okay, lady, fun is fun. You're lucky I don't haul you over and go through your whole load." He waved her on her way.

Earlier on, Great-great-Grandmother Matilda Scott had heard the children come in. Her room was across the hall from Paulus's and they had been quiet. But sleep, with her now, was like the flight of a butterfly, peaceful for a moment, then alive in the air on wings. Here, there, and back again.

Lying here resting after the shock of this morning's terrible news, she had managed to come to terms with grief and loss, as she had always done. As she had had to do, because, at ninety, she had seen so many of the best of them go. And because you are faithful, she told the secret voice of Time, ticking, ticking, softly in the wall behind the head of her bed. You can be depended on to come creeping, after a while, and take them away. And nothing I have done has ever helped it.

"I wish," she had told Cora early in the evening, "you would stop flock-of-hens-ing around in here and go to bed." She loved Cora dearly, but it was hard to when Cora was nervous. And Cora was. She was afraid Gran would get out from under her thumb and do too much; she was worried about the kids—where on earth were they? Gran had hurt her feelings, but she still insisted on sitting up in the Morris chair beside the bed. After a time, Gran had given out a few sensible-sized snores, so that Cora, her mind relieved somewhat, had settled back in the chair and had gone sound asleep. Snored, too.

After the children had come in and had been quiet for

some time, Gran had got up, slanted her door so that the light would shine across the hall, and had looked in at them.

She saw George, with his baseball bat, the defender, and, God bless him, who could wake him up, whatever danger came? And they had, somehow, got Henry away from Gladys. She went quietly back to bed.

They didn't tackle a bear with an ax, she told Sarah Thomas, silently, for it seemed that that brave and stubborn presence had somehow come quite close to her now. They tackled something worse. Because there's nothing more frightful on earth than human evil. I hope you're where you can see and be proud of your ninth-generation grandchildren.

When the telephone rang, she woke up Cora, told her to answer it and to look into Polly's room on the way downstairs.

Pied Piper, yes, Gran thought, overhearing Annabelle's quiet words. Polly is. He's like Dennis all over again. My dearest Dennis. Who always had a troop of children at his heels and couldn't think why. Who couldn't understand why animals and even birds loved and trusted him. She smiled a little, recalling his astonished face the day the chickadee lit on his head and tweaked out one of his hairs to build a nest with.